Bottom Feeder

by James A. Davison

ISBN 978-1-64663-670-9

Published by

 köehlerbooks™

3705 Shore Drive
Virginia Beach, VA 23455
800-435-4811
www.koehlerbooks.com

BOTTOM FEEDER

JAMES A. DAVISON

VIRGINIA BEACH
CAPE CHARLES

I am eternally grateful for a loving and supportive spouse whose intelligence and smile light up my universe.

1

Martin Landry blinks rapidly and forces his eyes to close, vigorously digging the knuckles of his index fingers into his eye sockets. The bright image seared into his retinas persists, mocking his efforts.

"What the hell was that? I'm still here, so a Russian ICBM didn't destroy Barksdale," he mutters, referring to the US Air Force base about twenty miles west of his home in Minden, Louisiana.

As the afterimage finally begins to diminish, he glances at the framed front page of a local newspaper, the *Sunday Shreveport Times*, from January 12, 1969. In full color, it illustrates local civil defense zones, evacuation routes, and fallout shelter locations for North Louisiana. He licks a finger and runs it over the metal frame, removing accumulated dust. Since he hasn't been turned into radioactive debris, he knows the flash of light, accompanied by a minor ground tremor, was not a nuclear attack.

"Well, earthquakes don't have flashes of light. I still have electricity, so lightning didn't hit the house. A plane hasn't crashed into the bayou—"

A wall-mounted phone next to his back door interrupts his musings. He sighs and reaches for it. With the afterimage no longer an issue, he blinks again, and that's when the debris, strewn in a semicircle where the water meets the land, comes into focus.

"What would do that?" he wonders aloud as he picks up the phone. "This is Martin. Who is this?"

"Martin, it's Timmy. Did you see that shooting star? I bet it fell in the lake! Think there's money to be made if we can find it? Sell it to a collector? Or maybe the government? I bet NASA would buy it! I hear them things are magnetic. I can git my brother's big ole boat magnet and johnboat, and we can go drag the lake until we find it. We'll make a fortune!"

Martin pivots the phone away from his mouth and squints at the bayou. He can still hear Timmy Johnson, a local ne'er-do-well drug dealer and gun nut, babble on about his plans for becoming rich and famous. Martin's blood pressure spikes. He knows that whatever made the noise and flash of light is right there, in his backyard. With his eyes fixed on the bayou, Martin is casual in his reply to Timmy.

"Yeah, uh, I heard it, but I bet it was just a B-52 outta Barksdale. Did you actually see a fireball? Because that's how the term 'shooting star' came to be used. Was there a fireball?"

"Yep. I saw it, came right over my trailer. Kinda sounded like a jet, but it wasn't, you know, huge. There was blueish and black smoke behind it. Could it be a bomb that got away from one of the Barksdale jets? The B-52? The way I figure, it was headed right towards the lower lake or the bayou behind your place. If it hit the forest, it mighta started a forest fire. You see anything on fire over your way?"

Martin laughs at how Timmy pronounces "fire," which sounds much more like "far," though he is intrigued with his description of the trail of smoke. *Blueish? Space debris would burn after going through the atmosphere. If it's a meteorite, this could be my lucky day. I need to get out there and see if it held together on impact.*

"Look, Timmy, it could have been a small meteorite. By the time it went through the atmosphere, though, it probably got reduced to the size of a pebble. To be honest, if it was big enough for anyone like NASA to care, the impact would have killed us all."

"Serious?"

"Totally serious. So, it's a good story to tell your friends, but there's just no way what you saw survived going through the atmosphere and an impact with the earth. We get hit by space debris thousands of times a year. I've heard experts from NASA say that at least ninety-five percent of what does make it through our atmosphere just disintegrates. Sorry, but there's no space-debris pot of gold at the end of that rainbow."

Martin hears Timmy groan and decides to cut the conversation off. "Look, I gotta run; there's food on my stovetop. Catch ya later."

"Sure, Doc, talk to ya later. Thanks for burstin' my bubble."

Martin hangs up but keeps his eyes on the bayou. He knows the nickel and titanium found in most meteorites holds real value to scientists and collectors. Mentally, he starts to organize his thoughts. But first, he looks out the window again and begins to consider his options.

He goes to the closet that houses his nuclear-war gear and sets aside a one-piece zippered suit with attached rubber boots. Taking a small tank of compressed air, he connects a full-face scuba mask. Martin glances towards the bayou, making sure no tripod-legged Martians, like those from the *War of the Worlds* radio broadcast, have emerged on a mission to kill all humans. He twists the knob to start the compressed airflow to the regulator with a smirk and mentally calculates his consumption rate.

"Timmy was right, some meteorites are magnetic, but I don't have a big magnet. Oh man, what if there is some kind of microbial life on it? That could be huge!"

The gravity of what he has just said hits him squarely. He stops and realizes it could be unhealthy to jump into the bayou and retrieve whatever it is by hand. He'd seen that movie *The Andromeda Strain* last year. Though the science was skewed, he knows that if this is from deep space, it could be bad. Very bad. *Especially for me.*

He digs through a corner filled with discarded equipment and comes up with a medium-sized glass box he once constructed to hold an experiment.

The box has a cover with a handle and a latch that will accept a master or combination lock. It is also airtight. Another sobering thought crosses his mind, and he resorts to his habitual one-sided conversation.

"Huh, maybe I should bring a gun?" He scoffs at the notion and instead looks around for a tool that provides protection and perhaps help grab whatever is in his bayou.

"Perfect," he mutters as he grabs a metal fireplace poker with a pointed end and the large set of metal tongs from an old set of fireplace tools against the wall. He looks at the glass box, takes a no. 2 pencil from his pocket protector, and slides it into the latch in place of a lock. "I am such a genius."

Suited up, he heads out to examine whatever it is that has landed in his bayou.

Stuck in the muck at the bottom of Martin's bayou, is the rock that fell to Earth. The tiny life-form, born in another universe and more than a billion years old, is awake. The newcomer basked in the heat generated as its home soared through the layers of Earth's atmosphere. Now, after so long alone in deep-space stasis, it senses life. It also experiences acute hunger.

Anger wells up in the aftermath of the collision, which has damaged what is left of its tiny dwelling. The temperature around it increases as heat transfers to the muddy, cool liquid into which it fell. It feels a measure of comfort and warmth, so the anger abates somewhat, but the hunger remains. It is confused because there is a strangeness here. Ghost-like, ancient memories of the liquid universe that was once its home flood in.

All the newcomer has known for so long is the weightlessness of space, so it takes a tentative step to adjust its molecular structure and finds a measure of stability. The pain caused by its exposure to Earth's gravity lessens.

As the steam from the vaporized bayou water dissipates, the creatures of the local ecosystem resume their own everyday life-and-death struggle. The newcomer expands its senses and is pleased to find that there is food here. It explores slowly and takes its first substantive meal with a tentative move. Though the taste is odd, hunger overrides all other senses, and it tries to take another. However, the targets of its attacks, alerted to the presence of a new predator in the bayou, prove too quick for reflexes still burdened by the newness of gravity. The fact that it has been in deep space for a substantial portion of its existence is a contributing factor to its failure; another meal will not be as easy as its first.

The newcomer uses the soft tissue of its victim as needed and discards what it cannot digest. It also adjusts its molecular structure to enable growth, a result of the stimulation caused to its system by the meal. Somewhat satiated, it rests and considers its next move. Billions of years ago, it accepted a lonely and perhaps deadly fate. Now it hopes to have encountered a place where it will not just survive but thrive.

It spreads out on the bottom of the bayou, resting, then senses movement. Given the waves emanating through the ground, something significant approaches. What comes? Predator or prey? Still too weak from its long slumber, it retracts. While it waits, it becomes frightened and moves to take up residence once again inside its original home, which, though broken by its impact with the earth, provides a sense of safety. This action brings momentary calm.

Standing five feet away at the edge of the bayou, Martin is amazed. The spot in the cattails where the meteorite impacted is easy to see, dirty mud and reeds arrayed in a perfect semicircle.

"Well, I'll be. For once, Timmy was right!" Martin places the glass box at the edge of the bayou and opens the lid. The water is disturbed and too murky for Martin to see the bottom. He decides scientific curiosity outweighs the possibility of meeting an angry Martian, and with some measure of caution, he wades in. Keeping his eyes open for anything out of place, he probes the water with the tongs.

The newcomer waits, unsure about what is happening. Since there is no way to predict what comes next, it chooses patience. Then, without warning, its home begins to shift.

Swishing the fireplace tongs through the water, Martin pauses when they hit something and make an odd noise, as if scraping against a craggy rock. There are no rocks in his bayou, so he uses the tongs to explore just how big the thing in the water might be. Satisfied that it isn't too large to handle, he closes the tongs around it, applies just enough pressure to secure it, and carefully lifts. A scorched-looking rock sheds mud, duckweed, and water as it breaks the surface. Martin eases the ovoid thing, about the size of a shoebox with the edges rounded off, into the glass case and quickly closes the lid, sliding the no. 2 pencil through the latch. He runs to the shed and returns with a shovel.

The newcomer clamps down on fear and tries to remain calm. Hidden inside its home, it resolves to examine its options once the upheaval stops. There is a sudden thump, accompanied by more of the luscious liquid into which it had fallen. Unharmed, it makes no effort to retaliate.

Martin tilts the box back and forth to be sure it doesn't leak. Satisfied, he kneels into the grass at the edge of the bayou. He stands, removes the mask, and turns off the flow of air. "Man, this is huge! I wonder if Timmy was right? Would NASA be interested?"

He bends closer to the box. "Welcome to Earth, little fella! Where did you come from? I guess you want me to take you to our leaders, don't ya?"

While Martin laughs at the worn-out science-fiction movie joke, he has no idea just how close to the truth he is.

Unsure of what has just happened, the newcomer notes the turmoil has stopped. Through the millennia of its life, there have been many challenges to its continued existence. It has endured the death of its species, being thrust into an entirely new universe because of a murderous black hole, hunger, uncertainty, and now this new set of circumstances. It senses that this new structure it has been encased in is one that it cannot penetrate. The molecular peculiarities of the glass box confound its abilities.

It feels the danger of this unknown environment and the large predator that has removed it from where its journey among the stars ended. Deep inside, though, it has confidence; it has never faced obstacles that could not be overcome. It has learned that patience always presents an opportunity.

One overarching thought remains active. It is still hungry.

2

"Son, listen to me. There are things here that can hurt you, so I need you to be careful and keep your hands to yourself. Don't touch anything."

Oscar pretends to listen while he contemplates the plans he's already made to get away from his father. He would do anything to leave the lab—its fluorescent lights that flicker and hurt his eyes and the chemical smells that always give him headaches.

"Oscar Michael Landry, are you listening to me?"

Oscar turns and smirks. "Yeah, Dad, I hear you. Don't touch anything in here, don't play with anything, don't have any fun . . . I think I understand."

"I just want you to be careful. That is my only point, to be careful. Of course you can have fun, but everything in here is significant."

Oscar squints at the cages of animals against the wall.

"Even the rabbits? What about the guinea pigs?"

"Yes."

"Kind of mad-scientist-like if you ask me." Oscar knows this insult will hurt his father.

Martin shakes his head. "You know, son, we're not alone in the universe. When the rest of the world comes to their senses and realizes that we are killing the earth with our pollution and garbage, we'll need ways to exist without the things we take for granted. That's just one way my research is important. I promise you, soon, I'm going to be famous and rich, and then, I'll buy you whatever you want, and we won't need your grandfather's money or his friends."

Oscar doubts any of what his father has just said is true. Oscar's mother is quick to tell him that his father is the world's biggest liar. Plus, his grandparents already buy him anything that he wants, so he sees no real need to be nice to his father. The only reason he's here today is because the domestic relations court forced him to spend time with his father. But, of course, that's also something his mother says to him. He lets out a long sigh.

"I get it, Dad. You don't need to lecture me about how everything you do in your lab is important to humanity."

That ex of mine. She's filled Oscar's head with lies about me. I should have done something with her when I had the chance. He smiles at the thought. *People disappear in the bayou all the time.*

While Martin contemplates killing his wealthy ex, Oscar moves closer to the glass case situated to his right. He saw it during a previous visit but didn't get close enough to be genuinely interested. This time is different. The last time he saw the case, it was locked and covered with a sheet. Today, there is no sheet, and it is unlocked.

He goes to it and puts both hands against the glass, which feels cool to the touch. Oscar slides his hands down to the same level as the muddy slime in the bottom and is shocked by the transition from cool to hot. *What in the world is Dad hiding?* He wonders if it's some kind of animal his dad has for research.

Inside the box, the newcomer pays close attention to this new intruder. It senses a difference. This one is much smaller in mass. The smaller predator touches the prison, startling the newcomer and awakening its curiosity. Two tendrils that resemble tentacles without suckers appear. They radiate from under a small piece of rotten cypress in the corner of the container and touch the glass. They mirror Oscar's hands. He screams in surprise, and before he can react or move, Martin jumps to his side and slaps his hands away from the glass.

"What the hell was that, Dad? What do you have in there?" Oscar yells. He rubs his wrists where his dad's hands chopped them away.

"It's big. That's all I can say. The past few weeks have been pretty exciting! When you understand what I have here, you will forget all about the lies your mother and her criminal family have told you about me!"

"The past few weeks? I saw it last time I was here. How long have you had this thing?"

Further explanation is interrupted when a phone rings. Martin doesn't move. Instead, he points towards a stool against the lab table.

"Sit there until I get back, then I'll get out the fishing gear, and we'll hike up the dam to the lake. How does that sound?"

"Whatever you want, Dad, but I don't know why you have an octopus in an aquarium without enough water."

"It's not an aquarium, and it's not an octopus. Look, sit tight. I'll be right back. And please, don't touch anything."

Oscar squints and nods, and his father goes to answer the phone.

With his dad gone, Oscar turns his full attention to the glass box. He wants to see what is hidden inside. Oscar slides his feet out of his sneakers and tiptoes to the glass case.

He hears his father in the other room, complaining to someone about repairs made to his Buick. Oscar sees that the combination lock to the case is open. He removes the lock very slowly and flips up the steel latch, which creaks slightly. Oscar pauses; then, with a glance over his shoulder, he uses both hands to lift the glass lid and a metal rod attached to the rim to prop it open. Sliding his arm in, he waves his hand over the biomass and sees movement.

"Come on out, little guy. I think my father loves you more than he loves me, so let's feed you to the rabbits," he murmurs to whatever is living under the muddy cypress log.

The newcomer senses freedom and acts immediately, shooting two tendrils out from under the log. Both contact Oscar's left hand. One tendril hopscotches up Oscar's right arm. In less than a second, it covers his nose while the other tendril slides up his left arm, headed for where the sound this predator produces originates.

Where the newcomer touches, Oscar is inflamed with unbearable heat. Oscar screams, shaking to rid himself of the pain. He grasps at the thing covering his nose, filling his sinuses and then his throat. He can't breathe. The cypress log slingshots up and slams into the side of the container as Oscar backpedals away and trips. Falling to the floor, he brings the entire case down on top of him. The glass box shatters, freeing the newcomer.

In the other room, Martin swears and drops the phone. *What has he broken now?* The worst-case scenario isn't a consideration until he rounds the corner and sees Oscar on the floor, broken glass from the case strewn everywhere. His face and one hand are coated by muddy-looking slime. Martin freezes. He knows exactly what's covering Oscar's face.

"Daf! Hep, iz nin mi mouff," Oscar screams, his ability to form complete words already affected by the slime that now occupies his throat. Martin remains frozen. "Ik hurtfz! Ey canf breaf!"

Martin does the only thing he can think of. "Hold on, son!" he yells over his shoulder as he runs to the garage to grab his oxyacetylene torch.

On the floor, covered in broken glass, every attempt Oscar makes to shed the brown, sticky substance is met with resistance. He hears his father yelling until the newcomer fills his ear canals. Using the energy from this exponential growth spurt, the newcomer easily overpowers Oscar. Inside the smaller mass, it discovers flimsy organs easily consumed to sustain its life and growth. It quickly fills Oscar's lungs, stomach, and intestines, digesting every organ. It knows true joy.

With its successful escape, the feeding frenzy stops. Empowered, it knows this new structure might be helpful in furthering its escape. It inhabits Oscar's bone structure and stands upright with little effort. There is an undeniable urge for sustenance and water in what once was Oscar. Millions of years of anger and hunger take control. The newcomer discovers that one of the augments this creature has, its eyes, are useful. Seconds later, the newcomer sees for the first time. It turns to take in its surroundings.

Though it doesn't understand anything it sees, it does know food is near. Lots of it. The animals cower in their cages, aware that an apex predator of unknown origin has suddenly appeared. The rabbits scream in terror as what once was Oscar moves to the largest cage and opens the door. Within a second, the rabbit is gone, and the newcomer is on to the one next to it. Oscar's eyes turn a yellowish red and get more prominent, allowing different light spectrums to enter, and they begin to see things no human eye can see. The newcomer turns and wants to follow the wave of humidity wafting in through the open door. It knows the place where its journey among the stars ended is that direction.

It takes a tentative step and then begins to lope like an uncoordinated baby animal into the sunlight. Raising an increasingly un-humanlike appendage to block the bright light assaulting yellow eyes that once were green, it sees the water and accelerates its forward progress.

Martin pushes the cart with the tanks and torch but stops cold when he sees something his son's size escape through the open door and head towards the bayou. He watches as it wades into the water and turns, making eye contact before it disappears below the surface. Martin screams Oscar's name and falls to his knees, sobbing. He knows there is nothing he can do. Oscar is gone.

In disbelief, he stares at the bayou. Something on the ground catches his eyes. Goosebumps form on his arms, and an involuntary shiver races over him. He sees what looks like small bones. Unsure if he is hallucinating, he stoops for a better look and is taken aback when he recognizes the intact bones of a human hand.

"Oscar," he blubbers. Then it hits him. The bones from every frog, fish, or squirrel he's fed his captive in the glass box were never digested, as if they were too alien for its extraterrestrial origin.

Looking towards the lab, he sees more bones. He follows the trail of bones back to the broken glass and total disarray of overturned equipment. His shoulders drop as he surveys the damage.

"Oh my God, Oscar . . . son, what have you done? What have I done?"

He retraces his steps back to the bayou. More bones, human bones, form a trail directly into the water. At the edge of the bayou, what looks like the top of a white baseball cap just barely submerged rocks gently as the wind moves across the water. Curious, he bends over to pick it up with both hands, but what he pulls out of the muddy water isn't a baseball cap. It is a human skull. Dirty water pours out of its mouth and eye sockets. Martin stumbles back and falls hard, dropping the skull. He sits in horror, unmoving, hardly breathing. It is clear to him what he's just picked out of the bayou.

The skull shifts, reacting to the pull of gravity on its most dense structure, and as it falls over, the jawbone rocks open. Even Oscar's skull mocks him.

"Oh my God, Oscar. Why did you have to meddle?"

Dragging a plastic bin, Martin gathers up every bone he sees. He is driven to find them all before he calls the police. Martin stops when he reaches 206 bones. As he lifts an Oscar-sized femur, he realizes the bone is lighter than it should be. *Even the bone marrow is gone.* Anger overwhelms him, and he remembers the oxyacetylene tanks and torch on the ground between the door and the bayou. He exits and, seconds later, rolls the tanks into the lab. He looks around with a heavy heart and spots a simple glass aquarium.

"That'll have to do for now," he mutters as he grabs it angrily and puts it on the floor near the cypress log. There are several small samples, sliced from the original, still in his freezer.

Donning heavy gloves, he purges the oxygen and fuel gas lines on the oxyacetylene setup. He ignites the torch and feathers the gas and oxygen needle valves until a perfectly brilliant, blue flame appears and the hissing stops. Gritting his teeth, he approaches the log, trying to tamp down the destructive rage surging through his body.

As he unleashes his anger, Martin feels galvanized. He grits his teeth and aims the torch at some of the most explosive parts of the lab. The fire begins to lick the walls, and he points the torch at the cypress log. He hopes something is left of the creature that once lived beneath it as he reduces the debris to ashes.

3

Martin slaps the mosquito on his arm. He glances at the bloody remnants and wipes the mess on his pants, then reaches for a canteen full of water and splashes a small amount on both his hands. Rubbing them together, he removes a handkerchief from his back pocket to dry them.

The construction foreman standing to his right reacts with, "They're pretty big this year. Out early, and they all seem hungry."

Martin replaces his handkerchief and nods. "Yeah, they have their place, but that doesn't mean I have to like it." Martin isn't interested in small talk, so he points towards the thick set of blueprints laid out on the table in front of him. "So, what was it you needed to see me about?"

The foreman frowns and flips through the pages, looking for a particular section. Finally he stops at a cross section of what appears to be a room within a room.

"This right here. I don't quite understand your design requirement for the valve system that starts inside this room. According to the plans, the room is designed for negative-pressure operations. But this valve connection with the outside world could negate all the work we're doing, and all the money you're spending. Are you sure this is what you want to do?"

"Yes. One hundred percent sure. And you don't need to worry about how this valve might affect the negative-pressure room construction.

Once engaged, the stem packing, valve connection seals, and body seals will handle the negative pressure created for the room."

"But what is it for exactly? How will it be used? It's almost like those automatic vacuum-cleaner lines people have been putting in new-home builds, but it's too big for that. By the way, that's it right over there," he says, pointing towards a large, wooden crate that was dropped off a week ago. "I've looked at the specs for it, and to be honest, it's constructed out of the strongest steel I've ever dealt with. So, before we pour that section of the build this afternoon, I wanted to go over the details."

Martin saw the trench dug in the ground when he arrived and hoped that meant the valve and piping would be laid that day. Before exiting his car, he made a note to call his contact at NASA about the chlorine trifluoride he was trying to acquire.

"That section will be done this afternoon?"

"Yes. And if I understand the plans, the pipe will terminate in an outbuilding that isn't even built yet!" He points towards an eighteen-wheeler that has been parked at the edge of the road since construction started. "And why is that reefer truck over there? It runs twenty-four hours a day. Should I be concerned about what's inside? Is it some bizarre experiment that has to remain frozen until we get this crazy cement palace built? Some of the men are superstitious about what you're building here."

Martin is shocked that the foreman has gotten so close to the truth.

"The men do what they are hired to do. Let's be clear: they do what you tell them to do, or else they get replaced. That includes you," Martin spits out. "It's their job to build what I have designed. It's your job to manage the whole process and build this structure built to my exact specifications. No questions asked. I must insist that what I have designed be followed to the most minute detail—no cutting corners. No cheap materials to shave costs. No questions regarding a purpose or reason. Honestly, I fail to understand why I continue to be asked questions like this."

"It's just that this project is so *odd*. We've done similar buildings in Shreveport and Bossier, but those two were an ice plant and a cold-storage facility. Anyone who takes the time to thoroughly examine your blueprints will ask questions that I can't answer. In fact, the Webster Parish code-enforcement guy wants to speak to you. Look, I understand it when you say this has to be built to your specs, but you also can't fault us for asking questions, especially about why we're deviating from normal building practices. I know this building is a hybrid model, kind of a mix between residential and commercial, but still, we have to get everything inspected by the parish, so I need to know what I need to know."

Martin shakes his head. After Oscar's disappearance, he endured weeks of investigations by the local police, the FBI, and one which was far more painful and intimate, conducted by his ex-wife's family. Unable to verify or disprove his story about Oscar being kidnapped, eventually they left him alone. An emboldened Martin razed what was left of the original house and removed all the wooden structures on his property so that he could start with a clean slate and build an impregnable fortress.

He doesn't know if Oscar's changes can be reversed, but he hopes to be given the opportunity. And that opportunity will only come to fruition if his facility is up to the task. The design he settled on for his new laboratory is one best suited for both containing and possibly repelling the creature that killed his son.

His thoughts are interrupted when the foreman continues.

"We are dealing with concrete and steel. Add a fully sealed foundation and roof, and the details get very confusing. You must understand that this project is odd enough to cause some unique problems for the construction crew. All I ask is that you cut me some slack. As I have said before, I'm following your construction requirements, but we are also required to follow the housing and construction codes of Louisiana and Webster Parish. I cannot just turn a blind eye to everything that has to pass inspection. Frankly, that could cost me my license. So, now that the initial phase of construction is nearing completion, are there any more modifications that I need to know about?"

Martin considers the request. He has made a few modifications to improve his odds of survival should what once was Oscar come out of the bayou, but he has no plans to speak about them.

"Look, all I need is for them to pour the concrete as it comes. Then, insert the rebar properly. Plumb the steel pipes to where my two outbuildings will be located. Check and double-check the window openings to be ready to receive the bulletproof glass once it is delivered, and leave at the end of each shift. It's just that simple."

"You forgot no working in the rain or thunderstorms." As soon as he's said it, the foreman regrets it, but before Martin's ire can build, he forges ahead with another topic. "And this guy, Timmy Johnson, the one you recommended. He keeps showing up drunk or high, and I think he's been selling weed to some of my younger workers. I just can't have that on my job site."

"I know he smokes marijuana, but you say he's been selling drugs on my property? Okay. Fire him if you haven't already done so."

"Done. Now, something else, and this is just between you and me; you have almost every cement truck in the parish coming here, delivering the concrete we're using on your building. Add to that the steel I-beams coming this afternoon for the ceiling and the bulletproof glass—I mean, to be honest, that's how rumors get started."

Martin snorts his answer. "Like I care what anyone in town thinks."

Man, how I hate this guy, the foreman thinks sourly. However, the foreman is unwilling to lose out on the bonus money Martin promised everyone if the job is completed on time, so he shoves his frustration with Martin into a box in his mind and presses on. He points to the road, where three workers are framing a small building around a water well, and asks, "Regarding the two outbuildings you just mentioned, one is that shed."

"What about it?"

"Can you at least enlighten me on why the shed over your water well is to be built out of concrete and rebar to mimic what we're doing for your house?"

Martin begins with a well-worn phrase he's thrown towards his foreman dozens of times.

"First, it's a laboratory, not just a house. Second, protecting my well water is just as important to me as protecting the materials and experiments in my lab. I must have access to pure water that is not corrupted by anything in the bayou or nearby waterways."

"What's in the bayou that could corrupt the water coming from your well? Everyone around here gets their water from a well, and no one complains about it being corrupted."

"Good for them."

"Right. Well, about that bulletproof glass . . ."

"Yes? What about it?"

"Come on, it's just weird. Like I said, what you're doing here is how you get rumors started in town. When the glass is delivered, will we be installing it, or do you have someone else in mind for that installation?"

"A firm over in Dallas is constructing the windows. I understand the glass will be shipped the day after tomorrow, which should dovetail nicely with the placement of the steel ceiling joists and the pouring of the cement roof. It should take another day to get here. I expect you to be ready for them when they arrive. And their installation is critical to the sealed, protective envelope of my building, so when the windows arrive, the technicians to install them will also arrive. I need your men to pause their work while the windows are installed. Once they are finished with the installation, your men can return to the jobsite."

The foreman flips the blueprint back to the page for the windows and mutters, "Oh, we'll be ready for a break, but trust me when I say they'll get right back to work. Every man here wants that bonus you've promised. Now, if you'll excuse me, I've got six more cement trucks arriving soon, and I want to meet your deadline as much as anyone."

With that, he closes the blueprints, grabs a cigarette, and walks away from Martin. As his strides add to the distance, he makes a mental note to look in on his buddy Jerry, the Minden city marshal. He can't wait to tell him all about Martin Landry and his cement lab with the bulletproof windows.

4

Adjusting the focus on his trinocular biological compound microscope, Martin holds his breath and introduces the perfect drop of a chemical compound onto the slide. Relaxing for a moment, he reflects on the events of the past year. Finding the meteorite and the creature living inside it, losing Oscar two weeks later, the FBI investigation, and the beating he endured at the hands of his father-in-law's thugs flash through his memory. He looks up and sees his reflection in the polished metal of the lab table.

Thankfully, he was able to flash freeze what was left of his discovery after the incident. Otherwise, he'd have nothing to work on here—well, if he didn't count Oscar out in the bayou.

With a shrug, he returns his focus to the microscope. The slice he is manipulating is too small to pose any real danger. Martin believes he is much closer to understanding the life-form that fell to Earth that day. He relaxes for a moment, imagining the cheers as he holds up the Nobel Prize and the medal he'll receive from the president. He smirks. "Whoever that may be, because I know Tricky Dick won't be president; he might even be in prison! My story will make a great Hollywood movie. Maybe Steve McQueen will play me!"

He shakes his head, blinks away tears, and his vision returns to normal.

Not yet, Martin. Stay focused.

Thoughts of worldwide acclaim are forever coupled with regrets for what he will never have again. Once again, Martin focuses on the task at hand. Using the thumb-activated, time-release cable attached to his Nikon F2 35mm single-lens-reflex camera, he snaps two photographs using the "bulb" setting and smirks again at a thought. *Glad I have my darkroom. I bet the camera shop would ask a ton of questions if I had them develop these photos.*

His scope and associated laboratory equipment sit on a faded, government-surplus metal table next to the large glass box containing his dream of scientific stardom. Thunder in the distance breaks his concentration, and he leans back from the eyepiece, rubbing his neck, face, and finally his eyes. He digs his knuckles into his eye sockets, triggering a kaleidoscope of black and white stars. He blinks, and his vision returns. With a chuckle, he recalls something his eye doctor once told him—that if he was going to rub his eyes, he should only use his elbows.

His head hurts, and he feels tired. The strain of his scientific endeavors, watching life begin and end on a microscopic level, has taken a toll on him.

Another glance at the glass box, and a heavy sigh escapes his lips. Given the horror that occurred last year, this box has bulletproof glass, constructed by the same Texas firm that manufactured and installed his bulletproof windows. The muddy slime and water twitch ominously with each low roll of thunder from the approaching storm, reinforcing Martin's recent hypothesis that this life-form hates thunder.

"I wish I knew why," Martin says out loud. "Have to figure that out at some point. Perhaps something to do with the waves of sound or harmonics? Genetic memory?"

The next clap of thunder is closer, and he is grateful for the bladed mesh titanium screen inset into the top of the box, separate from the box's bulletproof construction. It has prevented his experiment from escaping several times, given that it apparently cannot reconstitute itself after being cut into a thousand tiny pieces. Regarding his captive with some affection, Martin speaks to it.

"You've never learned that lesson, have you, little guy? You still try. I can understand. I'd also be trying like hell to escape my prison cell."

Martin's curiosity overrules his other desires with a storm approaching, and he decides to go outside once the rain starts. With practiced motion, he turns the keys on top of the box to lock it and hangs them on a nearby hook. The thick cover on the screen takes two keys to remove. He got the idea from a movie about nuclear warfare showing how it takes two keys to launch a nuclear missile.

He stands back and surveys the two new sections he's added to the bulletproof box. He thinks of the larger one as the "kill box," which he has set up to use should it become necessary to kill the creature. The smaller one he uses to feed it.

Standing, he runs a hand through his graying hair and walks to the tiny window next to the front door. Lightning throws weird shadows from the foreboding sky through the steel security bars. He glances back at the box and its lethal contents, and guilt overwhelms him for a moment—guilt for what he has lost due to his stupidity and negligence.

Another flash. A fast reply of thunder shakes the building. Martin shivers with the knowledge that, tonight, someone is going to die.

"And not a thing I can do about it. Yet."

He walks into the next room and adjusts the volume on the television. His favorite weatherman, Al Bolton over on Channel 12 out of Shreveport, is talking about today's heat index, which is so high that the thunderstorms headed towards Martin have grown in both intensity and severity.

This storm will certainly bring Oscar out of the water.

He casts his eyes—no more than a swift glance—at the small but complete 206-bone human skeleton hanging from a display hook on the wall. At its feet are the skeletons of two rabbits and one nutria. He mutters with a clenched jaw, "What? Stop looking at me like that!"

and returns to the microscope. Back at his table, he removes the slide he's been studying and pauses. Then, feeling another tinge of guilt, he glances back through the doorway at the tiny human skeleton and speaks to it in a halting, emotional tone.

"I'm sorry I yelled at you, son. I didn't mean it. I love you. I miss you so much."

Thunder tries to shake the windows free of their frames as a pressure wave propagates through the forest. Next to him, the glass box vibrates in harmony with the wave. Martin grimly stows the slide in the tiny, slide-filled box and places it into the freezer, closing and locking the insulated door.

He rests both hands on the cool metal table and sits quietly for a moment. Memories join the drum of rain on the windows. The hum of the fluorescent lights above adds a metallic buzz. He can still see Oscar's face, fearful and yet hopeful that his dad can fix what is happening to him. A flash of lightning, followed by a sharp and instantaneous clap of thunder, snaps Martin back to the present. The lights flicker, and raindrops the size of coins begin to splatter against the metal bars and windows.

Oh no.

He grabs his stopwatch from the counter and activates it. Retrieving a yellow rain slicker from where it hangs by the door, he dons it and jingles the right-hand pocket, making sure his spare set of car keys is still there. *Can't be too careful, might need them.* He grabs the big Maglite off the counter by the door, clicks it on, and exits the lab. He makes a point of shutting and locking the door behind him . . . *Just in case he shows.*

Taking cautious steps to avoid slipping in the wet grass and becoming incapacitated, he makes it down to the edge of the bayou that backs up to his lab. The heavy rain makes it challenging to see the earthen dam a few hundred feet away that separates his tailwater bayou from the large recreational lakes on the other side. The small overflow spillway at the far end of the dam gurgles as the lake on the other side works to rid itself of the rainwater. He cinches the hood closer around his head.

Sweeping the surface of the bayou with the flashlight, he muses, "Nothing yet. I suppose if he's here, he'll be out in the deeper section."

The rain subdues the beam of the flashlight. Martin holds it above his head, trying to get a better angle. He grasps it in both hands and twists the lens to produce more of a spotlight, pointing it where the water is deeper. He stops when the rain begins to run down his arms and under the slicker.

The wind and rain whip the forest. Martin stands still. He hears limbs break. Tiny waves lap angrily against the red clay and matted grass at his feet. He swallows hard and steps back from the edge, apprehensive. Under assault from the storm, Martin absentmindedly taps his left foot and calls out to the bayou.

"Why did you have to visit when I was so busy? Why did you play around with my experiment? Why couldn't you just leave everything alone and do what I told you to do?"

Realizing the water has risen enough to enclose his foot, he takes another tentative step backward and tries to calm himself. His heart thumps. The noise of the rain on his slicker gets louder and more forceful as the raindrops increase in size and number.

With emotion rising in his voice, he yells to the wind, "I'm so sorry this happened to you. I should have paid better attention to everything. Please forgive me, son. Please forgive me."

The thunder quiets for a moment, and a shiver runs through his body. The hairs on his arms stand up. Martin backs up further, aware his level of danger increases with every drop of rain slapping loudly onto the bayou.

He glances down at the waterproof stopwatch. Rain pools in the palm of his hand.

Ten minutes.

The newcomer, stirred awake by the thunder, rises from the bottom, sensing it has company. Perhaps the time for revenge has finally come. It breaks the surface, driven by anger and hunger.

Martin hears splashing, as if a bull alligator has surprised an inattentive deer at the water's edge. He holds his breath for a moment, clenches his hand, and inadvertently clicks off the stopwatch. He slings the hood away so that he can hear the noise coming from the bayou. Looking across the water, he can't help being impressed.

"Well, hello, Oscar. I hoped you would still be here."

A dark shadow rises slowly from the water. The rain slows for a moment, and the beam of light finds it.

The newcomer sees him and blinks.

Martin tries to control the flood of emotions when he sees what Oscar has become. *Only one eye? What happened?* When it escaped, it had both of Oscar's eyes. *Is this some form of mutation because the original isn't from Earth? How does only one eye help him? What did it do to my Oscar?* "Do you still know me, son?"

Martin searches his memory for the last time he saw Oscar. In the distance, it moves.

"Oh man, it can swim!"

Turning, Martin breaks into a sprint that takes him around his lab, towards his Buick. Reaching into the pocket for his keys, he hears a noise from the bayou. As the water gets shallower, the sounds gets closer.

Splash. Squish. Thump! Squish. Thump!

He glances over his shoulder and marvels at the changes in Oscar. *How is it getting through the water?* It looks like it's dissolving to move, then reconstituting once on solid ground. *Is that even possible?*

Fumbling for his keys, he curses loudly when he almost drops them. Martin knows he'll be killed if that happens, so he slows down and manages to insert the car key into the door lock. He gets in and slams the door shut, locking it, then cranks the key in the ignition so hard he almost snaps it in half.

Martin guns the engine a few times as he addresses his emotional state. "Calm down; you don't know that he's coming for you. Last time you saw him, he wasn't very stable on land."

THUNK! A heavy limb lands in the center of the hood. Martin yells in fear and wonders if the impact will affect the engine. That could mean his end. He shifts the car into drive but hesitates. His curiosity about Oscar's current form overwhelms the desire to leave. That is, until he sees Oscar turn the corner around the lab.

"Oh man, it kept Oscar's legs. No, no, no, no," he chants, but hidden inside his words lurks another emotion. He is fascinated. "I guess he's still subject to some kind of mutation." The father in him wants to yell, "Oscar!" but he knows in his soul that if Oscar gets to him, there will be no escape.

He shifts the car into reverse and careens out of the driveway. Tiny, hair-like fractures spread out on the right side of the windshield as a tree limb strikes the car and slides off. Once on the hardtop asphalt, Martin stops. His fingers find the electric window buttons, and he puts down the passenger side window. Even as rain pours into the car, he is curious. He gasps as Oscar is illuminated.

The newcomer slows. Its quarry is in sight. Still working out how to use the legs it kept, it stumbles, regains its footing, and continues towards its torturer. Happiness overwhelms it.

"It's larger than it used to be. Wonder how that happened?" Martin asks the rearview mirror. Another flash. It's much closer than he'd like. He watches it stumble, slowing its approach, and pause as if planning what to do next.

"Wait, did it just smile?" he wonders aloud.

The smile doesn't last long, though. The large, yellow eye takes on a much more sinister aspect as the newcomer leans forward and begins to race towards Martin.

Martin's brain sends the "Stomp on the gas pedal, fool" signal to his right leg and foot, and both comply with gusto, sending the tires spinning. The car fishtails on the wet pavement, then accelerates away. In the rearview mirror, every flash of lightning reveals the horror that once was his son. Oscar, at one time a promising student and the only heir to an immense fortune, is now a monster.

Martin turns onto Parish Road 116, going slow enough to keep

Oscar in his rearview mirror. He comes to the intersection of Dorcheat Road and sits momentarily.

In a snap decision, Martin spins the steering wheel and turns north, away from town and away from his lab, towards the turnoff to Caney Lake, a popular recreational area. He slows the car for a moment because his brain has just made a critical connection. The overflow spillway that empties into his bayou flashes across his mind.

"Oh man, how did I miss that? Of course he's been getting out of the bayou. Caney Lake is . . . oh no. Lots of meals to be had up there. I haven't seen any gators lately. Maybe that's why he's grown so much. But no one has been reported missing from the lake, and I've not found any skeletons. I guess he's not eating water-skiers or fishermen yet. No doubt that would have made the news. I wonder if the state or the rangers ever count the deer and other animal populations?"

With another glance into the rearview mirror, he slows even further.

"Maybe he just wants me to try and fix him. I wish I knew how."

Something lands squarely on the roof of the Buick. It makes a terrible noise. Martin watches as the broken tree branch slides into the road behind him.

"Calm down, Martin. It's just another limb broken off by the wind," he says to the empty car.

He slows to a crawl and turns in his seat, searching for any signs of Oscar. Another series of back-to-back flashes flood light around the Buick. They also illuminate Oscar. Each flash is like a strobe light that shows the thing behind Martin, just a bit closer every time. It is clear that Oscar wants to catch him. Martin notes the eye remains slanted in anger.

He turns back around, shakes his head, and applies more pressure to the gas pedal.

"Sorry, son, you're not gonna get me tonight. I still have too much to do."

Racing away in the night, Martin wonders if this version of Oscar still plays with his food before he eats it.

5

The crappy headlights on Timmy Johnson's aging Subaru barely cut through the four feet of vertical rain and darkness that is his universe. He likes living in this remote wilderness. People leave each other alone, which means he can cook the crystal methamphetamine he sells to the motorcycle gang, grow his weed, and shoot his guns pretty much without anyone ever complaining.

As he drives far too fast for the conditions, the deficiencies of his Subaru are evident; one headlight is permanently stuck on bright and points straight up, which serves no purpose as a headlight. The other one points in the correct direction but is too dim to be functionally beneficial. The dim headlight flashes off a large puddle on the side of the road, and since he is very late, he decides to cut the apex of the corner onto Caney Lake Road from Dorcheat Road to save a few seconds. He's too high to know the puddle hides a new ditch the state prisoners created that afternoon.

He saw them working on the roadside when he raced around the corner headed the opposite direction twelve hours earlier. A corrections deputy had yelled at him to slow down, and Timmy flipped him the bird. The prisoners, all dressed in black-and-white-striped jail uniforms, also yelled at him about driving like an idiot. He didn't bother to flip them off since it is entirely possible that he will see most of them again, either in jail or buying drugs from him.

As his car hurtles into the rain, the ditches filled with rainwater and oily road runoff merge with the pavement, invisible and indistinguishable from the roadway.

Swerving to cut the corner, he hears an ugly, metallic noise, and the car tilts crazily as the new ditch reaches up and swallows the front suspension. All forward motion of the car stops, and his head and the steering wheel meet, the front axle of his car grinding a divot into the pavement and deafening him for a moment. It sticks.

Dazed and confused, he regains his composure and curses. He wipes blood from his forehead and fumbles under the seat for the flashlight he stole from a hunting camp—one of those Maglites the cops always use when they want to make a point. The impact must have knocked it out from under his seat. Twisting to the right, he dips down, grips the cool, metal body, and switches it on. He leans forward and reaches over the steering wheel to grab his favorite Shreveport Captains' ball cap, now lodged between the dashboard and the broken windshield when the car hit the ditch.

Opening the door, he exits the car, which isn't easy since it sits cattywampus with the driver side elevated an additional eight inches off the ground. Timmy grabs a yellow slicker from the back seat and slings it over his head, flipping the hood on to protect his eyes from the rain. Thunder roars, and Timmy gains a measure of comfort from the soft sound as he pulls the waterproof zipper all the way up to his neck.

Timmy contemplates the berating he will receive at the hands of his new girlfriend for not getting home earlier. Dejected, he kicks the car. He kicks it again just in case it didn't get the message the first time.

Flicking the flashlight onto his watch activates the remaining tritium in the dial, numbers, and markings.

"Dammit. How did it get to be 11:30! She's gonna kill me for bein' late again. She'll think I been at Shelia's, and I ain't even been near her." Thinking for a moment, which takes considerable effort, he finishes that statement with "Today."

Absentmindedly, he unzips the slicker far enough to reach into his shirt pocket to retrieve a smoke. His fingers are soaked as he fumbles with a matchbook and drops it. With grim displeasure, he watches it float away in a rivulet of muddy, red water mixed with road oil.

"Well, crap," he says, flipping the now-soaked cigarette into the water. Defeated, he shakes his head again, which jars a bit of helpful information from his brain. *I think I still have a couple road flares in the trunk. I wonder if them things work in a frog strangler like this one. Bet it'll light a cigarette!* However, the pack of Marlboros in his left hand is empty. He crushes it and tosses it into the water, then returns his attention to the possibility of the road flare. *Might as well look.*

Making his way around the car, he is careful to alternate the flashlight up and down the road for two primary reasons. First, in case some big log truck or a drunk redneck in a Chevy comes along and doesn't see him until it's too late. His second reason is grounded in real fear; people disappear up here from time to time, and he has no interest in joining that club.

He opens the trunk and shoves aside the stereo he stole from the same hunting camp where he acquired the Maglite.

"Oh yeah," he mutters victoriously to the single thirty-minute road flare.

Flicking off the protective plastic cap, he strikes the igniter against the rough tip of the flare, and it jumps to life. He feels much better with the orange-tinged flame radiating from its slender body. However, the sulfur makes him gag, which convinces him it wouldn't have been a good idea to use the flare to light a cigarette.

Don't have one anyway, so, dangit.

Raindrops hiss as they hit the flare. Timmy grasps the bottom of the flare and bends the two metal legs over his right hand, just as he was taught as a kid. Walking fifteen paces from the back of the car, he bends over and places the flare in the roadway, then stands back to admire his work.

Something in the distance catches his eye. He wipes the rain from his face.

"Yes!" he yells to the wind, thrusting both arms into the air as a set of headlights appears in the distance. "This is Timmy's day, screw you!" he screams at Mother Nature.

He moves to stand in front of his car and waves the big Maglite in huge circles, turning his body. When he glances down, the cockeyed headlight blinds him momentarily.

He rubs his eyes, trying to restore his night vision, and the oncoming car begins to slow just enough to be visible in the rain. Timmy thinks he recognizes the car as Martin Landry's. Everyone north of Minden knows Martin is a former medical doctor with money to burn. He lives way back in the woods near the lake. Whenever Timmy sees Martin in town, he's always buying dry ice. When asked about the dry ice, Martin constantly mutters the name "Oscar." No one continues the conversation after hearing that name. They all know the story of his kidnapped son, who was never seen again. After what happened last year, everyone just figures Martin went kind of crazy.

Timmy spreads his arms as wide as possible when it's clear Landry will not stop and help. The motion translates into "What the heck, Martin; come on, man, you gotta stop! Are you just gonna leave me stranded here?"

He sees that the passenger-side window is down as the Buick LaSabre slows and fishtails when Landry brakes on the wet pavement. The noise of the rain beating down doesn't alter or mute the words that Landry yells in his direction.

"You can't be here! He's coming! I can't stop him! I don't know how to stop him! Get back in your car, Timmy! You need to get out of here!"

Timmy is sure his pal Martin must be drunk. His outstretched arms fall to his sides like lead weights as he watches Landry accelerate away from the intersection.

"You drunken fool, you cud-a stopped!" he yells at the taillights that disappear in the rain. "And I can't git back in my car and git home cuz *my car's stuck in a ditch*, you moron!"

Timmy screams at the universe, which makes him feel better as he jumps up and down in the road like an eight-year-old child. Part of him thinks it weird that the man is driving in the opposite direction of civilization.

"Wait, what did he just yell? 'He's coming?' Who's coming? What an idiot! He's as weird as everyone says he is, that's for sure!"

Shaking his head, Timmy hears another sound. It reminds him of the sound his cowboy boots make at the rodeo after a significant rain. Water mixed with blood, manure, and soil creates a peculiar sucking sound when you step in it, and he's stepped in it far too many times.

With the lights of Martin's car disappearing into the night, the newcomer is aware it is not alone. It stops running and waits. Then, taking tentative steps, it moves closer for a better look. Beneath it, the gravel makes odd crunching noises.

What the H-E-double-L is that? Timmy wonders as the rain slackens for a moment. Now it sounds like someone dragging something through the gravel lot across the street. A metallic clanging adds to Timmy's discomfort.

He spins on his heels, and the circle of light from the Maglite sweeps across the road, the trees, the gravel parking lot, and the building. Martin searches for the noise source and sees the metal roof flashing as it twists in the wind at the abandoned strip club once known as Beaver Cheeks. He hears the crunching again, from in front of the decrepit building. As he moves the light to see, the rain increases once more, and the building disappears in the downpour.

Nervous, he reverts to the annoying habit of talking to himself out loud whenever he faces an unusual situation, which frequently involves women, liquor, losing money on the horses at Louisiana Downs over in Bossier City, or a combination of the three.

"Can an animal make that noise? No, if it were a big cat, it would be snarling. Maybe a bear? No. No animal I know of is gonna be out on a night like this. That crazy old coot has me freaked out."

Turning his face towards heaven, Timmy directs his angst into the storm. "Hello! Anyone out there? I need some help here!" Directing his anger at the universe, which must hate him, he adds, "And hey you, upstairs, can you make it rain just a bit *harder*? I'm not completely soaked yet!"

On cue, the rain increases substantially in volume.

Timmy hangs his head and shakes it. Water flies from the rain slicker hood as if even it doesn't want to be near him. "Great. Now I've pissed off God."

Just across the roadway from Timmy, the newcomer is distracted as it revels in the perfection falling from the sky. It sits back, eye closed, and takes in as much as it can handle.

In most thunderstorms, Timmy loves watching lightning flashing everywhere, imagining the demons or aliens who might be riding the waves of light and sound. But only when he is tucked away in the comfort of his trailer. The sound the rain makes on the metal roof is as mesmerizing as a good rock guitar solo, especially when he's high.

He opens the door to his car and sees the muddy water seeping into the car's passenger side. "Aw, dammit! Man, that mud is gonna stink in the morning."

As he slams the door shut, the hair on the back of his neck stands up. He shivers and straightens. His hunting instincts tell him that he is no longer alone on the dark roadway. Someone or something else is here with him. He wants to run, but where? A wave of fear ripples through his body, and he tightens his grip on the flashlight.

"Dammit, yet another great night not to have my pistol."

Timmy musters as much bravado as possible and reopens the car door. He reaches in and pulls the twelve-inch machete from its hiding place in the fabric above the sun visor. Turning slowly, he raises the flashlight and wields the machete like some redneck caveman about to slay a predator for dinner.

The beam of the light catches something across the street that looks like an eye. A large eye. It appears to blink in reaction to the brightness. As the beam deviates away from it, the eye disappears. *What kind of animal has a huge yellow eye like that? Just one?* Timmy's brain tries to alter his original evaluation. *Am I seeing things?*

He reorients the light and sees nothing. There it is! Then, it's gone. But the lightning provides an assist. What it reveals frightens Timmy beyond his ability to control his emotions.

"What the hell are you?" he screams as the shadow with the eye closes the distance between them faster than Timmy thought possible. Another bolt of lightning streaks across the sky, and Timmy is speechless. Standing less than a foot away is every monster nightmare he's ever had. The flashlight wavers, and the eye reforms, transmitting an emotion of regret mixed with anger.

Another powerful bolt sears the afterimage into Timmy's retinas. The eye changes shape. Timmy blinks to remove water from his eyes. So does the eye. A giant, sloppy, brown hand uncurls from the darkness. Timmy reacts, slicing at the thing with the machete. A small piece of it falls to the pavement and slides towards a pothole filled with rainwater. The creature pauses its advance. Timmy is unsure of what he just witnessed. *Did that piece I just cut off crawl over to that pothole?*

This thought freaks Timmy out even more, but it also makes him hopeful that whatever this thing is can be killed, so he raises his arm for another strike, this time aiming for the eye. Trying to manage the flashlight and the machete, Timmy reorients his grip and drops the machete. He tries to catch it but grabs the sharp side, which deeply lacerates his palm. The machete falls and lands in the roadway with a wet, metallic clang. Timmy sticks his wounded hand under the opposite armpit and screams.

The long fingers of the newcomer take advantage of this and wrap around his body, squeezing him like a tube of Timmy toothpaste. One long, extra-slimy finger goes down his throat and stops his scream. His legs leave the ground. The flashlight drops from his hand and rolls wildly on the pavement. The circle of light splashes across what looks like a mud puddle with legs before the flashlight wedges between the roadway and the back tire. As the slimy hand squeezes, the pressure ruptures Timmy's organs. The tendril down his throat dissolves everything it touches, turning Timmy into sustenance. His eyes register that a mouth is opening, and he's headed right for it. His brain tells him to scream, but he no longer has lungs, throat, or vocal cords.

Then, everything goes black, and he is no longer Timmy.

A tiny rivulet of blood from his palm mixes with the rainwater as he disappears into the newcomer. The red streaks join the red puddle under Timmy's Subaru.

Satiated by the large meal, the newcomer considers looking for the part of it that was sliced off but decides to let that piece begin its own life, so it turns and disappears into the ditch of muddy water rushing in the direction of its home. Behind it, Timmy's yellow slicker is carried away to a new home of its own.

Inside the Subaru, a small whirlpool of mud and water forms. Old coffee cups and other debris circle the stick shift. The car takes on a forlorn and abandoned look. Twenty minutes later, darkness returns as the rain slows and the flare self-consumes.

6

Andrew McLean, a stout, fifty-five-year-old law enforcement officer, shifts his Chrysler into reverse. He inches back until he feels the familiar thump as the trailer hitch meets the Shasta camping trailer. His son, Colin, jumps down the porch steps and offers to help just as Andrew secures a twelve-foot johnboat to the top of the car.

"Hey, Dad! Are we still going camping this weekend?"

"Yes, we are, son. I think we left most of the fish in the lake two weeks ago; we need to catch the ones we left. And we've not had much time to fish since I started this new job, so I thought we'd take a few days off and go have some fun."

"That's awesome! I can't wait! When do we leave?"

His father points towards the house. "Go ask your mother. Tell her the trailer is ready. All we need is to pack the clothes and cooler. Why don't you go help your mom? Then we might be able to leave a little earlier."

Colin bolts into the house, up the stairs to the hallway, and into his mother, who has her hard-shell Johnsonite luggage in hand. The look on her face is not a happy one.

"Colin, slow down! You know you're not supposed to be running inside the house. You almost knocked me over!"

Colin screeches to a halt. "I'm sorry, Mom. Dad told me to get packed. I'm gonna get my swimsuit and some shirts! He said we're going camping and then fishin'! I was just in a hurry to get them so we can leave!"

"We still have to pack the cooler." She waves a finger and continues, "And no more running in the house. You could have killed me! Now, go finish getting ready. And when you're done, come back in and help me with the cooler."

"Yes, Mom," Colin says as he walks calmly into his room, wondering if running in the hallway could really kill someone. He resolves to ask his father later. Grabbing a small tote bag, he stuffs his old swimsuit and several T-shirts in with three pairs of underwear. Snapping his fingers, he looks for the new swimsuit his mother gave him for his birthday a month ago. Colin digs through the clothes until he unearths the brightly colored suit. With a smile of satisfaction, he crumples it into a ball and drops it into his suitcase.

This is a calculated move on his part, given that his mom always asks them to bring something better than "lake clothes," as she calls them, to attend Sunday services held at the lakeside outdoor chapel. *I can wear my swim trunks to church with a clean T-shirt.* That way, when the old country minister finishes singing the last, off-key verse to "Amazing Grace," he can run right to the boat.

The idea of wearing multipurpose clothes to church is so perfect that Colin wonders if he is the first ever to think of it. He contemplates for a minute and decides that someone else must have thought of it too, given it is—what is the word he heard recently? *Oh yeah, genius!*

Now packed for the week, he opens the door and announces, "I'm not running" as he starts a slow, not-running dash towards the back porch and the outside world.

His mother's voice resonates from the kitchen. "You better not be."

With Colin's bag in the trunk of the car, Andrew says, "Alright, son, go help your mother with the cooler. Make sure she takes the milk out of the freezer to thaw. Tell her to remember the heavy-duty aluminum foil too."

Colin nods and heads inside. Once there, he feels the need to bring up a pressing topic.

"Mom? Do you think Dad will let me sleep outside yet? I love his hammock! I could put up mosquito netting and sleep in my sleeping bag. That would be awesome!"

During World War II, Andrew had been in the Navy, and when the war was over, he brought his hammock—or rack, as he called it—home. He'd used it all over the Pacific during the war, and the hammock found new life when the family started camping. Tied between two trees, it quickly became everyone's favorite place to relax. Last year, Colin asked if he could use it to sleep outside, which his mother met with little enthusiasm. Even his father said no. Finally, when Colin pressed the subject, his dad stated that he was too young to sleep alone outside.

One year older now, he hopes his father will agree to it.

"Colin, I don't know if you'll get to sleep in your father's hammock outside. What if it rains, or what if a snake crawls up the tree and decides the hammock looks comfortable?"

Colin frowns. "Mom, everyone knows that snakes can't climb trees." Seeing the look on his mother's face, his eyes get larger. "Wait, they can't climb trees, right? Right?" he asks with emphasis.

Her reply is already in the air as he finishes that last question.

"Do you want to find out?"

Colin is quite sure he doesn't want to. "No, I don't. But there's no way snakes can climb trees," he mutters. Doubt creeps into his young mind. He mumbles again, "No way," as he stuffs the cooler with ice from the ice maker. In the corner of the freezer, he sees the frozen milk and remembers to tell his mom to pack it.

"Dad wanted me to remind you not to forget the milk. Hope it thaws before breakfast tomorrow!"

"Is there still room in the cooler?" his mother asks, retrieving the milk.

Colin shoves the bacon, frozen, and the hamburger meat, even more frozen, aside and turns them sideways. He reaches into the icy water and swirls it around, turning a few pieces of frozen fried chicken entombed in thick aluminum foil sideways in the process. Doing so makes a perfect, milk-container-shaped hole in the cooler.

"There. It will fit now if you hand it to me."

"You and your father, two peas in a pod. Only the two of you could figure out how to make a full cooler give up more room. One day I know you will do something great with that brain of yours. Now, help me take this out to your father."

Colin lifts his side of the cooler. Even though it's snapped closed, he is careful not to spill its contents as he walks down the hall, through the back porch, and down the concrete steps to where his father waits. As his mom goes back inside the house, Colin watches Andrew methodically place the cooler inside the trailer, snugging it up against the seven-horsepower Johnson motor they use with the johnboat. Colin is always impressed with how his father is with shapes and fitting things that generally don't belong together into a small space. He hopes one day, when he is all grown up, to be as intelligent.

Andrew closes the door to the trailer and looks towards the house with a hopeful gaze. Colin sees it and smiles. His father shrugs. "I bet your mother isn't ready."

"I bet you're right!" Colin says enthusiastically. He glances behind the loaded trailer at the Vivian Marine, a twenty-four-foot bass boat that isn't making the trip. "When I'm old enough to drive, maybe you'll let me drive Mom's car and pull the bass boat? It'd be fun to get to fish and then maybe do a little skiing!"

Andrew smiles at his son's infectious ambition to grow up.

"One day, you'll be old enough and skilled enough to do that. When that day comes, we'll bring the trailer and the bass boat. Not sure I want that to happen so soon, though, because it means you'll almost be an adult, which also means you'll be going off to college, then you'll get a job, get married, have kids, and then I'll be a grandpa. So, I'm not ready for all that yet. But, yes, of course. One day, that's what we'll do."

Colin mulls his father's answer, curious about the description of his future transition from being a teenager eager to get a driver's license to getting married and having kids. Colin figures it's best to keep his thoughts to himself, so he keeps quiet.

Sensing that perhaps he's freaked his son out a little, Andrew begins to repack the trunk while Colin fidgets. He knows how anxious his son is to get on the road, so he smiles and says, "Well, let's go see if your mother is coming with us."

"I'm here and ready to go," Margery announces as she steps out of the house. "Just had to grab a few things that I forgot last time."

"Great," Andrew says, taking the large suitcase from Mom. The look on his face says he isn't sure if it will fit in the trunk, so he hefts it and walks to the trailer, sizing up the remaining room carefully. He leans inside the trailer and reorients the cooler and outboard motor to make room. Satisfied, he eases the suitcase in.

"I don't want my suitcase and all my clothing smelling like gasoline when we get there," she says, unhappy to see her luggage on the floor next to the outboard motor.

In anticipation of such a comment, Andrew is quick with his reply. "Oh, it won't smell like gas. There's none in the motor. It's in the gas can, which is under the trailer."

"It might smell like Jonson seven-horsepower engine oil, though," Colin offers, which earns a semi-fake stern look from his father.

Andrew knows it's necessary to head off any potential issues.

"He's just kidding." He locks the door to the trailer.

"Why did you lock the door?"

"Can't have it swing open on the interstate and everything fall out! Crucial, important things like your mother's suitcase or our fishing gear!" Without turning around, he continues, "Is the house locked?"

"No, I didn't know if you needed to go back inside before we left."

Andrew looks at Colin. "You need anything inside?"

"No, sir."

Andrew takes a set of keys from his pocket and pulls the back door to the house shut, locking the deadbolt. "Well then, let's get going!"

He cranks the Chrysler and begins to pull out of the driveway when Colin's mother turns her head and asks, "Aren't you going to say it, Colin?"

Colin grins and responds with his mother's favorite one-liner regarding their travel plans. "We're off like a herd of turtles!"

With a smile, his mother nods and says, "Okay, now we can leave."

Colin sits back in the seat and is soon lulled to sleep by the motion of the car, into a world where he flies through the air like a bird and battles aliens from another dimension.

7

Clipboard in hand, Louisiana State Police captain Clinton Ward doesn't look up as a car slows to a stop behind his. He called for assistance a few minutes ago. The crackling of the police radio as the driver exits his vehicle is drowned out by a voice he recognizes.

"What is one of the most decorated troopers in the great state of Louisiana doing next to an abandoned car in Webster Parish? There must be something else, something much more ridiculous, for a dedicated and illustrious trooper such as the one who stands in front of me to undertake a simple abandoned vehicle case."

The nature of the question is not unexpected, given who poses it. Clint knows the questioner just by how he pronounces "Deck-err-ated."

Before he can answer, though, it is followed by another question.

"Well, whatcha got to say for yourself, Clinton? Or shall I just shorten it to Clint and ask if you've started carrying a .44 magnum like your wannabe best pal, Dirty Harry?"

Clint chuckles and turns to address Jerry Thomson, the city marshal for the nearest actual town, Minden. He and Jerry have been friends since childhood and frequently spend time together on and off duty. Jerry's penchant for ridiculousness is well known, so Clint decides to address the least ridiculous parts of Jerry's questions.

"Well, Jerry, why don't you just call me whatever you like. However, the powers that be in that ivory tower down in Baton Rouge think a .44 magnum might scare lots of people, so instead, they give us these," he says, patting his holstered Smith & Wesson K-Frame Model 66, chambered in .357 magnum.

Jerry tilts his head.

"Yeah, that may be true." Jerry smirks and feels it necessary to rib his buddy a bit more. "I see you guys are still using that silly swivel holster."

A rueful smile crosses Clint's face.

"It broke at least three times this month. Just last week, it broke during a traffic stop. Fell right off my hip onto the road. I had to stop, tell the lady not to drive off as I retrieved it, and take it back to my police car. All before I could even tell her why I stopped her." Clint shakes his head as if the memory of the event is too embarrassing to even think about. "It was absurd, like Keystone Cops."

Jerry laughs, pats his holster, and offers, "We've talked about this before, my friend. My semiauto in a retention holster hasn't broken and fallen onto the roadway. We can send more lead downrange, it's much sturdier, and I'm happy not to carry two or three speed loaders in my pockets."

"Yeah, I hear the armory boys at headquarters in Baton Rouge are testing some semiautos right now." Switching gears, Clint decides to answer his buddy's question. "So, to answer you, I was just out for a leisurely drive on this lovely morning and heard that someone had left a perfectly good, wonderfully chartreuse Subaru out all night, so I came right over, hoping to meet the owner. I mean, someone with a car this color must be an exceptional individual."

Jerry smiles. He expected nothing less than a smart-aleck answer and doesn't hesitate with his reply. "Well? Is it?"

Clint furrows his brows. "Is it what, Jerry?"

"Perfectly good?" Jerry asks with some enthusiasm.

Clint looks doubtful as he shakes his head. "No, it doesn't appear to be perfectly good at all. It's been here all night, judging by the mud line inside and out."

Jerry walks around Clint and opens the driver's door to confirm. It's easy to make out the high-water marks inside the car. "Yep. I guess the car was at least partially filled at some point last night." Jerry recognizes the car but doesn't say so. Instead, he asks, "Any sign of the owner?"

"Nope again. All we got is that spent flare in the roadway, about fifteen feet away from the back of the car, this machete," he says, holding up an evidence bag, "which was in the roadway, and"—holding up another evidence bag—"this big ole Maglite."

Clint puts the bags down and goes back to filling out the tow form.

"The owner is Timmy Johnson," Jerry finally offers.

"You recognize the car?" Clint says, not surprised.

"It's Timmy's, alright. Any indication of why he abandoned it here?"

"Looks like he ran off the road. The front end of the car is dug into the asphalt. I guess the ditch was filled with water and looked like a normal puddle when he cut the corner. I found the machete about where you're standing and the Maglite, still lit, under the back tire."

"Had to make a hell of a bang when the front axle hit the pavement." Jerry bends down and looks under the car. "Even with the rain last night, there's quite a bit of mud. Man, his whole front end is dug in." He stands, glances inside the car, and continues, "Yeah, I know him. Don't see many cars around here that color whose owner hasn't been beaten to smithereens by the locals. Timmy's a huge pain in my butt. If his name sounds familiar, it's because of that big illegal fireworks thing ATF had back last summer. Remember it? Over near the old ordnance plant? Timmy was part of that."

Clint pauses to stop three trucks pulling fishing boats. He motions for them to either turn around in the old strip club parking lot or pass him very slowly. One turns around while the other two pull into the oncoming travel lane and proceed around the two police cruisers and the Subaru.

"Hold on," he says to Jerry as he pushes the transmit button on his portable radio. "Twenty-One Bravo, Webster dispatch."

"Twenty-One Bravo, go ahead."

"Twenty-One Bravo. Can you have a couple of Webster scout cars come my way for traffic control?"

"Twenty-One Bravo, ten-four. I have two units coming to you."

"Twenty-One Bravo, ten-four. Thank you."

Turning back to Jerry, Clint says, "Sorry, but if you're here to help me with this, we can't keep turning our backs to traffic. Sooner or later, some good old boy who spent all night at his favorite bar will come barreling up Dorcheat and kill us both. Now, what were you saying?"

"I was going to ask if there was anything else in the car?"

"Just an old stereo in the trunk, some weed and drug paraphernalia."

Jerry focuses on the Maglite and the machete. He is intrigued.

"You say the Maglite was still lit?"

"Yep. It was wedged against the front tire. Batteries almost dead, which, if the batteries were fresh, gives us an approximate time of the accident."

"Yeah, they burn, what, maybe nine or ten hours on new batteries?"

"What I figure."

"That's pretty weird. And the machete? Thoughts on that one?"

Clint shakes his head. "Nope. If there were foul play, I guess we'd have evidence of a struggle, though the heavy rain overnight would have washed any blood away pretty thoroughly."

"Does seem like we'd at least have a body if a gang was involved."

"You talking about motorcycle gangs or some other gang?"

Jerry rubs his chin as he answers. "Motorcycle. Timmy was one of their local cooks. I heard that he was supposedly pretty good at making crystal meth."

Clint nods. "Maybe they got tired of him? But isn't it kind of odd to just snatch him and leave his car on the side of the road? I thought they were always looking to make a profit. If they took him, wouldn't they have taken his car too? If nothing else, for the parts alone. I mean, it's gotta be worth a couple thousand. Kinda weird."

"Yep," Jerry acknowledges. "Weird."

"All I seem to roll up on lately, the weird ones."

"But no sign of Timmy? And let's say, for the sake of argument, he wasn't snatched by a motorcycle gang. If he wrecked his car and set off on foot, I don't get why he'd leave the flashlight or the machete."

"Right. I mean, if you're gonna stroll off in the middle of a severe thunderstorm, wouldn't you take the one thing that could save your life in an animal attack and the thing that could be used to flag down another driver?"

Jerry chews his lower lip for a moment. Then both turn and face two more cars that have idled up to the scene. Clint gestures to the drivers to turn and go back in the other direction. He watches quietly while both cars pull into the gravel lot across the street and head towards town. Jerry considers moving his car to block the road.

Instead he asks, "Will you make contact with his girlfriend? They still live in a trailer at the far end of Parish Road 814 and that old logging road."

Clint nods. "Well, now that I know that information, I'll go there next. Wanna join me?"

"Thought you'd never ask," Jerry laughs.

"Just waiting for Johnny's Towing to show up. We'll stick the car in impound until Timmy shows up asking about it."

An older Honda Civic crests the hill to the east of the intersection, blazing at top speed right for them. The nose dips as the driver brakes just before reaching the intersection, and it screeches to a halt, almost striking the Subaru. Both men jump back a step or two, not sure what to expect. *Maybe it's the owner?* Clint thinks.

Unlike Clint, Jerry recognizes the driver by her expression and purple hair. He lets out a long sigh and shakes his head.

"Oh man, that's Becky, Timmy's psycho girlfriend," he offers just loud enough for Clint to hear. She puts her car in park, throws open the door, and starts yelling.

"Where is Timmy! He never came home last night. If he been with Shelia, I'm gonna kill him! You can testify that I said that at my trial, too, because he's as good as dead when I get my hands on him if he's been with that ugly witch!"

She points towards Clint's car and hollers, "Have you got him in the back of your car there? Was he drunk and fell asleep after wrecking that god-awful thing of his? I want to give him a full piece of my mind before y'all haul his butt off to jail again. Where is he? Lemme at him for just a few minutes! He'll regret he ever treated me like this! I'm seriously gonna kill him, I'm tellin ya!"

"Now, Becky, we don't have Timmy. All we got is his car, abandoned here in the ditch."

"What do you mean you don't have him? His car is right there!" she says, pointing over Jerry towards the Subaru.

"I know that's his car, but Timmy isn't in it. It looks like he must have run off the road and got stuck in the ditch during the big thunderstorm last night. We don't know where he is."

"You don't got him?"

Now Jerry is concerned. "You say he didn't come home at all last night?"

"No, he did not." Becky holds both hands to her mouth, and a horrified look crosses her face. "Maybe he started to walk home and got ate by a bear, or a mountain lion! You know we have them around here! What if it was so dark he got hit by some drunk, and they just tossed what was left of him into the woods?"

She inhales as if blowing up the largest balloon in the world, her voice rising several octaves with every word as they clamp together like one very long sentence: "He coulda been hit and throwed off the road! My Timbo might be somewhere right now, dyin', and we'd never know it! We gotta do something, get a search going; y'all have them K-9s that sniff out bodies. My baby could be off in the brush dyin' right now, and y'all just be standing here doing nothing!"

Clint and Jerry shake their collective heads and, without saying a word, share a look that grudgingly admits she might be onto something.

"Well, I guess he could have gone under a big tree to get out of the rain since his car was flooded."

"And if he'd been drinking, he could still be asleep," Jerry adds.

Clint nods. "Look, Becky, as soon as I get some help here, we'll organize a search party and comb through the bushes nearby—"

Clint's portable police radio comes to life, interrupting him.

"Twenty-One Bravo. Troop B."

Relieved at the interruption, Clint takes the radio off his belt and pushes the transmit button. "Twenty-One Bravo, I copy Troop B; go ahead."

"You still on that ten-forty-six at Dorcheat and Caney Lake?"

"Ten-four."

"We just got a call from the superintendent over at the church campground. They found some clothing on the beach there. They also found some . . ." The dispatcher pauses for a moment and then comes back on. "Twenty-One Bravo, are you signal three?"

Now both Jerry and Clint are on full alert. *Signal three? What the heck is going on? They only use that when they don't want the people who pass the time listening to police scanners to hear details about finding the bodies.*

Clint keys the transmit button. "Troop, Twenty-One Bravo. No. Please stand by."

"Ten-four."

Looking at Becky, he points towards her car and in his sternest voice says, "Do not go near Timmy's car. You are not to touch anything. In fact, sit your butt down in your car, shut the door, and don't move until we come back."

When she hears the severity of Clint's commands, the blood drains from her face. She nods and, without saying a word, returns to her car. They both hear her sniffle, trying not to sob.

"Something bad has happened to my Timbo. I know it," she says as she starts weeping and closes the car door.

Clint and Jerry go to the rear of Clint's cruiser.

"Troop, Twenty-One Bravo. We are signal three. State your traffic."

"Twenty-One Bravo, ten-four. At the church camp over on the lower lake, one of the caretakers said he was surveying damage from the storm last night and found some clothes. He says there was a shirt, pants, underwear, and an undershirt on the beach this morning." The two men look at each other. Both are thinking, *So what? It's just clothes.*

"Clothes? Is that it?" Clint voices.

"When he found the clothes, there were also remnants of what looks like blood on the clothing, and a, well, what he described as a bunch of bones. The superintendent believes they are human bones. Webster SO has been notified and are en route. The coroner has been alerted and is on his way. They ask you to tape off the car and any other areas you believe might be involved so that forensics can process the car and the scene. You are now working what appears to be a homicide."

Stunned, both men are quiet for a few seconds.

Jerry mutters, "Homicide?"

Clint shoots him a look as he keys the mic on his radio.

"Dispatch, Twenty-One Bravo. How do we know the remains are tied in with my abandoned vehicle?"

"There was a wallet in a hidden, zippered pocket of the pants. Belonged to Mr. Timmy Jonson, Rural Route 814, Minden."

"Yep. That's Timmy. Never trusts people. Too scared of thieves and pickpockets. He has a hidden pocket sewn into every pair of pants I've ever had the bad fortune to search. When he went over to the Bossier strip, he'd carry his real wallet in those hidden pockets and a 'pickpocket wallet' in his back pocket. It even had fake money in it." Jerry looks down Dorcheat Road and finishes with, "Guess I'll reposition my car and get the tape outta my trunk. You wanna tell Becky?"

"No. But guess I need to."

Jerry goes to his car, starts it, and executes a deft three-point turn to block the road. Getting out, he directs two more cars to turn around as he opens the trunk and retrieves yellow "crime scene, caution" tape. In the distance, sirens pierce the calm. Lots of them. Wrapping the end of the tape around a fence post just behind his car, Jerry strings it across the road and around more posts on the opposite side, leaving open the entrance to the gravel lot to use for turning traffic.

"NO! NO! NO!" Becky begins screaming as she pounds the steering wheel with her fists.

Jerry puts the tape dispenser in his cruiser and looks over at Clint, who guides Becky out of her car and is actively trying to console her regarding something he doesn't know enough about yet to confirm.

Turning, Jerry checks himself quickly to avoid a glob of what looks like mud in the middle of the road. "Dammit! What is this stuff?"

He thinks about kicking it into the ditch but doesn't want whatever it is on his freshly shined boots, so he steps over it. He makes a mental note to tell the tow truck driver to shovel it off the roadway and into a nearby ditch.

The slimy ball of mud extends a tiny tendril and attaches itself to the Subaru's undercarriage. Sending another tendril into a puddle of water just inches away, with one motion it pulls itself free of the car and plops back onto the wet pavement. It stops moving, though, given the unpleasant taste of the ditch water full of old road oil and gasoline washed away by the heavy rain, and it returns to the warmest part of the car's metal frame. Scared, it stops moving. Unsure of what to do next, the small slice from the original newcomer decides to be patient. Perhaps time will present a better set of circumstances.

A tow truck arrives, and the driver walks under the yellow tape to stand just a foot or so away from Timmy's car, bringing Jerry back to reality.

"Hey, Marshal. I'm Dennis, from Johnny's Tow Service. Remember me from that eviction and impoundment you guys did last week?"

"Oh yeah. Good to see you, Dennis."

"You need me to hook this or what?"

"You'll have to cool your heels, Dennis. This is a crime scene. If you wouldn't mind, I need you to back up a few feet. In fact, why don't you go sit in your truck. We're gonna be a few with this . . . situation."

Two Webster Parish sheriff deputies arrive. Without a word, one repositions his car to block the road thirty feet from Jerry's car, near the second entrance to the old Beaver Cheeks gravel lot, which impresses

Jerry. He watches with interest as that deputy walks up to the police tape and holds it high enough so the other can drive under it. That deputy parks his cruiser across the road in the other direction, thirty feet north of the intersection, effectively blocking all traffic.

Jerry nods to both deputies in acknowledgment.

"You primary?" one asks.

Jerry points towards Clint. "He is."

Both share a look of mock amazement. "The cap? Man, that never happens! Must be a *very* slow day for the Louisiana State Police!"

"Settle down, you two," Jerry says as they all share a conspiratorial snicker.

The deputy nearest Jerry walks back to direct traffic and stops. Something just off the road has caught his eye. He steps over the ditch and into the tall grass.

"Hey, Jerry! There's something over here!"

Intrigued, Jerry walks under the yellow tape and turns to the tow truck driver. "You, stay put." A minute later he joins the deputy in the grass. "Huh. Weird place to leave a rain slicker."

"I don't get it: why would you take off a perfectly good rain slicker in the middle of a rainstorm?"

"Dunno." Removing a Bowie knife from his belt, Jerry reaches down and with the tip lifts the slicker. He turns it to the deputy and asks, "See anything written on the inside?"

"Yep. In blue ink, though it's runny. Two initials . . . there's a *T* and a *J*."

"Oh man, that's Timmy's."

Behind them, Dennis is very intrigued now. "This is gonna be good! Please tell me that it's another weird murder!"

The only reaction he gets from Jerry is a raised eyebrow.

"This one's all yours, Marshal," one deputy says as he turns to address the growing number of cars headed to the lake for some weekend recreation.

The tow driver feels that something big is going on and wants in on the secrets.

"Are there bones? I heard rumors round town 'bout some folk disappearing up here. Just bones and nothing else." Seeing what he thinks is doubt on Jerry's face, the driver continues, "Yeah, man, bones! Nothing else! I heard there's some wicked, weird voodoo happening up here in the woods!"

Dennis the tow driver stands on his toes, trying to see if any bones or body parts are strewn about. Jerry makes a mental note to look into his background and, when the opportunity arises, to softly interrogate him some point soon.

8

The forty-mile trip from South Shreveport to just outside Minden is uneventful until Andrew decides he doesn't like all the eighteen-wheelers on Interstate 20 and exits onto old Louisiana Highway 80 at Dixie Inn. Colin wonders how fast his father is driving. He leans forward just enough to glance over the front seat and sees the needle on the speedometer.

Seventy-five! Wow! I can't wait until I'll get to drive that fast!

Colin is happy they exited the interstate because it means he will see, and once again try to mention, the spray-painted sign propped up against a large pine tree just outside Minden. The four-by-eight-foot sheet of plywood is painted black, and in large, bright-red, easy-to-read letters, the landowner has written, *Speed on, brother—hell ain't half full,* which Colin always finds quite hilarious. He knows about hell from the Bible and church and wonders if people in hell even have brothers.

Conversely, Colin's mother takes a dim view of the author of the phrase and her son's obsession with it. She sometimes wonders if her husband takes this route on purpose. She sighs when she sees the wooden sign in the distance and turns just enough in her seat for Colin to hear and understand her next comments.

"Colin Andrew, don't you dare do what I know you are thinking of doing."

Colin tries his best to look innocent of the crime he's just dying to commit, but he also knows his first and middle names are reserved for use in situations involving potential or already committed serious infractions of "Mom's law," as he calls it.

"But, Mom, I wasn't . . ." Colin mutters while he slumps down in his seat. His fake pout scores no points.

"Colin, I never want to hear you speaking like that. We raised you better than whoever put that terrible sign out for everyone to see."

Andrew looks over his sunglasses at Colin in the rearview mirror.

"Your mother is right, son. At first glance, it might appear to be humorous, but in reality, the author of that sign is probably not very intelligent or has severe mental problems." Seeing his son mulling over his comments, Andrew continues, "I bet that whoever spray-painted that phrase is a troublemaker. You don't want to ever be that person, nor do you want to encourage someone like that. You've said that you want to go to college and get into the Marshals Service, like me. Well, I guarantee the person who wrote that sign could never become a marshal."

Colin nods. He is close enough to young adulthood that he comprehends his father and appreciates being spoken to as an adult and not as a child.

"Okay, Dad. I understand."

The speed limit drops to thirty-five, and Andrew slows as they enter the City of Minden. Colin likes downtown Minden because it means that the lake, and all the fish he's going to catch, are close. At a stoplight, he notices a yellow ribbon around a light pole. Creosote from the pole has stained the ribbon like dirty tears.

He knows all about creosote, and he hates it. There is a creosote plant not far from where he rides bikes with his friends on a railroad line, next to a place that everybody calls "Slack." His father says it's an abandoned Army Air Corps base from World War Two. Colin and his friends ride their bicycles on the old runway, which is more than a mile long. The pavement is frequently stained with side-by-side tire marks from teenagers drag racing. It always stinks near the creosote plant, and everyone coughs and their eyes sting if they ride through the grayish smoke the plant belches out.

"What is that yellow ribbon for?" Colin asks as the light turns green and his dad accelerates through the intersection. Before one of the adults can answer, he spots one more. This one has a poster of a young man stapled to the light pole.

"Hey, there's another one. This one has some kind of poster on it too!" he blurts out.

Without turning, Andrew answers. "Well, son, that poster is about someone who has disappeared without a trace." He smiles and glances over at his wife. She gives him the "Don't you dare" headshake, but he plows forward anyway. Andrew uses his best "spooky" voice and offers, "Some think that there might be some kind of monster on the loose."

This, of course, is huge news for Colin, who has a fascination with science fiction, monsters, and all things spooky. "You mean, like the Fouke monster! *Wow*, that would be pretty cool!" Colin exclaims loudly. "I would love to catch him and put him in a zoo!"

In a voice Colin can't hear, Margery protests, "Do you have to joke about a 'monster'?" Genuine concern creeps into her voice. "How are you sure we can be safe?"

"It'll be fine. Besides, I have a gun."

She shakes her head in mock disgust. Andrew shakes his head too, but not enough to draw her attention. His wife is a native of a state that Southerners would describe as being on the "wrong side of the War of Northern Aggression." As such, she's never shown any aptitude with nor interest in his guns, his love of hunting, or his friends who do both.

At least she likes the outdoors. Camping, hiking, cooking the fish we catch.

Andrew lowers his voice to reply. "Anyone who tries anything stupid around my family will suffer the same fate as all my enemies did in the war."

Margery goes silent. She has never successfully gotten her husband to talk about his time in the Pacific during World War Two. However, she knows he was shot twice, killed the enemy, and all these years later holds hardness in his heart for those who attack the innocent or prey on the weak and vulnerable. The outward scars and his tattoos are her constant reminders of what he faced every day, but what was tattooed inside Andrew's soul remains unseen.

Dad refocuses his attention on Colin in the back seat.

"No, son, it's not the Fouke monster. We're too far away from Fouke. No one knows what's going on. I guess they're just hoping it stops soon."

Colin is even more intrigued. "Dad, what would you do if it is the Fouke monster?"

Margery looks at her husband. She has a good idea what he might say but waits for his response. The hunter in him wins the internal battle. Looking at his son in the rearview mirror, he answers, "Well, son, my most honest answer would be that everything can be killed. Even monsters. However, if it is not hurting people, and it's not trying to hurt us or anyone we know, then we don't need to kill it. We should just let it be."

"Just like when we're huntin', and you let some deer walk by the stand without shootin' them, and after they leave, you talk about how beautiful and regal they look?"

This is news to Margery, who raises her eyebrows and looks at her husband with renewed hope that one day he'll grow tired of hunting and stay home.

"Yep, son, just like that." He smiles as he speaks, knowing that his wife will misinterpret this new information. "And to answer your question, if it is hurting people, then, yes, it needs to be hunted and stopped."

"Maybe if it's bad and we stop it, we could eat it, right?"

Andrew laughs. "I don't know about that. I'm not sure monster meat would be good with biscuits and gravy."

Mom has heard enough about killing. "Son, let your father drive." She reserves a somewhat unhappy look for her husband.

Oblivious to his mother's displeasure, Colin opines, "I bet Mom could cook it. She can cook anything!"

Her son's compliment brings a smile to her face. "Thank you, Colin, but I'm certain your father is right. And I'd rather not have to figure out how to cook monster anyway. What would go with it? Corn? Potatoes? Green beans? Now, enough of that talk. We'll be at the lake soon."

Colin sits back, his interest in the disappearances heightened.

Nearing the turnoff to Caney Lake, traffic slows to a crawl. Lots of vehicles, most pulling boats or trailers, are going the opposite direction. As their car rolls to a stop, it's clear that every vehicle in front of them is being told to turn around in the gravel parking lot of an old, abandoned strip club.

"Hmm, what's going on?" Colin wonders aloud.

Andrew shrugs as he waits his turn. They stop about fifty feet from a shockingly green Subaru in a deep ditch. Beyond the yellow police tape, deputies and state police officers take measurements and photographs.

Colin's head bobs up and down. "Oh man, this is a crime scene! Look at all those cops, Dad. What do you think it is? Do they need your help?" Then, in a hopeful voice, he wonders aloud, "Has the monster that's been taking all those people been here?"

This question gives his mother goosebumps and upsets her stomach.

"Settle down, Colin. Let your father talk to the deputy. We're next in line."

Colin sits up to pay attention as his dad eases the car to a stop next to a deputy turning around every vehicle. Behind the young deputy is another very serious-looking state trooper.

"Sorry, sir, this road is closed. You'll have to turn around. I see you've got a boat and trailer. Going to the lake?"

"Yes, we are, Deputy. We're going to spend a few days fishing. I just started a new job and thought the family needed a bit of rest and recreation." Andrew's cop senses are piqued, so he is unhappy to ask this question within earshot of his wife, but he feels it's necessary. "Is this just an accident, or is there any reason I should be concerned for our safety when we get to the lake?"

The deputy looks towards the Subaru in the ditch.

"Where are you going? Upper or lower Caney?"

"Upper."

The deputy leans in close so his words can't be heard by the back seat. "So, maybe stay on the upper lake. We're not sure what we have here, got a guy who's just disappeared, left his car here in a huge thunderstorm that happened last night, and hasn't been seen since. Keep an eye on things, have a good time, and y'all will be just fine."

Behind the deputy, realization hits the trooper, and he takes a step towards Andrew.

"Sir, excuse me for interrupting, but aren't you Andrew McLean?"

Andrew nods. "Yes."

The trooper turns slightly and whispers to the deputy, who bobs his head in acknowledgment. When the deputy returns his attention to Andrew, he stands just a bit straighter and makes furtive movements to straighten his uniform, gun belt, and hat.

"Sir, I'm sorry you can't come this way; we're going to have the road blocked for a while. But if you're going to Caney, the east entrance to the lake is open."

Andrew considers this advice for a moment. "So, what's happening here isn't connected to the lake, and the lake is currently open?"

The deputy considers the two parts of Andrew's question. "Uh, sir, as far as I know, this is just an accident. And, yes, sir, the lake is open for business. Once you turn around, go back to Church Camp Road . . . uh, belay that; it's closed too."

"Church Camp Road is closed too?" Now Andrew is suspicious.

Behind the rookie deputy, the trooper steps up to help.

"Sir, the road to the camp is closed as a result of storm damage from last night. There were some trees across the road and such. However, you can go back to Minden, go through town, and take Lewisville Road up to the lake."

Andrew nods his understanding and shares a smile with the trooper that says, "The deputy is a rookie, isn't he?"

"Okay, I appreciate that, trooper. Thank you."

Taking notice of the two large tattoos, one on Andrew's left arm and the other on his right forearm, the deputy inquires, "You were Navy, sir? And the one on your left arm, is that a Seabee tattoo?"

Andrew looks down. "Yes, it is." He shoves the short sleeve up farther, revealing the entire tattoo. "Navy Combat Demolition Unit."

"Pacific?"

Andrew nods. If possible, the deputy stands just a tick straighter, snaps a quick salute, and offers, "Sir, thank you for your service. Your generation saved America. My dad was regular Marines; he was there. His stories about how you guys worked miracles with dynamite, bulldozers, and your bare hands are always the star of the show when he reminisces about his wartime service."

"Well, Deputy, it wasn't an easy job, but someone had to do it."

"Thank you again, sir." The deputy bends down and addresses the rest of the family. "And you folks have a great day. Enjoy your time on the lake." He directs them across the road to turn around.

"Honey, I'm not sure it's a good idea to do this," Margery mutters under her breath.

"It'll be fine. You heard the deputy. It's probably just some drunk kid who wrecked his car and wandered off."

"Hey, Dad, what did that deputy say? Why did he salute you like that?"

"His father was in World War Two, like me. It was just a sign of his respect for my military service. We're going back to town and will take another road to the lake; this one is closed because of that accident up ahead."

"But we're still going, right?" Colin asks.

"Yes, we are, son. Now sit still."

Colin sits back, happy. He relaxes, taking in the trailer parks and woods as the car accelerates back towards town.

His mother, though, is now quite uncomfortable. Her husband's lack of concern bothers her. In her experience, that's about the time when things go completely awry.

9

Clint rolls his window down as he pulls into the church camp driveway. The sheriff's deputy on guard duty recognizes him, waves, and lifts the yellow crime scene tape that has been slowly twisting in the breeze. Jerry follows in his marked cruiser. Both park on the surface lot in front of the mess hall. They stand there for a minute.

"I haven't been here in a long time."

Clint nods. "Yeah, last time for me was when . . . what was his name, uh, the Landry kid disappeared."

"Oh yeah. Oscar, if I recall. Kidnapped, or so his father said."

"Yes. Shreveport and Bossier PD scrambled their dive teams to assist the sheriff's office. I was here as divemaster, but the divers never found anything in either lake. Mr. Landry kept babbling on about people kidnapping his son, but he could provide no proof other than he looked like he'd been beaten up pretty good and his place was pretty much burned to the ground."

"I remember that. We did a dragline on both lakes several times over and never found a thing except a few guns and some car parts."

"Tragic."

"Yep. Seems to be a thing lately," Jerry agrees as he skips to another topic. "It's weird that we're not hip-deep in families, campers, staff, and children. Can you imagine if this place was full? Especially if this guy was murdered here on the beach."

"Yeah, I know what you mean. I used the radiophone to contact the camp superintendent on the way over, and he said they are closed for a week to do some repair and maintenance on the septic system."

Clint immediately regrets mentioning the septic system when he sees the look on Jerry's face. "So, you're saying if I have to, you know, go, I gotta act like a bear in the woods?"

Shaking his head, Clint grabs Jerry by the elbow and replies, "Come on, let's find everyone before you cause trouble."

They take a stone pathway that slopes down to the lake, chasing the faint sound of motorboats, water-skiers, and children from the upper lake echoing off the buildings. Noise is filtered by stately pine trees that sway in the breeze. The distant chatter of police radios piercing the otherwise peaceful setting provides a general direction.

"Webster homicide gonna take this one off your hands?" Jerry asks.

"Well, that sounds like a good idea. The superintendent said Sheriff Hancock and someone from homicide are headed here, so I'd be happy to hand this off if that's what they want. One hour ago it was just an abandoned car."

"Yeah, murder can complicate the most routine report of an abandoned car, can't it?"

"Yes, it can," Clint mutters as the woods thin and a large beach comes into view. Yellow tape cordons off the entire area. Clint and Jerry emerge from the pathway and observe several sheriff deputies and state troopers mingling. One man in a blue jumpsuit is on his knees near the water's edge, a camera around his neck and *Forensics* emblazoned in yellow block letters across his back.

Clint points at the long pile of bones stretching at least ten feet to the water's edge.

"Looks like they lead right into the lake."

"If I were to put on my crime-scene-investigator hat for a moment," Jerry mused, "I'd have a few thoughts. I guess an alligator could be responsible, but a gator would have stuck the body underwater in a hole or under a log to marinate for a while, and no gator I know of can clean bones like that. Those bones appear spotless. If this is Timmy, there is no way for them to have been picked that clean by scavengers since last night."

"Anything else strike you as weird?"

"Well, how in the world did Timmy get here from his car, which was stuck in that ditch, more than a few miles away?"

"In the middle of a severe thunderstorm," Clint finishes Jerry's sentence.

Both watch the forensic deputy lie on his belly to take a low-angle shot of the bones from up on the beach. Satisfied, he repositions and continues, taking at least two photographs from every other angle. Next, he wades about four feet in the water and turns to face the bones. They two friends share a bemused look.

Clint squats over the clothes strewn across the beach.

"Looking for anything in particular?" Jerry asks from over his shoulder.

"No, just curious about the nature of all this."

They are joined by Don Hardin, a sergeant in Clint's command.

"You get tired of traffic control?" Clint asks with a smile.

"The deputy I was with is a rook just out of field training, and he was happy to be in control of the situation, so I let him have it."

The three of them walk to where the sand-and-pebble beach meets the lake.

"These bones are weird. It's as if they were laid out like that on purpose," observes Hardin. He pauses, then continues, "Clothes too, though they're not as perfectly placed as if to get our attention—more like they were just left there."

Clint hadn't considered that. "You don't think they're posed, do you? By a serial killer, like that guy out in California? Man, that'd be very bad for business."

"Very bad for business," Jerry echoes.

Hardin remembers his interaction from the morning and has to share it with Clint and Jerry. "Oh hey, guess who I met over by Timmy's car. He was with his family, pulling a trailer, headed to the lake to go camping."

"Who?"

"That new US marshal, Andrew McLean."

Clint is surprised. "The guy who just got appointed a couple of months ago from over in Texas?"

"More importantly, you mean the guy who last year walked in on a bank robbery over in Dallas and killed all three robbers with just three shots?" Jerry adds.

Hardin nods vigorously. "The same. And I learned something else about him that I didn't know."

"What's that?"

"He had on a short-sleeve shirt, and I spotted a US Navy emblem on his right forearm, and above the elbow, covering his entire left bicep, is a colorful Seabee tat. Get this, the guy was in a combat demolition unit in the Pacific during World War Two!"

Jerry, a master chief sergeant in the Air Force during the Vietnam War, whistles softly. "Seabees, huh? Man, that's interesting information. Wonder if he's still proficient with explosives."

"They say once you've been bitten by that bug, it never goes away," Clint offers. "Might be a good thing to remember about the guy. You say he was going to Caney?"

"Yep. Had a kid in the car, and his wife. Little silver, teardrop trailer, and a johnboat on top of the car. Brand-new Chrysler sedan. Seemed like a nice guy. Reserved, though."

Clint and Jerry share a look, but Jerry speaks first.

"Well, we should go over there when we leave here, just to introduce ourselves."

Clint nods. "I agree. A combat demolition unit? That's pretty hardcore. I'd like to meet this guy."

The forensics guy stands and joins them. "Couldn't help but overhear you guys. Those combat demolition guys were the talk of the war in the Pacific. Built airstrips in the middle of shootouts with Japs, repaired buildings and military facilities literally on enemy lines as bombs fell on them. I heard of one group repairing an aircraft carrier as kamikaze pilots dive-bombed it! They were badass beyond badass. If he was truly a Seabee, then he's a good man to have on your side."

Clint, Jerry, and Don remain silent, so the forensics deputy begins reviewing the steps he's taken. "Alright, so, after sweeping the water with a steel sieve—"

Jerry interrupts, "A steel sieve? Why in the world do you have a steel sieve?"

The deputy looks pleased to explain. "It's the newest thing for water investigations and evidence recovery. I guess I've never used it when you've been divemaster. Soon as I heard of it, just made sense that we should have one, so I talked to the sheriff, and he said to buy it."

Jerry looks unconvinced, while Clint's expression transmits the humor he sees in the situation. Looking at Clint, Jerry shrugs, laughs, and asks, "What? It's a legitimate question!"

Clint smiles as the deputy continues, "Right, so, after sweeping the water all along the beachfront, I found no bones or clothes there. What we did find here, by my best estimation, is a complete human skeleton. All 206 bones, even the little ones. And before you question me on that, I counted most of them."

Even though he knows the answer, Clint asks, "Male? Female?"

Bending to one knee, the deputy points at what looks like a pelvis.

"See how closed off the pelvic bones are? The female pelvis is wider, with more space between the interior of the bony structure. This tells me it's a male."

"Any marks on the bones? Like, teeth marks, or anything that indicates predation?"

"While I haven't put each bone under a microscope, just my cursory examination shows nothing out of the ordinary. No teeth marks, either human or animal."

Clint and Jerry share a look at that remark.

"And no weapon use indicated. The bones are pristine, like they're from one of those medical-school skeletons used in a classroom. The only thing that looks weird is the slight red tint to them." He laughs briefly. "It's like they'd been soaked in some Red River mud for a while. The white material in his underwear, shirt, and socks have that same redness to them. I don't know if he got dragged through the mud last night or yesterday or was caught up in a flash flood of muddy water, which doesn't make much sense, but you know, crime frequently doesn't make sense at first blush."

"Well, the lake isn't red, right?"

"Not completely. I guess the bottom might be in some of the shallower spots over where there are cattails. The little bayou off the lower-lake spillway feeds into a bayou marshland. I bet it's muddy there."

Clint considers this information. "Seen anything like this before?"

The forensics deputy shakes his head as he answers. "Nope." He appears unconcerned though. "Once I collect the bones and clothes, I'll run them over to your lab in Bossier City. It should be easy enough to identify the discoloration at that point. I can also make some calls to other departments, see if they've had any cases with just bones and clothing."

Clint nods in agreement. "That's a good idea. Keep me informed if you come up with anything." He then turns to Hardin, who was tasked with delivering the news to Timmy's family down in Minden. "How'd it go with the family? You learn anything useful from them?"

"No. Timmy's family is as baffled as we are. Said Timmy stopped by in the evening yesterday, just before it started to rain. He was pretty hyped up. Told them that he'd won three hundred dollars in the Louisiana lottery. His mother said he was going to the track later this weekend."

"I don't play the lottery. I wonder how the lottery pays out winning tickets. I'm guessing in cash?"

Hardin shrugs and replies, "I don't play either. I never win anything, so why try?"

Jerry pulls a pair of black gloves from a rear pocket and dons them, then goes to the evidence bag containing Timmy's personal effects.

"Jerry, look for—well, let's make this easy: three one-hundred-dollar bills in his wallet."

Jerry rummages through the clear plastic bag and comes up with an alligator wallet. He smiles and holds it up for Clint and Hardin to see.

"If it was a gator that got him, maybe it was payback for this hideous wallet. Might have been a cousin!"

Clint shakes his head and smiles but presses the question once again.

"Focus, Jerry. Three hundred dollars." Jerry produces three new hundred-dollar bills from the depths of the wallet. A condom also falls out, as does a business card with the phone number written in felt-tip pen. The card stock is stained pinkish red.

"Well, at least he believed in safe sex."

Hardin snickers. "He'd need to if that card has Shelia's name on it."

Jerry picks up the business card. "Smeared as it is, I can still read the name," he says with a grin.

Clint gets worried. "Maybe we don't tell Becky about this. She might think Shelia was involved in his disappearance and do something stupid. But, also maybe, someone should go talk to Shelia. She needs to be told that Timmy is dead. Maybe she saw him yesterday after all."

Hardin wears a resigned expression. "I suppose I'll go do it since I talked to his family."

Clint nods. He certainly doesn't want to; besides, his captain's bars outweigh Hardin's sergeant stripes. He's just glad he didn't have to gently shove Hardin towards conducting the interview.

"Great idea. Thank you. Just file a supplemental to my original report when you get done. Include anything you think might be interesting or pertinent."

"Will do," Hardin says and turns on his heel, heading back up the hill to the parking lot.

Jerry sidles up to Clint. "Well? What now?"

Clint squints and contemplates Jerry's question. With the toe of his left boot, he rolls pebbles on the edge of the lake. "I'd like to know what other local unsolved homicides might match what we have here."

Concerned, Jerry says, "Well, that's in your ballpark or the sheriff's.

I can guess that there are always unsolved cases. We don't have too many in Minden. I seem to recall bulletins on cases where only bones were recovered. Some here, some in neighboring parishes. I think there have been a few cases down south, and with the FBI, over in Texas. I recall seeing something over the teletype about it."

Clint nods. "Same here, but the murders stopped, if I recall. Almost like the criminal got religion or went to prison. While I'm not too keen on the media getting ahold of the details on this particular case, I'm curious about how these similar situations have escaped the notice of the press. They're usually all over disappearances and murders."

Jerry shakes his head. "Maybe the details are so bizarre even they don't believe them?"

"Bizarre? You mean, like what we have in front of us right now?"

Jerry looks his way and nods.

"Well, okay then. I guess I need to get up to speed on these other cases. Maybe we can head to your office when this wraps up."

"Sounds like a plan. Say," Jerry says to the deputy, who is packing up his gear, "you said you're taking all that back to the state lab in Bossier?"

"Yep. It should be a few days before we get any results. It will be almost impossible to determine cause of death or even time of death. There are no tissues to sample for temperature, no way to get a toxicology screen, either. I don't even think the bone marrow is still there."

Clint is stunned silent at hearing this fact spoken so casually. Jerry beats Clint to the punch: "What do you mean the bone marrow is gone? How can you tell that?"

The deputy holds up a large bone and responds, "Every connective tissue is gone from the bones. No tendons, no muscles, nothing. Take this femur, for example. It's the largest and strongest bone in the human body. All the big, heavy bones here are too light. Marrow accounts for about five percent of the total body weight on the average human." The deputy hefts the bone and holds it out with both hands. He casually tosses it about a foot in the air like a high school baton twirler would a baton. "These bones are way too light. Honestly, I bet it will be difficult to do the normal due diligence we'd give a dead body."

Clint shakes his head in disbelief. "Back to the marrow. What can do that?"

"No idea."

"Seen it before?"

The forensics deputy shakes his head. "Nope. In some instances of cannibalism, flesh is cut from the bones, focusing on the larger muscle groups. Then, they break the bones apart to get at the marrow, which is fat-rich and quite nutritious. However, that's usually a last-ditch effort to survive."

Clint and Jerry share a skeptical look and silence for a few seconds.

Jerry offers a few thoughts. "Well, first, remind me not to spend the apocalypse anywhere near you because what you know about stripping the flesh from bones kinda freaks me out. And next, can you tell if this is human predation? What story can the bones tell about the victim or the murderer?"

"Honestly, I don't have an answer right now. Though, I don't see any blade marks on the bones, which you'd need to get them this clean. We should eventually be able to tell what this red tint is. I bet we can get a ton of information from the clothing. I'll put a priority rush on them since that's the best source we have. My partner is still over with the car. Something in there might be helpful."

"Great," Clint grunts. "Thanks. I'd appreciate it if you could get anything important over to me as soon as you can."

Everyone glances up the hill towards the parking lot as the beeping of a large vehicle rolls through the woods to the beach area.

The deputy says, "Guess the meat wagon is here."

"More like the meatless wagon, if you ask me," Jerry quips, pointing towards the pile of bones on the beach. "The bone wagon?"

Clint rubs his temple and tries his best to look offended. "Seriously, Jerry?"

Jerry shrugs and raises both arms at the same time. "What? Was it something I said?"

Shaking his head, Clint replies, "You know, when I was a kid, I always wondered why, when I ate cantaloupes in the summer and swallowed the seeds, a cantaloupe didn't grow inside my stomach."

"Yeah?" Jerry asks, curious about this latest gem of Clint wisdom.

"Yeah. Sometimes I wonder if maybe you stuck some cantaloupe seeds into your ears, and one grew where your brain should be."

Every cop within earshot laughs.

Jerry laughs too and has only one answer. "You know, if, and I say *if,* I had done something like that, then my brain would be pretty tasty. If only that were true, I'd always have a snack handy!"

Clint laughs and takes Jerry by the arm. "Come on, troublemaker. Let's take that brain of yours over to the campground and introduce ourselves to the new US marshal. If we get the opportunity, we can bounce some of the details about Timmy's murder off him. It might be helpful to get a federal marshal's take on the crime.

10

Andrew and Colin have just finished wrestling with a mesh tent designed to keep bugs and mosquitos from swarming over the picnic table when Colin sees two police cars slowly roll into the campground.

"Hey, Dad, look who's coming our direction," he says as he pounds the last tent stake into the ground with a hatchet.

Andrew lifts his head. "I see them, son. Why don't you go help your mother get the rest of our things out of the trailer?"

"Okay. Do you think they want to talk to you?"

"If they stop here, you'll know the answer to that at the same time I do." *Maybe this is a courtesy visit from local law enforcement.*

As the cars inch in his direction, he notices one is a state trooper, the other a local marshal. As a matter of protocol, he's met the Shreveport city marshal and the city marshal across the Red River in Bossier City, but not the marshal from Minden.

The two cars slow, which draws the attention of the campers in nearby trailers and tents.

Clint and Jerry chat on a sideband to the police radio channel inside their respective cars.

"So, how will we recognize him?" Jerry asks. "I don't expect he'll have a big shingle out with the US Marshals badge on it. Knowing some of the people who camp up here, that wouldn't be the best idea."

"Well, Hardin said he was driving a brand-new Chrysler, had a silver teardrop trailer. Those are what most of us in law enforcement call clues. Kinda specific clues."

"Oh yeah, clues. I've heard of those before," Jerry drawls.

Clint smirks as Jerry's voice comes back over the radio.

"I know you're smirking; I can hear it from here."

"You're right."

"Figures. Hey, wait. Is that the car and trailer there by the water?"

Clint nods and then keys the transmit button. "Yep. Look, even has a Louisiana-shaped cutout with their names already hanging from a tree."

Both men slow their cars, shut off the engines, and get out. Andrew looks for his wife, who has just stepped out of the trailer with items destined for the picnic table.

"Andrew? What's going on?"

He shakes his head and shrugs. "Part of the job, honey. You heard that trooper at the roadblock who recognized me. I guess he must have mentioned seeing me to his boss, who thought it okay to come say hello. I'll talk with them for a few minutes and send them on their way."

She hands the items in her hands to Colin and points at the table. "Colin, put these on the table, please." She adds with some emotion in her voice, "And be careful with those knives." Satisfied that Colin will do as she has requested, she looks once more at the two cars and then steps back into the trailer.

Clint and Jerry smile as they approach. Clint speaks first. "Marshal?"

Andrew nods and holds out his right hand. "Andrew McLean. How are you gentlemen doing today?"

"Clinton Ward, Louisiana State Police, but please call me Clint." He turns to Jerry, who adds, "Jerry Thomson, city marshal for Minden."

Andrew offers, "I've met your counterparts in Shreveport and Bossier, but I haven't ventured over to Minden yet. It's a pleasure to meet you two. What brings you to Caney Lake Campground? Hope this is a social call and not official business."

The men share a look which telegraphs "Not quite," and Andrew's cop senses kick in. Concerned, he moves away from the campsite. Both men fall in with him as he heads towards the trunk of Clint's cruiser and leans against the cool metal.

"Okay, what gives? I assumed this was just a courtesy call. Is there something that I can help you with? Something on your mind?"

"Well, Marshal—"

"Call me Andrew, please. I'm not on duty. We're in a campground. I'm not wearing my gun, nor do I have my credentials in my back pocket. Just Andrew, please."

"Alright, Andrew. We came to see you sort of as a courtesy and sort of on official business."

Huh. Well, this should be interesting.

"One of my on-the-ball troopers recognized you over at the checkpoint."

"Yes, I know. I appreciate that he didn't broadcast that fact to everyone."

"Yeah, he's a good man. Solid cop. But listen, you recall that greenish little Subaru that was in the ditch? Right in front of where you were directed to turn around?"

Andrew nods but says nothing.

Jerry picks up the conversation. "You see, sir"—the look on Andrew's face makes Jerry reframe his words—"uh, Andrew, Timmy Johnson, the man who owns that car, is a local troublemaker. He went missing in the thunderstorm that happened here last night."

"Correct me if I'm wrong, but missing persons aren't usually top priorities for a city marshal or a state trooper, right?"

"You are correct on that assumption. However, the lines of responsibility get a bit grayer when the owner of that car is found murdered."

Clint pauses as "murdered" lingers between the three men for a moment. He continues, "His bones were found strewn across the beach over at the church camp on the lower lake."

Andrew replies, "You're telling me there was a murder over on the lower lake?" Andrew starts to point towards the spillway and dam separating the two lakes but stops short, given that his wife might be watching. "That's not quite a quarter mile away from where we are standing. I assume the forensics team from Webster Sheriff must have worked the area of the murder. Did they get anything useful from the body? Have you identified any suspects?"

"Well, you see, that's where we hit a bit of a snag. We did locate Mr. Johnson, but fact of the matter is there was nothing left of him but bones. All 206 of them. Oh, his clothes were there too, but not much else."

Andrew is intrigued now. "Bones? No meat, tissue, muscle, internal organs?"

Jerry and Clint shake their heads almost in unison as Clint replies, "All gone. The only thing left of our victim are his bones, which, I would add, had an unusual tint to them. The crime-scene guy thought that fact was interesting, but he can't conclude anything until the state lab examines the bones in Bossier City. He did say that all 206 bones from the human body were there. He also thinks that even the bone marrow is gone."

"You said the bones had no marrow and a slight red tint?"

"Why? Does that sound familiar to you?"

Andrew nods slowly. "Maybe." He shifts his position against the police car. "Sounds like a couple of cases I heard about over in East Texas. One at Lake O' the Pines and another on the Texas side of Caddo Lake. For some reason, I think there's been something like what you described over near the Mississippi line, too. I know the FBI worked the two I mentioned in Texas because there was some belief that the perp crossed state lines to commit the crimes."

"You don't say?" Jerry wonders aloud. "Wonder why we haven't heard about these."

Clint opines, "Jerry, it's the FBI. I'm sure they took over the investigation and never did anything about it. Who knows why they do the things they do?"

Andrew laughs in agreement. "I see you've met them."

"Yes, and I'd prefer not to involve them in what we have here, given their propensity to swoop in, take over, and then do nothing."

"Sorry to say this, but given what you described, the circumstances seem similar enough that there might be a connection to those older cases. We thought we had a fugitive serial killer on our hands, which is how the Marshals Service got involved. But whoever was committing the crimes stopped or moved on." Andrew scratches his chin. "My wife's not gonna like this. She was already a little skeptical about staying here after my son pointed out the 'missing' posters in town."

Jerry's face clearly expresses his unhappiness. "Yeah, I wish they'd stop putting those things up where the tourists can see them."

Andrew contemplates what to do next. "Alright, this is just between us for the moment. If my wife finds out about this, we'll be packing up and heading back to Shreveport in record time."

"Well, we won't tell her then," Clint says with a conspiratorial whisper.

"Agreed. Mum's the word from me!" Jerry concurs.

A look of concern crosses Clint's face. "By the way, are you armed? We can certainly provide you with a firearm or two, at least to protect yourself and your family as we sort this out."

Andrew smiles wryly. "I'm a typical cop on vacation. I brought two pistols and a twelve-gauge shotgun, and enough ammo to hold off a small army. But don't tell my wife: she'll say that doesn't seem to be very camping-friendly."

Jerry and Clint share a look that conveys their approval.

"Hey, one last thing."

Andrew cocks his eyebrow. "Yeah?"

"Well, the trooper who recognized you was pretty impressed by your tattoos. How long were you in the Navy?"

"Did twenty years. Once I separated, I went right into the Marshals Service. Got appointed to my current position six months ago. Before that, I was chief deputy marshal over in Dallas."

"Yes, we, uh, know about your time in Dallas," Jerry says with a slight chuckle.

"What about the other tattoo?" Clint inquires.

"You mean this one?" Andrew says, rolling up his sleeve to reveal the large, colorful tattoo of a yellow jacket with a machine gun.

Clint and Jerry admire the artwork for a few moments.

"Seabees, huh? Man, I bet you saw some of the action," Clint says. "I was a drill instructor for the Coast Guard during the mid to late sixties, and Jerry there was with the Air Force Office of Special Investigations in Nam at about the same time."

Andrew is impressed that both men served and directs his first question towards Jerry.

"OSI? That's great. I knew a few OSI agents when I was attached as an instructor at the Federal Law Enforcement Training Center over in Georgia. I'm curious, what did OSI do in Vietnam—that is, if you can talk about it?"

"Since we've declared victory of sorts and have moved on, I guess I can talk about my work there. My primary job was to secure and remove classified payloads and hardware from aircraft that had been shot down."

Andrew raises his eyebrows. "Behind enemy lines?"

"Yes sir."

"Seriously? That was a job? I would have thought we'd have self-destruct mechanisms on aircraft for situations just like that. Couldn't the pilot just set fire to the plane and call it good?"

"Some could, but if the pilots did not survive the crash, or they ejected and didn't have time to destroy what the Russians or Chinese might get their hands on, they'd send my team in. We'd do whatever it took to either retrieve or destroy whatever the pointy heads up in DC told us to retrieve or destroy."

Jerry considers that Andrew is not used to his off-kilter sense of humor and finishes with "Uh, you know, the big-head, ivory-tower guys who run the show from the Pentagon. The guys with little-to-no combat experience or knowledge. Those guys."

Andrew laughs and decides to plow ahead with his next question. "Well, Jerry, I know we just met and all, but if you don't mind, exactly how did a, well, a Black Air Force OSI special agent end up in Minden, Louisiana, and manage to get himself elected city marshal?"

Jerry doesn't hesitate. "Yeah, it's been interesting. I grew up just south of Shreveport, in a small community called Keithville. Played football, which is how Clint and I met. He was a safety; I was a wide receiver. After high school, I got drafted, and my test results said I would make a good military policeman. I was thrilled, given I wasn't interested in being a pilot and I didn't want to get stuck loading things that go boom onto fighter jets."

Jerry pauses and chuckles, which makes Andrew curious about what is coming next.

"I always figured the only reason I got the classified job was because I was a little bit more expendable than some of the White soldiers. But we all fought the same enemy over there, so eventually, they just saw my Black colleagues and me as soldiers. As you can imagine, some didn't like that I had a badge and a gun, but to be entirely clear, most of the men I put into handcuffs were criminals or had ties to a certain white-sheet-loving group.

"Honestly, in the Air Force, the color of my skin was never a consideration. Could I do the job and do it in such a way that I got results that didn't embarrass the brass? Yes. And that's what mattered. When my last tour in Vietnam ended, I asked for and got assigned to OSI Region Eight, located over at Barksdale. I was thrilled to be back home, even though some citizens hated us for being over in Vietnam. At Barksdale, I was the senior agent, running a team whose job was to try and defeat the security of our nuclear weapons storage. We were also tasked with corrupting local airmen at bars, getting them to reveal classified information about nuclear weapons, tactics, aircraft, and storage security details to hookers or strippers, stuff like that."

Andrew cocks his head sideways and raises an eyebrow. Jerry continues quickly since he knows where Andrew's mind has gone.

"The hookers and strippers were also OSI, brought in from another office so no one would recognize them. When I retired, I just wasn't ready to stop the cop thing. As far as getting elected, Minden isn't the backwater redneck heaven some would think. Sure, I faced resistance. The good ole boys who still fly the battle flag of the Confederacy were concerned, but they also had only ever had a White marshal. Everywhere I campaigned, I stressed my experience. It's not Jim Crow days anymore, the times are changing, and I hope the handwriting is on the wall regarding discrimination based on skin color. Eventually, the agitators who only complained about the color of my skin accepted me or moved on to their next stupid crusade."

"Well, I am pleased to get to know you. We have lots of Black veterans in the Marshals Service, so I'm sure your experiences in Vietnam and then with OSI make you a pretty awesome city marshal. And I'd love to chat you up someday about your operation to 'corrupt' airmen. I bet that was a lot of fun!"

"Indeed, it was."

Andrew turns to Clint and asks, "And what about you, Mr. Drill Instructor?"

"Enlisted right out of high school. Eventually made my way to the Coast Guard Investigative Service, where I spent the majority of my time until I transitioned over to the academy. Finished my hitch as a master chief petty officer."

"You gentlemen have some impressive credentials to be roaming around North Louisiana. I believe with you two on this case, the suspect doesn't stand a chance."

"Thank you, Andrew. Now, what about you?"

Andrew crosses his arms, showing thick muscles which strain at the fabric of his shirt.

"Well, I was three years into college when the war began. I went to enlist in the Navy but was talked into joining ROTC and completing my degree. I graduated and went to Navy recruit training and then right into Officer Candidate School. After OCS, I attended the Naval Construction Training Center and the Advanced Base Depot schools. The instructors at both did as much as possible to prepare us for wartime construction operations through instruction in trade skills, military discipline, and advanced combat training."

"How'd you end up with the Seabees?"

"My father's family was in construction, and I knew earthmovers, dirt, and dynamite. I was around all that my whole young life. After OCS and all the Navy schools, I got assigned to the Bureau of Yards and Docks."

Seeing puzzlement on both faces, Andrew feels a quick explanation is in order. "They're responsible for building and maintaining Navy yards, dry docks, and other facilities relating to ship construction, maintenance, and repair. It was a good job, but I heard rumors that the government was forming construction battalions and sending them to the Pacific theater to rebuild places destroyed by the Japs. Frankly, against the wishes of my father and family, I couldn't sign my name on my transfer papers fast enough. In my mind, a duty station near a beach was a great idea—I grew up around the water. I guess I hadn't thought through the fact that the enemy was going to be shooting at us the whole time.

"Anyway, I was immediately transferred to a new command, the construction battalion." Andrew pauses for a moment. Clint and Jerry see his war experiences playing out in his mind, behind his green eyes. They wait patiently.

"I was attached to one of the first five Seabee battalions the Navy deployed. After training, we were immediately sent to the Pacific. Although technically designated to support combat operations, we frequently found ourselves under fire and fighting once we landed and started to work on restoring airfields, piers, ammunition bunkers, supply depots, hospitals, fuel tanks, and barracks side by side with the Marines."

"Did you spend most of your time on dry land?"

"Not entirely. We split the detachments into commands, and I ended up on the USS *Enterprise*, working to repair her even as she engaged enemy ships and dive bombers." Andrew chuckles. "We worked to repair the forward elevator while she fought and sank the Jap carrier *Hiei*. I'd like to say that earned us shore leave, but in reality, we just moved on to the next impossible task."

"Guadalcanal?"

"Yes. We were all over the central and northern Pacific as our forces pushed back the Jap army and navy. The sixth Seabees detachment even worked with the scientists who assembled the bomb used on Hiroshima."

Clint's voice goes up an octave. "Really?"

Andrew nods. "That team built the facility used to store and assemble the bomb components. They also stood guard duty to protect the scientists while they worked. When the bomb was loaded into the *Enola Gay*, it was at an advance base the Seabees had constructed for the sole purpose of delivering the bomb to our enemies." He pauses, laughs, then continues with "I'm sure you guys have heard the old saying 'Marines will be guarding the gate to Heaven, but the road there was built by Seabees.'"

As Andrew's voice trails off, it's clear he's finished discussing his service. Clint and Jerry both hold out their hands. Andrew grasps Clint's first, then Jerry's, who smiles and says, "We're honored to have met you. It is unfortunate to be under these circumstances. However, we will follow up with your office. If we have anything of interest, we'll circle back to you with it. How's that sound?"

"Sounds like a solid plan. We're here all week, so if I'm not here at camp, I'll be on the water with my son."

The door slams on Andrew's trailer, and Colin runs to his father's side.

"Clint, Jerry, this is my son, Colin. Son, say hello to our new friends."

"Nice to meet you," Colin says as he shakes their hands. He eyes the badge on Jerry's belt and asks, "Sir, your police car says Minden on the side, but I see the star of a marshal on your belt. But you don't work for my dad, do you?"

"No, Colin. I'm the city marshal for Minden. My job is a lot like your dad's, but not for the federal government. My office protects the city courthouse and the judges. We conduct arrest warrants, do civil papers." Colin looks confused, so Jerry tries to explain. "Civil papers are when someone sues someone else, or a landlord wants to evict a tenant who hasn't paid rent—things like that."

Colin nods his understanding, so Jerry continues. "Sometimes, we assist the local police departments or the state police with traffic control. And, like your dad, we also focus on criminal fugitives. Honestly, we do a little bit of everything."

"Son, according to Louisiana state law, the marshal is the executive officer of the court. They have the same powers and authority as a sheriff as they execute the orders and mandates of the court. One difference between his job and mine is that he was elected by the voters in his city, so he had to campaign and convince people to vote for him, just like a mayor, or a governor."

Colin looks newly impressed and offers, "Oh. That's cool. That must have been hard to do." Turning to Clint, he says, "And I've never met a Louisiana state trooper before. It's nice to meet you both. One day, I want to be a US marshal, just like my dad."

"That's great, Colin. With a man like your father guiding you, you'll have what it takes to become a marshal."

Colin nods his acceptance of this future challenge and looks at his father. "I was told to come get you. Mom is counting on frying fish for dinner."

Jerry and Clint laugh as Andrew claps his hands and says, "Well, men, I have my orders. Time to go fishing!" Seeing Jerry and Clint's concern, Andrew adds in a low voice, hoping Colin can't hear, "Of course, we will be careful while out on the water."

"Good deal. Like I said, if we come up with something, we'll be back in touch. Have fun fishing."

"Thank you," Andrew says, turning back to camp. With some enthusiasm, he pats Colin on the back and says, "Well, son, you ready to hit the lake?"

"You bet!"

"Great, why don't you go ask your mother for two Cokes. My tackle box is still in the trunk. I'll go get it and meet you at the boat."

"Okay, Dad!"

As Colin retrieves two Cokes, Andrew goes to the trunk of his car. Reaching into a canvas bag, he retrieves his holstered Colt Series

70 forty-five-caliber sidearm and a leather pouch that holds two extra magazines. He puts the gun and magazines in the bottom of the tackle box and closes the lid.

"Always be prepared isn't just for the Boy Scouts," he mutters to himself.

11

Dennis honks the horn on his tow truck and waits in front of the chain-link fence at the Minden Police Department's impoundment lot, just off Highway 80, west of town. He's about to honk again when an annoyed-looking security guard comes out. The guard's expression lightens and when he's within earshot he asks, "Dennis, whose car did you repo this time?" Before Dennis can answer, though, he laughs because he recognizes the car. "Oh my God, is that Timmy Johnson's car you have hooked?"

Dennis nods to confirm the guard's suspicions and hands over the paperwork.

"Yep, this ugly thing belongs to one Timothy James Johnson, whereabouts currently unknown. But I can tell ya where his car is."

The guard looks startled. "What do you mean, 'whereabouts currently unknown'?"

"Man, Timmy is capital M-I-S-S-I-N-G. You didn't hear? He's, like, goners. Outta here. Flew the coop. Trooper found his car abandoned over on Dorcheat, near the Caney Lake Campground turnoff. No sign of Timmy."

The guard whistles and arches his eyebrows. "Oh man. Please tell me Becky showed up and made a scene."

"Yes, she did. And, wow, despite the years and the drugs, she's still a looker!"

"Nice," the guard mutters with a lecherous smile as he begins turning a large metal hand crank to open the gate.

"Don't tell me that darn motor is broke again. Can't the city mechanical guys figure out what's wrong with it?"

"Yeah, the motor burnt out couple of days ago. The kicker is it's so old the parts aren't available anymore. I hear they might have a new one on order from someone's cousin, might even fall off a truck, you get the gist. Anyway, get in here and drop that car, Mr. Tow Boy."

"Drop that car, Mr. Tow *Man*," Dennis replies. He becomes all business as he hands a clipboard to the guard. "As this here paperwork says, the car is an impoundment from the state police. Want me to back it up to the fence over in the corner there?" he asks, pointing towards the back corner of the lot.

The guard hands the paperwork back to Dennis. "Yes. Don't take too long. The Dodgers are playing the Pirates, and I got a bet with one of my guys."

"Gotcha." Dennis executes a three-point turn and backs up. Seconds later, he feels the Subaru softly push into the chain-link fence. Pulling up about a foot, he shifts the tow truck into park, gets out, and manipulates the controls to drop the Subaru gently onto the pavement. The sound of a small spring-fed creek catches his attention, and he peers through the fence.

"I forget Cooley Branch is there." He stops and revels in the gurgling of the water as it slips over the rocks and other debris.

"What'd you say?" the guard asks, unsure if Dennis is trying to be friendly.

"Just saying I forget that Cooley Branch is there. It runs right through town to the gravel pits over in Dixie Inn, doesn't it?"

"Yep. Clean, clear water too. I hear the shine it makes tastes pretty good too."

Dennis laughs. "Don't know anything about that, for sure." Jumping into his tow truck, he puts it into gear. "Yet another awesome job by Dennis." Exiting the lot, he waves a friendly goodbye to the security guard.

"See ya later!" he says. Turning right out of the lot onto Highway 80 he adds, "Hope you lose the bet on your game."

The security guard smirks as he pulls the gate shut and locks it.

Underneath the Subaru, the piece of the newcomer severed by Timmy's machete awakens. It senses this is a new place. Liquid is close, which bears investigating. It drops to the warm pavement and luxuriates in the heat for a moment but knows that the surface, made of the same material on which it was first separated from its original, is hot and has a bad taste. The subdued heat also drains moisture and strength.

Slowly, it manages to slide under the fence and slip into Cooley Branch without a sound. The water is indeed cool, and it hurts somewhat, but it spreads out to minimize the pain as it floats just below the surface along with the current. It adjusts and rests.

The water ahead is disturbed when a raccoon wades in, searching for crevices on the banks where small prey could be hiding. With the quick snap of a tendril, it surprises the raccoon, who fights but eventually becomes the prey. It slowly disappears into the thing that resembles a simple clump of mud drifting just under the surface of the water. Soon bones and fur accompany the other debris that floats downstream, subject to the whims of the current.

12

Evan Wilson looks in the rearview mirror to make sure no one has followed them. His Ford F-250 four-wheel truck easily tackles the one-lane dirt track cutting deep into the piney woods just south of the Minden city limits.

"We going back to where we was before?" his best friend and regular partner in crime, Earl, asks from the passenger seat.

Evan nods but doesn't say anything. He keeps driving until he is deep enough in the trees to escape discovery, then backs up to a wooded area of bamboo and scrub pine. A cloud of red dust envelopes their feet as they exit the truck.

"Alright, let's get to work. Don't want to be here longer than necessary."

Not too far away, moving lazily across the bottom of the deepest spot in this section of Cooley Branch, the piece of the original newcomer severed by Timmy's machete tastes something awful. It recoils in pain. Too young to have grown an external shell for protection, the slice thins to its limits in an attempt to minimize exposure to this new threat. Doing so, it looks more like a thin piece torn off a brown paper grocery bag than the alien predator it is. The pain is intense, and in desperation, it lifts off the bottom and tries to alter its molecular structure. Unfortunately, since it is a mere slice of the whole, it lacks the molecular genetic memory and knowledge to fully complete the very complex task necessary for its survival.

Twenty feet in front of the slice, Evan and Earl prepare to dump the second load of their homemade pesticide and wood preservative onto the ground next to the stream. They had hoped to use the stuff in a start-up landscaping venture, but no one had hired them, and Earl's spouse was clear regarding the noxious liquid; it went, or she did.

"Man, I can still smell that last batch we dumped," Earl says as he scrunches up his nose.

"Yep, it's just over there," Evan says, nodding towards the dark splotches on the ground twenty feet away. He works to loosen the plastic cap on one of the 1,000-gallon containers in the bed of his truck. "You sure you ain't told no one? You're not turnin' snitch on me, are you? Remember, snitches git stitches!"

This gets Earl riled up. "Of course not! Hey, I didn't ask the first time, but why can't we just dump this stuff into the creek?"

"You know how the first batch almost burned the barn down 'cause you tossed your lit butt too close to the some we spilt on the floor?"

"Yeah."

"Well, this stuff is just too dangerous. It caught fire easily. I bet that even if we dump it in the water, it could still catch fire. Besides, this gets in the water, I 'spect it will kill anything it touches. Don't want to be the person who kills a buncha fish downstream. So, it stays here, in the woods. Eventually, it might make it to the water, but wet dirt after all that rain should prevent it from sparking. I figure it'll also dilute enough so it's not that toxic."

While he explains his thoughts, Evan removes the cap on the second bladder, and more of their sort-of-coal-tar creosote spurts out of the tank. The thick, oily liquid, somewhat amber to black as the sun strikes it, sloshes away from the truck. The truck creaks and the springs groan a bit as the load eases.

"Good thing you got them heavy-duty springs installed. I bet this stuff weighs a couple thousand pounds."

"Yep. I figured we'd be hauling some big loads—lumber, old railroad ties, bricks or pavers, stuff like that."

"I'm glad we didn't end up spraying this on someone's house or barn. I think they'd have told us to take it off cuz it stinks!" His brain is working on a problem as he speaks. "But can't it still catch fire if it sits in a puddle like it is?"

"Well, the way I see it, this ground is mostly soft clay and sand. It's porous. This stuff will sink in and get covered by the trees, limbs, pine straw, and whatever else is out here. Won't anyone ever know it's there."

"I don't know, but I think the ground is red clay. And red clay won't suck up all this liquid. It's gonna run off into Cooley Branch anyway. It's gonna kill some animals or fish," Earl mutters as he points towards the stream just beyond the stand of bamboo and pine trees.

"Shut up, Earl. You overthink things sometimes," Evan says.

Ten feet away, the dark liquid flows down a depression in the clay and directly into Cooley Branch. The chemicals form a discolored circular pattern on the water's surface, which adheres to leaves and other debris and sinks to the bottom, bringing oily death to the previously clear creek.

Just below the surface, the newcomer slice encounters more of the toxic mess. It recognizes some of the material that resembles the building blocks of its own life, but the subatomic structures are tainted, twisted. Something is seriously wrong with the taste as well. It has never encountered such material in its short life. It exerts too much energy in anger and not enough towards survival.

The luxury of the liquid it has been surrounded by is replaced by corruption and death. Too late, it realizes whatever is destroying its liquid medium also affects its metabolism. It is engulfed in the hateful, dark liquid and tries to move. It cannot. Sunlight breaks through the trees, and it is further immobilized by the rays as they dance around the water column.

With immense grief, it realizes there may be no way to survive, so it tries separating its parts into smaller pieces in hopes that something of it will continue to live, only to discover it is too weak from the initial exposure to successfully complete the action. As its life ends, it merges completely with the messy black goo. Eventually, pieces of it separate from the whole, but they are entirely dead, left to tumble in the stream with the other lifeless things killed by Evan and Earl's illegal dumping.

On land and unaware of what their chemical is doing, Evan tilts the plastic bladder and empties the last of the chemical onto the ground. He sees the dark remnants pool in a depression, so he tosses a few downed pine tree limbs over the puddle. As an added measure, he shovels some dirt over the whole mess, then replaces the cap on the bladder and looks around. They are still alone. Every minute they linger increases the possibility of being discovered.

"There, see? I told you we'd be okay. Now, let's get out of here before someone comes along on a four-wheeler and starts asking questions!"

He jumps into the truck and turns the key, gunning the engine. He spins the tires just as Earl closes his door. Racing down the dirt track, they spread dust and debris in their wake. He smiles as the large, off-road tires bite into the ground and the truck lurches.

"Yee-haw!" he yells out the open window when they careen onto William Brown Road and out of the woods. Evan makes the turn towards town, intent on acquiring much more beer and weed. Earl fires up a roach, inhales deeply, and passes it to Evan, who also takes a deep hit of the weed. Both feel invincible.

"Hey, Evan, how much more of this stuff we got squirreled away?"

Evan works through the gears, screeching the tires each time. "A few thousand more gallons. I got it hidden where Old Man Peters sometimes hides his shine. Under that big Quonset hut that's falling apart, back of his property. I figure we keep it just for fun."

"Never know when we're gonna need to burn some shit down," Earl agrees with a nod. He sits back and takes another slow hit of the roach.

They have no idea that their handiwork may have just saved thousands of animal and human lives and accidentally killed an apex alien predator.

13

The light mist begins the transition to actual rain as Jay Bob from Cincinnati steps gingerly over the steel railroad tracks and onto the ballast stone. He eyes the dark wooden sleepers.

"Guess they musta just replaced these things. They stink of fresh creosote in this rain," he mutters to himself. Jay Bob follows with some railroad trivia he knows by heart. "I bet not many people know that these big ole railroad ties are called sleepers." He coughs and continues his verbal musings. "I could use a sleeper right now. Heck, I'd be happy with some dry ground."

He is careful with his foot placement. From experience, he knows that the steel rails, their curved tops smoothed by constant use, are slippery in the rain.

After leaving Cincinnati, he'd jumped on a southbound train. When the freight train finally stopped rolling just outside Little Rock, he caught a ride with a trucker to Magnolia, Arkansas. From there, Jay Bob set out on foot, walking for hours, and eventually made it to Louisiana. Just outside the small town of Springhill, he came upon the set of tracks he'd been following south ever since.

Jay Bob pulls a worn-out baseball cap further down on his scalp so that the rain doesn't get in his eyes. He smacks the walking stick he carved out of an old shovel handle against his open hand, recalling the events at the homeless camp up in Cincinnati that led to his current road trip. "People just got no respect for other people! No sir!"

Living in the homeless camp in Cincinnati had been an easy lifestyle until two bullies arrived one day. It wasn't long before they started stealing food and valuables from people. When they saw Jay Bob as their next victim, they'd underestimated his willingness to fight back. Using techniques he learned in Vietnam, he made quick work of the two thieves. When it became apparent that perhaps they wouldn't survive, Jay Bob gathered his meager belongings and fled.

Recalling the events, Jay Bob shrugs again, partly to adjust the backpack and somewhat to bolster his belief that his actions were justified. He stops for a moment, eyeing the terrain on the other side of the tracks. It appears to be high ground, which would be helpful with the rain beginning to pick up. He knows it's time to stop for the evening. Seeing no barns or outbuildings, he decides to set up a lean-to shelter with the old Army poncho he carries in his backpack. He scampers over the rails, jumps across a muddy, swollen bayou, and walks into the woods. To his delight, he spies an old metal deer stand leaning against a large pine tree.

"Oh man, that's great." He'll drape his poncho over it, cut a few branches and put them on either side and underneath for a bed, and be set until the rain stops or tomorrow morning.

He hangs his pack on a limb and slowly maneuvers the deer stand to the ground. Retrieving a large Bowie knife, Jay Bob hacks evergreen branches from every tree he can reach and fashions a floor for his shelter. Then he pulls the large camo Army-surplus poncho out of his pack and drapes it over the deer stand. He backs up to admire his handiwork as lightning and thunder rip through the woods. Rain transitions from annoying to heavy.

"Well, someone up there just opened the spigots of heaven." He grabs his backpack, crawls under his poncho, and settles gently onto the bed of evergreen boughs. The smell from the freshly cut limbs is pleasant. It reminds him of his youth, of Christmas trees and better times. He smiles as he rearranges the dry clothes in his backpack to use as a pillow and lies back.

"This is the life," he mutters. With a flashlight he checks for leaks in his poncho. Finding none, he turns off the light and relaxes. The rain drumming on the poncho begins to lull him to sleep. He closes his eyes and says a prayer: "Lord, those two robbers might not have deserved to die, but they attacked me first, so I leave it to you to deal with them."

In the distance, the newcomer stands perfectly still in the bayou behind Martin's lab, half out of the water, half in. It luxuriates in the liquid falling from the sky. Though this universe killed most of its species, it feels fortunate to have happened upon such a beautiful place, where the life liquid is accessible and even falls from above. It also knows that had it not escaped from its captor, it would be dead by now.

Thinking of its escape, it glances several times towards the place where it was held captive and tortured, aware that the darkness surrounding it means the evil one is not inside. Flashes from the storm reveal the yellow eye. The newcomer puts aside the anger and decides to address its growing hunger. Then, something in the woods draws its attention. There is a disruption in the darkness. Perhaps another animal? With resolve, it follows the small, muddy bayou that flows out of its home towards the flashes in the distance.

Under Jay Bob's poncho, the noise of the rain is unrelenting. Large drops from the tree limbs above make even louder plops. With his flashlight on again, Jay Bob rummages in his backpack, trying to find the Mountain Dew and beef jerky he stole from a 7-Eleven in Springhill.

"Ah-ha!" he says enthusiastically. The Mountain Dew fizzes and spews carbonated soda as he pulls the pop tab. After a deep swig, Jay Bob exhales loudly. "Man, oh man, I needed that!" Raising the can towards the sky, he toasts the 7-Eleven clerk who clearly saw him shoplift the food and drink and let him get away with it. "My kind of guy. Thanks, brother, for the meal."

The newcomer pauses. Though the flashing in the distance is new, it recalls a similar experience in its recent past, which resulted in the loss of some of its life force and the premature creation of a little one. That memory brings more anger to the surface. It hopes the immature one survived.

The odd light sweeps through the woods, so the newcomer slows its approach, curious about what lies ahead. The light emanates from just above the ground. It pauses, curious.

The rain lets up slightly, and Jay Bob wonders about dry wood. But he shakes his head to convince himself of the futility of going back outside and decides to wait until morning.

Jay Bob closes his eyes but is startled back to full alertness when he hears what sounds like an animal splashing in the small bayou stream fifteen feet below him.

"Dammit, this is why I should have a gun!" he exclaims. He flicks on the flashlight and waits for the next sound, hoping it's just a passing deer. He knows he stinks, which might work in his favor and help drive a wild animal away.

"Bet I taste pretty rank," he mutters with mock glee. To demonstrate that he is something too large to mess with, he starts hitting the sides of the poncho and making guttural screeching sounds. With the flashlight in one hand making crazy swirls in the air, the light waving around the confines of his camo-green poncho shelter reminds him of the disco craze from the sixties and early seventies.

"Man, those were the days. Party time every minute of every day," he says with a smile. He relaxes somewhat, though he transitions back to high alert when the splashing gets closer and closer. He holds his breath for a moment and calls out loudly to whatever is out there. "Just keep on walking. Nothing to see here, nothing you want . . ."

He clicks off the light, holds his breath, and waits. He strains to hear any new noise through the rain. Gathering his inner reserves, he takes his knife in one hand and the flashlight in the other and slowly lifts the poncho.

The newcomer stops as the light source disappears. It senses sustenance, but it is hidden somehow, and the desire to feed drives it to inch closer just as Jay Bob lifts the edge of his poncho shelter, hoping to scare off whatever is out there in the rain. As he clicks on the flashlight, the beam sweeps across the newcomer and stops at the eye. Jay Bob freezes, unsure what kind of animal has only one eye. He brandishes the big Bowie as the newcomer swiftly covers the distance between them with speed that surprises Jay Bob.

In a single motion, the newcomer covers Jay Bob's face with one large, brown hand and pulls him from under the covered deer stand and back out into the heavy rain. Flashes of lightning, like the disco strobes in the clubs of Jay Bob's past, reveal the newcomer in all its glory. Jay Bob tries to scream but is unable to do so. The knife in his hand sweeps towards whatever is holding his face. He strikes out in fear and anger.

His body tenses, and his grip on the knife slips away in the heavy rain. It drops tip first and impales itself three inches into the wet earth. The metal blade shines as lightning flashes across the heavens, marking where karma has finally caught up with Jay Bob from Cincinnati. Life escapes his body as the newcomer feeds. The flashlight, still lit, rolls down the hill and disappears into the muddy water, leaving the scene of the crime like a miniature submarine.

Satiated, the newcomer sits back, reveling in the fullness of a good meal. Then, as the rain dwindles, it sheds what it can't use, turns, and makes its way back to the bayou it calls home.

14

Jerry hangs up the phone as he waves Clint into his office. He isn't surprised to see his buddy on a Saturday. He knows how driven Clint is about doing his job.

"Good morning, sir. How are things on this glorious Saturday? And before you answer that question, A: you know I shouldn't even be here on a Saturday, and now I'm sure that I shall regret the fact that I am. And two—or 'B,' if I was a rule follower—shouldn't you be home with that lovely wife of yours, planning your eventual retirement to the mountains of Wyoming, Montana, or Idaho?"

"Well, good morning to you too, Jerry. I would be home, and in fact, I was home until I saw the *Shreveport Journal* and the *Times*. Not to mention the calls from John over at KWKH, someone at Channel 12, and that new weekend-news anchor over at Channel 3."

Jerry sits back in his chair and crosses his arms. "The one that just came up from Alexandria? Diane Chase?"

Clint squints. "I don't know, Jerry. Yeah, I guess that's her. Why?"

"Well, first, her reputation precedes her. A buddy down in Alexandria called me when she moved up here, said I best watch out, that she had a nose for news, especially small-town, cop-related news." Jerry holds up copies of the weekend papers Clint mentioned. "I see that the papers got the story, which tells me that at some point, you might be face-to-face with Ms. Chase regarding the bones of the former Timmy Johnson."

"You're right. Wait, *I* might?" Clint asks.

"Hey, you're the captain. I'm just a simple country lawman," Jerry says with a smirk.

Clint shakes his head as he laughs.

"Have to figure out a way to redirect her attention towards Rudolph."

"Rudolph? The red-nosed reindeer? Is he involved too?"

Clint laughs. "No, Mr. Smarty Pants. Rudolph, the deputy sheriff. The homicide detective over in major crimes."

Jerry smiles and laughs too. "I know. And that's a good idea. Let Rudy deal with her."

"Yep, but I can't worry about her right now. If she has the story, she has it. I wish the sheriff could control his people. I didn't talk. I know you didn't talk, but I suppose eleven different deputies couldn't wait to get on the phone to their favorite reporters and spill the beans. I have to admit, though, it might make things easier for us, all the details out in the open and stuff like that."

"Maybe," Jerry acknowledges. "But how we found Timmy's remains was bad enough. All we need is a bunch of gun-toting rednecks driving around, suspecting our murderous cannibal is a nutjob Yankee still fighting the Civil War. Someone will think it funny to scare their friends and end up getting shot fifty-seven times by twelve different people."

"Yeah, I suppose that's possible. Plus, if I have to start avoiding the press today, I'm not going to be a happy camper!"

"You think they might come out here? Aren't you also the 'public information' officer?"

Clint laughs at Jerry's air quotes. "Whatever. I figure someone will call as soon as we tell dispatch what we're doing, and eventually, the media will show up."

Jerry throws a skeptical look at Clint. "What exactly do you mean by 'what *we* are doing'?"

Clint ignores the question and plunges ahead. "Saturday is the slowest news day, and those weekend news crews have to justify their continued existence. You've heard the old saying 'If it bleeds, it leads'? Well, that's how the media over in Shreveport operate on an hourly basis."

Not wishing to get Clint further wound up about the media over in Shreveport, Jerry changes the subject.

"I expect you to eventually answer my question regarding your 'plans,' but for now, let me tell you something interesting. When you walked in, I was finishing a conversation with Timmy's mother. She's been to his car out in the impound lot and was curious about some of his personal effects that she says were not there. Unfortunately, the medical examiner doesn't have them either, so she called me."

"Like what?"

Jerry looks down at his notes as he answers. "His tennis shoes were not in the car or on the beach. They're a pair of red Keds with white stripes on the sides. She said that when she last saw him, he was wearing a pinky ring made of twenty-four-carat gold with a tiny diamond inset, his favorite Shreveport Captains' baseball cap, a bracelet with his momma's name on it, and his gold Rolex watch."

"Gold Rolex watch? Please tell me it's one of those fakes."

Jerry nods. "Oh yeah, it certainly is. But Sheryl—that's Momma, by the way—says none of those items were in the car or given to her at the funeral home."

"How do you have a funeral for a bunch of bones?" Clint wonders.

"Beats me, but she's pretty hot about those missing items, so I'm going back to the scene to maybe have a look around."

Clint smiles. "Me too, and I appreciate that you volunteered." Before Jerry can argue the point, he changes the subject. "Any news from the forensic folks yet? I realize it was just a day ago, but I seem to recall they said they'd get 'right on it.' So, I kind of expected they'd be true to their word and get right on it."

Jerry shakes his head. "Nope. Not a word from them. However, as I pointed out just a few moments ago to my good buddy Clint, perhaps he doesn't realize it's Saturday. Some people try not to work on Saturdays. And, you know, if those big-brain types even think about work today, they're going to put in for overtime or comp pay. So, I wouldn't get your hopes up too high. I bet we don't hear from them until Monday afternoon at the earliest."

Clint sits next to Jerry's desk and feels like he needs to say something positive.

"Yeah, I know it. But I can have hope."

Jerry leans back in his chair and takes a deep breath. Clint recognizes these actions and knows that a nugget of Jerry's odd wisdom is about to enter the room.

"You know, the other day, just before that big storm, I heard the weatherman over on Channel 6 say, 'We can have hope against hope that the storm will miss us.' Now, what in the world does 'hope against hope' even mean?"

Clint chuckles.

"Finally, you ask me a question I can answer. I'm pretty sure that weatherman isn't the smartest person in the world, but the phrase 'hope against hope' means that the person who said it is clinging to the mere *possibility* that something will happen."

Jerry frowns and rolls his pen between his hands for a moment, then shakes his head and says, "That's the most mush-mouthed, weird way to say something I have ever heard. If you want a storm to miss us, why not just say, 'I'd like the storm to miss us' instead of a phrase as dumb sounding as 'I have hope against hope the storm will miss us.'"

Clint sits quietly until Jerry's weather-related tantrum is over.

Jerry knows the expression on Clint's face.

"I guess you're hoping against hope that the forensics guys are working around the clock to solve the riddle of the red-tinted bones on the beach, right?"

"Jerry, if you put it that way, yes. I cling to the mere possibility that they might be working today on solving the riddle."

Jerry crosses his arms and with a smug expression replies, "Well, you can hope against hope all you want, but I'm telling you, they ain't working on a Saturday."

Clint knows his friend might be right, so he plows ahead with a different topic. "Alright, next item: do you know if the sheriff's deputies did any canvassing around the lake?"

Jerry shakes his head. "No idea. Yesterday I called Rudy and requested that he share the details if he finds anything. I guess he might go out there Monday. Technically, it's either within your jurisdiction or his, or both. It's not a city marshal thing at all."

Jerry recognizes the sly look plastered on Clint's face and sits back, clasping his hands together. "Unless the captain trooper decides it is a city marshal thing and requests activation of the mutual aid memorandum of understanding that exists between our two organizations."

Clint smiles and nods in appreciation of Jerry's ability to understand him.

"Well, about that MOU, I accept your offer to assist me in canvassing the area near where we found Mr. Johnson's car. Of course, I can submit my request in writing if the marshal believes that it may be necessary."

Jerry laughs as he talks. "I know that in one of the many pockets on your very impressive woodland-leaf-pattern outfit there is a written request form that has already been vetted and approved at none other than the great seat of state trooper power down in Baton Rouge."

Clint doesn't even flinch as he pulls a folded piece of paper from a large front pocket, unfolds it, and lays it on Jerry's desk. Jerry shakes his head and doesn't even pretend to read it. Instead, he pulls open the middle drawer on his desk, takes the paper, and drops it in. He then stands and grabs a baseball cap to follow Clint out the door.

"We are taking your car, I assume?"

"Yes, we are. I know it has more horsepower and more weaponry than yours does."

"You're not just right. You're one hundred percent right," Jerry says as he slides into the passenger seat of Clint's Dodge Monaco. "My car is the best the City of Minden can afford. I'm just happy it's not a pink Gremlin we repossessed from some crazy cat lady."

Minutes later, Clint pulls into the Beaver Cheeks gravel lot. When he shuts off his car, he notices a smile on Jerry's face and can't resist a bit of good-natured ribbing.

"Why the smile? Does coming here make you miss a favorite former Beaver Cheeks employee?"

"Man, the cases we used to get here were always epic. When I was with OSI, the sheriff would call us and say they'd heard rumors of airmen coming into town to start trouble. I'd have to come here with a dozen agents to help deal with the aftermath and the arrests. The base commander was never pleased. After I won the election, I'd see a lot of the same people in court. Drunk rednecks just love their favorite strippers. Made for some fun Friday and Saturday evenings. I was so happy when the state liquor board shut them down and pulled their license."

"Yeah, over in Bossier, we had our issues with the Bossier strip. More than once we'd bust a group who said that after they bond out, they were just gonna come over here to Beaver Cheeks. It was quite a nuisance. Too bad the building has fallen into disrepair. Someone with money should have opened a camp store or hunting outfitter kind of thing. A business like that, so close to the lake and the national forest, might be a money magnet."

As they exit the car, Jerry offers, "I guess it'd be a good business, as long as the clientele don't get murdered the minute their car breaks down in a thunderstorm and have their dead bodies get drug two miles away to a beach and then their bones stripped of all meat."

"Well, yeah, there is that. Might be problematic to the bottom line."

Jerry looks pretty pleased with himself and blurts out, "Say, Clint, you could buy the place and open one up as a retirement gig!"

"Oh, hell no. I hate people as much as anyone. Maybe even more! I'm the last person who should own and run a business where anyone can just waltz in off the street and act as if I'm supposed to care."

Jerry laughs, "Okay, Mr. People Hater, I was just trying to help you in your old age, but whatever. Now, let's talk about today. What's the plan?"

Clint spreads out a map of the area on the hood of his car, tips back his baseball cap, and starts explaining his plan. "Well, we are right here," he says as he marks their location with a red, felt-tip pen. "There are a few trailers over on Parish Road 11 and Regal Road, just south of here. We can see if anyone is home, saw or heard anything, and is willing to talk. We can hit the subdivision over on Church Camp Road after that."

Jerry runs his fingers over the map, following a rail line that transects the area.

"That train track is near enough to where we found Timmy's car that maybe we should give it a once-over."

"Okay. I think it's a KCS line. When we get back in the car, I'll have dispatch call KCS before we go wandering along an active train track. I'm not at all interested in getting run over by a freight train."

Jerry shakes his head in agreement. He removes his cap for a minute and scratches behind one ear. "Say, remember at the beach, when I said I hadn't been at the camp since dragging the lake last year for that kidnapped kid, Oscar Landry? Well, you may not recall this detail, but his dad, Martin, lives up against the dam on the Lower Caney bayou tailwater."

Clint examines the map while he ponders this information.

"Refresh my memory."

"Soon after the hoopla about the Landry kid being kidnapped, Martin Landry razed the house that had been there for a hundred years and built a place that looks more like a concrete fortress than a residence. Lots of rumors from the guys he contracted to build it. The new place has thick security bars on every window, and a buddy who oversaw the construction told me that all the windows are bulletproof."

Clint begins to recall the details. Anything out of the ordinary, like a concrete house with bulletproof windows, gets his attention.

"Bulletproof glass? I had forgotten all about that! And rumors? Like what?"

"Well, he wouldn't allow construction at night, especially if it was going to rain. If the forecast was for thunderstorms, no one was allowed on the property at all. No work at dusk. He would shoo everyone off the property and leave. He kept a reefer truck parked at the edge of the property. The rebar he used was larger than the normal quarter-inch rebar. He also had a good supply of some liquid he kept in a large container next to the lab, in silver cylinders. Some contraption attached to a heavy-duty hose that went back to the container seemed ready to spew a chemical into the bayou at a moment's notice. He also had coal-tar creosote on hand in a pit near the bayou. One guy I spoke with said Landry was constantly going over to the edge of the water and that he seemed pretty focused on it. Like he was looking for something he lost."

Clint sees the expression on Jerry's face. "There's more, right?"

"He installed a huge, industrial compressor in a concrete outbuilding that also houses his deep-water well. Drilled much deeper than necessary, by the way."

"Compressor?"

"I heard from one of my dive buddies, Kelsey. You remember him, right?"

Clint nods.

"Well, you may recall that Kelsey sells medical equipment used in hospitals and research centers. We were diving up at Ouachita one weekend, and he told me the craziest story about selling some guy in Minden a full-blown, medical-grade, negative-pressure room. I called him right before Timmy's mother called me this morning. Guess who the purchaser was?"

"Martin Landry?"

"Martin Landry."

"Huh. Talk about odd. This guy gets weirder every time I hear his name. A negative-pressure room? Why in the world would he need such a thing? Say, Jerry, when Landry reported his son missing, your dive team focused on the lake, didn't it?"

Jerry nods, looking up from the map and tilting his head. He thinks he knows why Clint asked that particular question.

"Yes. We didn't search the bayou behind Landry's place. Mr. Landry was clear; his son was taken out of the house by the kidnappers. A big fight ensued that destroyed the interior of the old house. His son, Oscar, tried to escape and ran out to the roadway, directly into the hands of more kidnappers. Landry said the side door to a blacked-out van opened, they snatched the kid, and sped off." Jerry stops speaking briefly, then asks, "Why? What are you thinking? That maybe he killed the kid and fed him to a gator or some equally awful thing, and the bayou is a murder scene that we never searched?"

"Jerry, you and I have met our share of bad people. I'd never say never when it comes to how evil one human can be to another."

"Okay. I agree. But kill his own kid?" Jerry looks thoughtful. "Look, recalling the details of the alleged kidnapping for you, I mean, now it sounds like a whole bunch of bull crap to me."

Clint nods in agreement. "It does seem like we may need to search that bayou. And I think we should do it with Landry there. Might be good to get him worried about what we could find."

"I think so. One thing bothers me still concerning what you said you'd heard from the construction crew. Why creosote? They don't use that in concrete construction, and the bayou isn't large enough or deep enough to install a dock, which to me is the only reason to have some of that stuff onsite."

"He also had what they described as some kind of military-surplus flamethrower. The man I spoke to said he had the feeling that Martin was trying to figure out a way to use the creosote and the flamethrower on or in the bayou for some reason. Still, no one knew what he was doing with it, since like you said, there was no need for its use in the construction."

"Homemade creosote and a flamethrower? Seriously? Man, this guy is peaking out on my total weirdo scale. Rumors, huh? I get the feeling there is much more at work here than we thought." Clint squints, then adds with a nod, "I remember him now—not too tall, frazzled hair. Kind of had that cartoonish, crazy-professor look in his eyes. I always figured he was just another killer who offed his kid, dumped the body somewhere to get back at the ex-wife, and never got caught. You say he lives right around the corner? In a concrete fortress? Well, now we absolutely must stop in and say hello."

"I'll hitch up the buggy!"

Clint shrugs. "How about we just take my cruiser?"

"Well, I guess we can do that too."

"Let's hit a few houses across the street before we speak with Mr. Landry."

"You're the captain!" Jerry says, shutting the car door as Clint cranks the engine. He casts a glance towards his buddy and asks, partly in jest, "Should we find a flamethrower or some creosote?"

Clint doesn't hesitate in his answer.

"Absolutely. Maybe."

15

"As far as the investigation goes, that wasn't entirely useless," Jerry says from the passenger seat of Clint's cruiser. "No one knew Timmy, no one saw Timmy, and no one wants to get involved in anything regarding Timmy."

"What, you were hoping for more dead—no, wait—more bones without flesh attached?"

"Well . . ."

"Just stop," Clint says as he looks both ways before he crosses Dorcheat Road onto Parish Road 116. "So, Jerry, do you believe everyone we spoke to just now?"

"I have no reason not to trust their responses. Now, I know I'm not a detective or a captain, but I did attend training at the FBI National Academy in Quantico."

"Do tell." Clint humors his pal. "What gems of wisdom did you absorb from those geniuses?"

"Well, one area they spent a great deal of time on was how to recognize what those in the lauded halls of federal law enforcement call 'clues.' And I've seen no clues that lead me to believe anyone has been less than truthful."

"I agree. Which, as I said, takes that whole side of the road out of the equation." Clint slows the car and pulls over about twenty feet from a set of railroad tracks.

"What gives?"

"I thought that before we leave the area, we should walk the rail line you identified."

"Good idea. We're slowly working our way from the original scene of the crime towards the place we believe is involved."

"Exactly," Clint says as he reaches down for the microphone to his in-car radio. "I'll have dispatch call and find out when the next train is due here."

"That is also a good idea."

"Troop B, Twenty-One Bravo."

"Twenty-One Bravo, go ahead."

"Twenty-One Bravo, can you call KCS dispatch and ask them when the next train is scheduled for their rail line just north of Minden? I believe it's a haulage line from Springhill to Minden. I'm interested in all rail activity that would be out or inbound."

"Ten-four. Will advise."

"Ten-four."

"Now, we wait," Clint says. He turns to Jerry with a sly look and asks, "Want a snack?"

"And to think that I thought you were just going to let me waste away over here! We've met, right? Of course I want a snack!"

Clint opens the door and clicks on his portable radio. Jerry does the same. Going to the trunk, Clint opens it and reveals a cooler.

"Clint, I always knew you were a man after my own heart."

"Care for a Coke and some smoked beef sticks? I also have peanuts."

"Such a feast!" Jerry laughs as he takes the Coke can from Clint and pulls up the small metal tab, taking a long swig with gusto. He also takes a careful bite of the beef stick Clint has offered and chews thoughtfully. "Such a treat on this gorgeous, humidity-filled day!"

"Jerry, the humidity is only 314 percent, which is entirely normal for a Louisiana summer."

"True that. Well, at least it's not raining yet!" Still chewing, he changes the subject. "Say, this beef stick. It's not a commercial thing. Where'd you get these?"

"It is good, isn't it? Buddy of mine owns a cattle operation up in Cotton Valley. When he takes the cattle to slaughter, I always score some beef he's smoked and turned into these beef sticks."

"How is it you've never introduced me to this buddy of yours so I can get my own supply of these wonders?"

"That is exactly the reason. I don't want you showing up at his doorstep with a shopping cart, asking where the beef stick aisle is located—"

"Troop B to Twenty-One Bravo."

Clint takes a swig of Coke, keys his radio, and responds, "Twenty-One Bravo, go ahead."

"Twenty-One Bravo, per your request, KCS advises there are no trains scheduled for the rest of the day on that track. They also want to know if you need KCS police at your location."

"Twenty-One Bravo. Let KCS know that at the moment, we do not need their police to come out. But tell them if we find anything, we will advise. Hold me and Minden city marshal Thomson out on an investigation here on Parish Road 116. We'll be walking the railroad tracks between Dorcheat and Parish Road 116, just west of Lower Caney Lake. Reference the homicide case at this location two days ago."

"Ten-four. Do you require Webster SO backup?"

Clint thinks about this request for a second. "Twenty-One Bravo, a couple of scout cars wouldn't be a bad idea."

Jerry shrugs and asks, "Could they hear me slurping over the air?"

Which earns him a smile from Clint. "I bet they could."

"Well, I was trying to slurp as quietly as possible. And I think it's a good idea to ask for a couple of cars."

Keying the radio once again, Clint continues, "Dispatch, 21 Bravo, if we need more units, we will advise. I will be on channel one."

"Twenty-One Bravo, ten-four. Troop B, out."

Clint looks Jerry's way as he loudly downs the last of his Coke. Jerry crushes the can between his hands and tosses it into Clint's trunk. "Well, sir, now that you've fed me, I suppose you expect to get a bit of work out of me?"

Clint laughs. "That's right. So, tell me if this makes sense. Why don't we each take a side of the track and walk up to where it crosses Dorcheat Road. We'll swap sides once we get there and work back to my car."

"Sounds like a solid plan," Jerry says. However, before crossing the road to the tracks, he unsheathes a ten-inch Bowie knife from his belt and walks over to a seven-foot-tall white oak sapling. Clint watches silently, curious. With one swing, Jerry cuts down the sapling and works to remove its tiny limbs. Once finished, he holds it aloft and swishes it in the air. He then beats in on the ground a few times to see if it breaks easily.

"Uh, Jerry, what in the world are you doing with that?"

"Snake stick," Jerry responds with a matter-of-fact tone. "Gonna beat this on the ground in front of me in suspect areas, kind of scare the snakes outta my way. You do know that my people are traditionally not very snake-friendly, right?"

Clint raises his eyebrows as his chin pivots downward. "Snake stick? Huh." He decides that a snake stick might be a good idea given the wooded, boggy wetlands alongside the tracks. "Lemme borrow that Bowie for a minute."

Jerry smugly hands over the knife and watches Clint duplicate his actions. Minutes later, armed adequately with snake sticks, they set out.

It's not long before Jerry calls out from his side of the tracks. "Yo, Clint? Next time you want to take a scenic walk alongside a railroad track, how about we do it in December?"

"Great idea."

"What?" Jerry asks.

"Nothing," Clint yells over the tracks.

Minutes later, they both come to a bridge constructed out of pressure-treated creosote pilings crossing over a small bayou. Something at the edge of the bayou immediately captures Jerry's attention. He stops and beats the ground around the area with his snake stick. Satisfied, he bends down to examine his find. He smiles, stands, and calls out Clint's name.

Clint answers with a somewhat exasperated tone, "Yes, Jerry?"

"Come on over, think I got something."

"Jerry . . . this better not be something weird, like a smoked beef stick poking out of your pants."

Jerry smiles, considering Clint's comment for a moment. "It's not, but that's a good idea. Maybe I'll try it next time. This is the real deal. Get over here."

Clint climbs the hill to the tracks and jumps across them. He finds Jerry standing next to a shallow, marshy, slow-moving bayou. Cattails and tall grass grow on its banks. The water is muddy. As if dropped from the sky, sitting on the bank is a pair of relatively new, red tennis shoes with what once were white stripes down the sides. They face upstream. Nearby is the skeleton of a small animal. Clint asks the question, but he already knows the answer.

"You said Timmy's mother mentioned that his red Keds were not with his personal effects, right?"

Jerry shakes his head as he answers, "Yep."

Clint thinks for a minute and then points his snake stick at the shoes.

"Timmy's?"

Jerry bends down, and with a deft move, he flips the snake stick around. Using the thickest end, he lifts one tennis shoe high and examines the heel. Both men see the initials *TJ* in blue ink, though the ink has begun to fade and run on the heel of the shoe.

"Well, well, well," Jerry says with a smile as he gently places the shoe back where he found it. He looks up the small bayou and offers, "You know, I bet the origin point for this thing is the larger bayou below the Lower Caney Lake dam and spillway."

"You mean Martin Landry's backyard?"

"Yep."

Clint keys his portable radio and tells dispatch to switch to channel four.

One second later, the dispatcher replies.

"Twenty-One Bravo, Troop B on channel four. What's up, Captain?"

"Contact Webster Sheriff's Office. We will need their forensic people and a couple more scout cars to respond to our location. Contact KCS and have them alert their police as well. Marshal Thomson and I are midway between Dorcheat Road and Parish 116 Road, on the western side of the KCS rail tracks. My car is parked at the railroad track intersection with Parish Road 116. We've just discovered evidence from the Johnson homicide two days ago. Once you contact them, have them step it up. The media knows we're out here and might show up. Given that I switched to the scrambled channel, I bet they're already headed this way."

"Ten-four. Stay on this channel, will confirm message delivery as soon as possible."

Clint puts the radio back on his gun belt and looks around.

"Guess we should step back. Don't want to contaminate a potential crime scene."

"Does this look familiar?" Jerry asks, pointing his snake stick towards the skeleton.

"Familiar? It's the woods, Jerry; lots of dead animals in the woods."

"Okay, I'll give you that, but do they all look like this? Perfectly clean with a slight red tint that looks unlike a normal bone color?"

"Are you suggesting this animal skeleton is connected to Timmy's murder?"

Jerry shrugs and looks up at Clint. "Well, I'm not sure how they can be connected, but, apparently, yes. Somehow, these events and this evidence must be connected."

"Seriously?"

Jerry looks thoughtful as he slaps his stick against the ground a couple of times.

"You know, nothing concrete yet, just a hunch. But I wonder, will we come across more of the same if we start looking through the woods here? Plus, remember our conversation this morning about Timmy's other personal effects. These are his shoes, so I have to wonder if the other missing items might be around here, somewhere."

Clint retrieves a handkerchief from a pocket, wipes the sweat from his forehead, and replaces his cap. "When we get a few more eyes out here, we should follow this little bayou."

Jerry squats down to one knee, his gaze following the waterway into the woods. "Which we both know will lead us directly to our mad scientist in his concrete fortress."

Clint nods. "Lots of things seem to point at Mr. Martin Landry. Now I think it's important that we interview him. Something isn't right, and if he's involved, then it might clear up a lot of questions people have about him."

Clint's radio squawks to life.

"Webster SO is ten-four on your request. KCS is ten-four also. Units from both are headed your direction. KCS police are responding from Sibley. ETA about fifteen minutes."

"Twenty-One Bravo, ten-four, thank you."

Clint sees the gears turn in Jerry's head but waits to inquire. It isn't long before Jerry speaks up. "Say, Clint, did you bring that map with you?"

Clint pulls the folded map from a front pocket and spreads it out on the rocks next to the train tracks. Putting a few stones from the railroad tracks on the edges of the paper to keep it in place, he stands back to give Jerry room to contemplate it. Jerry traces a finger to their exact location.

"Yep. This goes directly to the bayou behind the Landry place."

"Martin Landry's gotta be our main suspect. The question is how does he do it, and why."

"Well, not to make a snap judgment, but the evidence is mounting. Guess we should go back to your car to meet the reinforcements." Jerry looks around, memorizing the location. "Won't be hard to find once the crime scene guys get here. Lead on, my captain. I'll follow."

"You'll follow?"

"I believe you make a more attractive target for the snakes and gators."

Clint shakes his stick in the air. "I thought that's why we made the snake sticks."

"Yes, but we have the guns too, and we still made snake sticks . . . so, after you, sir."

Clint mutters under his breath. Shaking his head, he heads back to his car with Jerry taking up the rear.

The tennis shoes are photographed, measured, and bagged two hours later, as is the animal skeleton. Clint directs everyone to be careful as he has them fan out to search the woods. Ten minutes into the grid search, everyone hears a loud voice from deep in the woods.

"Hey, I got something here!"

As the searchers rush towards his voice, Clint and Jerry share a look. The deputy in question has been following the waterway into the woods.

"What you got?" Clint asks as he and Jerry stop next to the sheriff's deputy. Without a word, the deputy points towards what looks like a gold Presidential Rolex just barely visible at the muddy edges of the creek.

Jerry shakes his head. "Oh man. If it's Timmy's, it's not a Swiss movement, as real Rolexes are. It's got a cheap quartz movement. The crystal is also scratched, and the watch doesn't weigh anything like a real Rolex would."

Donning a glove and accepting an evidence bag from a colleague, the deputy picks up the watch. He bends to swish it in the water to remove the dirt and debris, but the forensics officer stops it.

"Hey, leave all that on the watch, please. Might contain trace evidence."

Clint nods in agreement while the deputy shrugs, puts it into the bag, and seals it shut. Giving it the once-over through the clear baggie, the deputy offers, "Just like the marshal said. It's one of those knockoffs you can buy at gun shows or flea markets."

"Timmy's?" Clint, already anticipating the answer, glances at Jerry, who nods.

"Gotta be Timmy's. He loved that watch, pretended like it was the real deal. I bet his cubic zirconia ring, set in gold, is here too. And his mother said he should have been wearing a gold bracelet with her name on. Spread out, boys. Let's see if we can find the rest of his stuff."

It takes ten minutes, but after a careful examination of the banks, they find the bracelet about fifteen feet away from where the watch was located. Their search yields more skeletons—one deer, beaver, and one alligator. Then, one of the KCS detectives shouts, "Hey, guys! I think I got human bones over here!"

Clint and Jerry grimly head in that direction.

16

"Oh man, this looks eerily familiar. Not another one," Clint says. Bones are scattered in a perfect line, beginning at the base of a large pine tree and ending near the bank of a muddy bayou.

"It's like the skin and tissue simply left the body," mutters the railroad detective as he resists bending down to pick up one of the bones.

Jerry shakes his head and spits out the only thing he can think at the moment. "The bayou is no place to die. Whoever this was, I bet they thought they were safe out here in the middle of nowhere." He shakes his head again, then points about thirty feet away. "Say, is that a deer stand covered in a camo poncho over there? Maybe he fell out?"

A deputy near the structure stoops down and examines it without touching it.

"Yep. Deer stand alright, but it's laid on its side like it was placed there, and a poncho is draped over it. There's a backpack and some snack-food wrappers here. I bet whoever this was might have been using the deer stand as a field-expedient shelter. There's also a nice Bowie knife stuck in the ground, knifepoint down. No rust on it; looks to be recently dropped."

"Seriously?" Clint asks, making his way through the brush towards the deer stand. Contemplating the knife, he shoves both hands into his pockets in frustration. "What in the world is all this?" He looks up at the deputy, who is now holding the backpack. "Any identification inside?"

The deputy looks through the pack's contents and, seconds later, pulls out a threadbare motorcycle wallet connected to a silver dog-collar chain.

"Got a wallet here, hold on." Opening it, he retrieves an identification card. "The card, and I guess the pack, belongs to Mr. Jayson Robert Betz of Cincinnati. This ID is only a year old, so it's current."

"This is getting weirder by the minute," Clint says under his breath to Jerry as the marshal joins him. "A dead guy from Cincinnati, the knife, these animals, the Rolex—"

"What about the ring?" Jerry asks. "Maybe Mr. Betz here is the killer, took the ring, shoes, and watch, found out it was fake, came back to his camp, and fell to his death accidentally. I mean, it could work out just that easily."

Clint shrugs. "Well, maybe. But is it ever that easy? The ring is so small it'd be easy to miss. But could an animal clean all these bones so quickly? The forensic deputy over at the church-camp beach crime scene said it wasn't possible."

Clint is perplexed. This abandoned-vehicle-turned-homicide case has taken a turn into bizarre territory, and it's only getting odder and more frustrating. Looking at the bagged remains, Clint shakes his head. "Well, I officially have no idea."

"Run him through teletype?" Jerry suggests softly.

Clint nods. "Oh, yeah. Great idea." He motions for the deputy to give him the identification. Picking up his radio, he pushes the transmit button and asks dispatch to run a twenty-nine on one Jayson Robert Betz.

"Ten-four. Will advise."

"I wonder if the bone marrow is gone on these new bones too?" Jerry speculates. He and Clint turn to the forensic deputy, who shrugs and nods as he's bagging the human bones.

"Could be. Have to wait until I get everything back to the lab to be sure, but they seem cleaner and lighter than normal."

Clint doesn't mind expressing his feelings. "I tell you, Jerry, this one is a stumper."

Jerry muses, "Timmy's car was abandoned in the heavy thunderstorm. No Shreveport Captains' baseball cap yet, either. Let's not forget that item is still missing."

"Right."

Jerry continues, "And his shoes were not on the tracks. They were beside them, next to the little bayou, which, I add, is where we found his jewelry. And now all this gear, the knife, and this new skeleton. To me, the bayou might be key to understanding what is going on."

The KCS detective interjects an opinion: "I could speculate that we have an itinerate killer riding the rails. It wouldn't be the first time. Maybe Mr. Cincinnati here was your killer, but if these bones are his, then he's clearly dead, and any new bodies that appear would not be his doing."

Clint asks, "Where does this line go?"

The KCS detective doesn't hesitate. "It's a short haulage line. Originates in the yard up in Springhill and terminates just outside Minden at the ordnance plant."

Clint considers the answer for a moment. "I don't know of any rail-hopper who'd be interested in such a truncated trip. Plus, no train-hopping hobo is going to clean animal skeletons like that. Add to that his own bones are cleaned. If he was the killer, how would he clean his own bones after his death?"

Jerry weighs in with his own thoughts. "Those tennis shoes we found were in good shape. Any hobo worth their salt would certainly have kept them to use as barter goods later, even if they were the wrong size. Like our mystery man from Cincinnati, someone could be camping here in the woods and preying on unsuspecting people. Still, these woods are as wild as ever. He never made a fire that we can see, and I don't smell campfire smoke. There are no trails broken through the woods, and as far as I can tell, no one has been here recently except Mr. Cincinnati and us." He looks perplexed as he finishes with, "I miss something?"

Clint shrugs slightly. "Look at the water. It's muddy. And somewhat like the coloring or tinting we found on Timmy's clothes. And we found Timmy's remains next to the lake, another body of water. And our new victim . . .

"Let's say the killer came from the direction we are traveling, and the waterway is how they hide their footprints. They killed Timmy and took his body for some weird reason. In the process, the killer dropped Timmy's shoes, watch, and bracelet where we found them, maybe by accident, maybe not. Then the killer took Timmy through the woods, up the dam, and along the trail that circles the lake, over to the beach at the church camp, where they stripped his clothes and—"

"And bones?" Jerry interrupts. Turning to the forensic deputy, Jerry asks, "Hey, in your professional opinion, how long does it take to strip the meat and tissue from a body? Oh, add the marrow, too, because your colleague said there was no marrow in the bones he collected. Did he tell you about it?"

"Yep, he did. He's pretty freaked out by that fact too. Let's see, you could simmer the body in water like a regular piece of meat, which would loosen up the connective tissue and the organs. But you'd need a huge pot and lots of salt. Kind of like a witch's cauldron. It would take anywhere from twelve to twenty-four hours for a large animal. Of course, I would need to dismember the body first. I don't see how you could do all that is necessary to fully strip the meat from a body, deposit the bones at the camp, and leave no trace."

Jerry shakes his head, remembering the similarly explicit explanation the man's colleague had provided. "You've clearly thought about this topic."

"Yeah, well, bodies are our business. There's even a facility up in New York where forensic scientists have put dead people who have willed their bodies to science and items that could be evidence in crimes—cars, guns, stuff like that—out in the elements. What we have here hasn't been out in the elements very long. They're too clean."

"Why would you put bodies out in the elements?" Jerry questions.

"To monitor the normal rate of decay, how long it takes for animal predation, how weather affects bodies left in the open, partially buried or fully buried. Stuff like that. It's fascinating reading their reports."

Disconcerted, Jerry says, "Remind me never to piss you off."

The forensic deputy shrugs and adds, "Now, to remove the marrow from, say, beef bones, you first cut the bones into three-inch sections. Then soak them in salty water for at least two days. On day three, you move them to a hot-water bath. Finally, you would use a thumb to push out the marrow. I just don't see how it could be possible. I mean, maybe some kind of *Star Trek* space alien might be able to do it, but a human? Just don't see it."

"Wait, you said you have to cut the bones into sections? Why?"

"Only easy way to get the marrow to move."

"Timmy's bones were completely intact, right? None of them had been cut to make it easier to access the marrow. And these new bones, completely intact, right?"

The deputy nods his agreement. "Yep. Which is yet another reason this case might be the weirdest one we've ever worked."

One deputy, feeling left out of the conversation, decides to throw his hat in the ring.

"Like he said, it could be aliens. Or a Bigfoot creature like the Fouke monster!"

"Yeah, aliens!" another says. "I saw an episode of *Star Trek* where they encountered a creature that sucked all the salt from people to stay alive. It almost killed Dr. McCoy!"

Clint looks unhappy with these additions. He rubs his temples with both hands and lets everyone know of his displeasure. "Just great. All we need is someone in town to overhear one of you repeating that our woods are full of bone-marrow-sucking aliens, and we'll have dozens of UFO and Fouke monster nutjobs up here."

Suddenly they hear what sounds like a gunshot.

"What the hell was that?" Clint moves his hand to the grip of his holstered sidearm by reflex.

"Gunshot. Maybe someone hears us, doesn't know we're the police, and is hoping to discourage us from trespassing on their property?"

Jerry looks at Clint, curious. "Clint, where are we?"

"Where are we? In the woods?"

"Whose woods? Who owns these woods?"

Looking at the tiny red flags still stuck into the ground where they found the bracelet and watch, Clint swats a mosquito. "Whose woods indeed." Turning to the KCS detective, he asks, "Hey, got another question for you. Where does the property line for your right-of-way end and the property line for these woods begin? Do you know?"

"Well, I guess you could simply measure twenty-five feet from the stone."

"Twenty-five feet from the stone?"

"Yeah. In general, our right-of-way extends twenty-five feet on either side of the track, as measured from the edge of the ballast stone on either side of the tracks." Seeing the question in Clint's eyes, he continues, "The ballast stone is the crushed stone that supports the railroad ties. Why?"

Clint looks at Jerry. "We're way more than twenty-five feet from the edge of that ballast stone. Everything we found today is inside the property line on this piece of land. I bet you a thousand dollars you and I know who the landowner is."

Before Jerry can answer, Clint's radio squelches to life.

"Troop B, 21 Bravo?"

He raises his eyebrows and brings the radio up to answer.

"21 Bravo, go ahead."

"Per the Ohio Bureau of Investigation, Jayson Robert Betz of Cincinnati is the suspect in two murders. There are two active warrants for his arrest. If you have him in custody, they absolutely will extradite him to Ohio. How should I advise the teletype operator? They are on hold."

Clint pauses, composing his answer. He also has a question for the authorities in Ohio. "21 Bravo. Ask Ohio if there are any distinguishing characteristics about Mr. Betz. I mean, is he missing an arm, leg, or fingers?"

"Interesting question," Jerry murmurs. The deputies nod in agreement.

"21 Bravo, stand by."

While they wait, Clint turns and asks, "After a quick glance, does anything look abnormal, bone-wise, on this skeleton?"

"Not that I can tell."

"Dental issues?"

"Oh, that's a good point, hold on." They all see a smile break out as the deputy answers triumphantly, "No teeth. Scarring of the gumline indicates poor dental hygiene. Maybe he even pulled his own teeth."

Before anyone can reply, Clint's radio comes back to life.

"21 Bravo. Ohio says identifying marks on the body would be several tattoos indicating service in Vietnam and Korea. They also say he wore dentures and had a broken femur from his military service."

Clint watches as the forensic deputy lifts a large bone. He examines it for a moment and nods. "Femur, broken and healed."

"21 Bravo, I copy that. Please tell Ohio I'm fairly confident that we have their suspect here. He is going to be part of our homicide investigation, but he is deceased, and they can close their case against him."

There is a slight pause, and then the dispatcher acknowledges Clint's message. Before Clint can put his radio away, the deputy watching their cars comes over the radio.

"Captain? I have two television cameras here and one guy from KWKH. One reporter, Diane Chase with Channel 3, says she called your office and was told you were here. She understands that you are here looking for evidence in the Johnson homicide. They all say they'd like a statement about whatever it is you are doing here. They also want something called 'B-roll' of you guys searching the woods. What should I do with them?"

Jerry laughs and slaps Clint on the back. "Well, boss man, I can imagine what you'd like the deputy to do with them. However, that's not a good idea and marginally illegal, even here in Louisiana. They're here, so I kinda think you have to talk to them."

Clint nods and looks around. "Okay, gentlemen, sounds like I've got to go deal with the media. In my absence, please make sure this area gets scoured for any more evidence." Turning to the forensic deputy, he continues, "Bag and tag everything. Take lots of pictures. I want to know where everything we found out here was located. It might be important, it might not, but I'd rather have it than not have it."

The forensic deputy nods.

Satisfied, Clint takes Jerry by the elbow. "I guess we better get out there. Can't have the media rooting around here in the brush. In no time, I'm sure they'd be crawling through the woods and end up stepping on a moccasin or a gator."

Jerry laughs again and holds out the snake stick still in his right hand. "You can bet they don't have snake sticks."

"Right," Clint chuckles, beginning the walk back to the train tracks. "Let me go take care of this." He turns to the other officers and deputies to give them a quick order. "I'm satisfied with what we found. I appreciate everyone coming out. I'll be sure to mention you all in my report. If I could get a couple of you to follow me, I know the media will want video of us pretending to search the woods."

Two deputies join, straightening their uniforms and combing their hair as they walk, which gives everyone a good laugh as they compare each other to their favorite movie stars. Clint waves for Jerry to walk beside him. In a voice low enough for only Jerry to hear, he says what's on his mind.

"Jerry, just to humor me. If you followed the evidence we recovered today, the tennis shoes, the bracelet, and the watch, remind me where are you likely to end up?"

Without hesitation, Jerry responds, "Martin Landry's backyard."

"Exactly. And that's twice in the last two hours we've concluded Mr. Landry is involved somehow. When I'm finished with the news media, we're going to pay him a visit—hopefully, without Ms. Chase hiding in the woods as we do it. Now, come on, you're going to need to look like you're searching for something."

"I'm not going to be on camera!" Jerry protests.

"Yes, you are. It's in the MOU you signed. Very small print at the bottom of the page."

"Dammit. I knew I should have read that thing. Okay, I'm right behind you."

Exiting the woods, Clint sees the television cameramen have set up tripods and are rolling video footage of him. The blinking red light on top of the video cameras reminds him of a warning light, just before the bad things happen.

"Good morning. How can I help you all today?" he asks as he tosses his snake stick in the high grass.

An hour later, finished with the interviews, Clint and Jerry watch as the news crews stow their gear and crank the engines on their vans to get the air-conditioning going. Channel 12 finally leaves, but the van from Channel 3 doesn't move, and they watch as Diane Chase opens the passenger door, steps down, and heads back towards Clint and Jerry.

"Oh brother, I knew she would have more questions," Jerry mutters. He turns away from her and continues, "You know, reporters of all stripes are never satisfied. They always need to ask that one last question they forgot to ask, and none of them ever want to ask it in front of the competition. Be careful, Clint. She's smart and persistent. I bet you she already has the home phone number of the city clerk. Dollars to donuts she'll know on whose land we found this evidence five minutes after she inserts two dimes into the payphone. Heck, she may just drive directly to the clerk's house."

Ms. Chase stops in front of Clint.

"Ms. Chase, was there another question you wanted to ask?" Clint asks.

"Well, Captain—and this can be off the record, no cameras, no microphones, but just for my deep background. I have heard there are similar MOs, if you will allow me to use a cop term, over in Texas, maybe over in Mississippi. After the news of Mr. Johnson's murder, I made a few calls locally, but no one would speak to me on the record. I heard the FBI took a similar case over in Texas and never came up with a suspect.

"My source in the FBI field office in Dallas was quite interested in the details of this case. He told me they'd turned all their evidence from the Texas cases over to a newly formed specialty group called the Behavioral Science Unit at the FBI Academy in Quantico, Virginia. He said there are ten agents in the BSU focusing only on homicides and sexual crimes that are unusual. He thought this one might fit their criteria for a special investigation."

When she finishes, Clint stands silent for a minute, then feels compelled to ask, "Is there a question in there somewhere, Ms. Chase?" as Jerry quietly snickers.

"In my experience, a crime like this is pretty unusual. But finding only bones and clothes? And his bones were found a distance from his car, which implies to me that someone took him and did those awful things to him somewhere else."

In my experience? Jerry wonders as he shakes his head. *I bet she's killed a few on her journey to the top of the heap of journalistic excellence.*

Clint looks entirely uncomfortable now, and he draws out his one-word answer into several syllables. "Okay."

"So, I guess I'm curious about what you found today. Is there a chance that there is a connection between the murder victim over on the lake, the bones of the guy you found today, and the area you searched? Are there any clues to the identity of the murderer that you can share?"

She sees Clint trying to come up with an acceptable answer and preempts him. "I wonder if the woods between this location and where the body, well, bones were found has been thoroughly searched? If your answer is no, when do you plan to search them?" She pulls out a business card from her wallet and hands it to Clint. "I'd like to be notified if and when you search the woods again. I may get out myself and search a bit with my cameraman, but I'm more interested in shooting video of you or your team of investigators doing it."

Clint wets his lips and tries to tamp down his desire to run.

"Ms. Chase, first, I'm not familiar with how the FBI investigated anything over in Texas. I've not heard of the FBI unit you mentioned, though it sounds like a great idea to have agents dedicated to those types of crimes. Second, yes, the car and Mr. Johnson's remains were separated by some distance. Regarding any evidence, either at the crime scene or recovered from the car or behind me in the woods, the forensic section is still actively involved, and you know I can't comment further on an open case. That's all I can say. Also, I feel it is necessary to strongly discourage you from undertaking any kind of search on your own."

"What about my cameraman and I following you next time you search the woods for evidence?" she suggests.

Jerry interjects, "Ms. Chase, let me interrupt for a moment. Let's say that we were to allow you to follow us as we look for evidence in an open homicide case, and you step on a gun used in the crime, or you step on human remains. Now you have become part of the crime scene. You'd be part of the chain of evidence. We'd have to subpoena your camera footage, your notes, and you, for every court motion filed and eventually for the case, should it ever go to trial. I'm pretty sure your bosses would rather you get the story and not become part of it."

Clint takes a tentative half step back as he formulates what to say. "Listen, I'm happy to call you when there is an update to the forensics or if we develop anything further that might be newsworthy. Is that acceptable?"

Diane Chase steps forward and holds out her hand. Clint grasps it and is shocked by the firmness of her grip. He also notes that even in the North Louisiana summer's heat, her hands are ice cold.

"I appreciate your cooperation, Captain." Turning to Jerry, she shakes his hand as well. "And I look forward to covering Minden's government too, Marshal Thomson. I've heard a lot of interesting things about you and your work when you were with the Air Force." Executing a quick turn, she walks to the news van, jumps in, and waves goodbye.

Clint and Jerry are stationary.

"I want to dislike her, but for some reason, I also find her drive admirable," Jerry mutters. "But part of me also wants to chop off my right arm before we let her ever see us in action again. I think she's trouble with a capital *T*."

"Agreed," Clint says, rubbing his palm on his pants. "I feel like I need to take a shower after speaking to her. That hand of hers was so cold I wonder if she even has a soul."

Jerry smiles. "So, maybe we should be investigating Ms. Chase? Perhaps she's a cold-blooded alien bone-marrow sucker?"

"That's hilarious. And, no, I don't want to know anything else about her," Clint replies.

"I assume we're not going to move until we're sure they are entirely out of sight and, say, in another parish, right?"

"Yep," Clint answers. "I want to see each one of them turn towards Minden, and even then, we'll still wait for a few minutes, just in case they double back and try to follow us."

Both men watch with feigned disinterest as Ms. Chase and her cameraman finally leave. Jerry decides to compliment Clint.

"That went about as well as I can imagine. I was particularly impressed with how you dodged the questions on any potential new evidence we might have discovered and if this was a tie-in to other cases."

"Glad you were impressed. Now, how about we do good cop/bad cop on Mr. Landry?"

"Which am I? Oh, I know, I'll be both cops! Or I could just act kind of crazy!"

"And I'm sure you don't even need to practice it," Clint says with a smirk as both men get into his car. Cranking the motor, he wonders what else will happen with this bizarre case. He clenches his jaw, puts the car in drive, and heads towards the residence of Martin Landry.

17

Martin is outside when he sees Clint's police car make the turn in to his driveway. Since the night of the storm, he's been afraid the investigation about what happened to Timmy would eventually find its way to his doorstep. Now Martin knows his fear was justified. He hangs his head just enough for Clint and Jerry to notice.

I should have stopped and picked Timmy up. I knew him. He was nice to me whenever I saw him in town. I just know Oscar killed him. He inhales forcefully, guilt rising to the surface.

"You can't tell them anything. Especially about Oscar," he says under his breath. "Make something up. You can handle this. You're smarter than they are."

He plasters a broad smile across his face and makes the bold decision to approach the two men without hesitation. He extends his hand to Clint as the captain exits the car.

"Sir, my name is Martin Landry. I own this property. What can I do for the Louisiana State Police?" He spots the badge on Jerry's belt as the other lawman walks around the car and comes to a stop behind Clint. "And the Minden city marshal?"

Clint jumps right into it. "Mr. Landry, the marshal and I are investigating the murder of Timmy Johnson a couple of days ago. Have you heard about it?"

Martin inhales again and tries to calm himself. He hopes that the sweat on his brow doesn't give him away. "Yes, tragic thing. I heard y'all found Timmy's body over on the beach at the church camp. Terrible news, just terrible."

Martin blinks a few times as he speaks, dips his head slightly, and rubs his chin with his right hand. Clint and Jerry take notice of Martin's body language. It is clear to both men that Martin is hiding something, so Clint decides to push Martin a bit to see if he'll break.

"Your place is close to where we found Mr. Johnson's car. It's also very close to new evidence related to the crime, discovered today over in the swamp by the railroad tracks. Not to mention that his remains were found just a short distance from here over at the camp. So, I hope you don't mind if we ask a few questions."

Clint's words send a chill up Martin's spine. His knees wobble, and his brain screams, *New evidence relating to the crime? What evidence?* Martin tries his best to look unconcerned but thinks, *Oscar, what did you leave behind for them to find?*

Behind Clint, Jerry recognizes the emotions playing across Martin's face and wonders just what Martin knows and why he isn't speaking up about it.

Martin hesitates more than necessary, shoves his hands into his pockets, and shrugs. He hopes his movements transmit indifference to their intrusion and potential questions.

"Yeah, I guess it's okay. I don't need a lawyer or anything, right?" Martin asks, looking off into space and nowhere near Jerry or Clint's face, which further convinces them that they are in the presence of someone connected to Timmy's murder.

"Well, Mr. Landry, we're just having a conversation in your front yard. Look, if we thought you were, let's say, involved—"

"Oh my God!" Martin forcefully interrupts. "Why would I kill him? Sure, I admit that I knew Timmy. He worked briefly on the construction of my lab. Since then, we've only spoken a couple of times. He was always trying to sell me marijuana, and I always said no, I don't do drugs! I need my mind as clear as possible for my work!"

Clint tries to calm him down. "Look, as I was saying, if we thought you were involved, this would be a very different conversation. We'd have come with lots more men and equipment. We'd be taking you to police headquarters in Minden, your Miranda rights would be read to you, we'd have a search warrant for your home and vehicles—"

Martin interrupts again with much more emotion and a tinge of anger in his voice.

"No! You can't have access to my lab! I forbid it!" He nervously backs up. Clint and Jerry recognize the action; most criminals who contemplate running from the police do the same thing. Jerry steps within inches of Martin's face.

"Martin!" he barks. "Martin, I need you to calm down! Stop with the emotions and get with the program, or else the next time you see us, we'll be here with twenty officers and the FBI. We can easily get search warrants to get a glimpse inside your little cement fortress, so don't even pretend that you won't allow it."

Martin jumps and almost trips as he backpedals. The mention of his lab is all it takes to elicit a small amount of cooperation. "I just, I can't let you inside. There are vital, fragile experiments inside that react to the slightest change in pressure, temperature, and light. It's a very controlled environment. So, I'm—I'm happy to continue talking out here, just, please, we can't go inside."

Martin's odd behavior convinces Jerry that every rumor he's ever heard about the concrete building and its owner is accurate. The man's voice trails off into a whimper, as if he's about to start crying. Jerry decides on a new tactic.

"Martin, look, a man is dead. His family needs closure. And to achieve that closure, we need to discover the answers to some pretty important questions."

"Questions? Like what?" Matin asks. His focus returns to the men in his front yard.

"Like, how did it happen? Why did it happen? We know the where and sort of the when. Most important to us, though, is *who* did it. Because when we know who committed the crime, then we can catch the criminal responsible and prevent it from ever happening again."

Martin is strangely quiet, but the look on his face screams for attention.

He's about to crack. What is he hiding? Clint wonders silently.

Our mad scientist/doctor knows who did it, doesn't he? Jerry is about to speak when something catches his eye and shoves him onto an entirely different course of action. With a covert motion, he moves one hand to the radio pager he carries. He activates the on-off switch with his thumb, and the pager cycles through a preprogrammed series of test tones.

"Uh, excuse me," he says to a puzzled Clint. Jerry walks back to the car, sits in the driver's seat, and pretends to have a muted conversation on Clint's radiotelephone. After a couple minutes, he emerges and calls for Clint's attention.

"Clint, hey, that was Channel 12. They say they had a tape malfunction, and they'd like to do your interview again. They'll meet us in town in front of the courthouse if that's okay with you."

"Okay. Tell them we'll be right there." Clint turns back to Martin and apologizes, "Look, we have to go, but I'd like to continue this conversation as soon as possible. The marshal and I will be back Monday morning to finish our discussion." Clint takes out his credentials, retrieves a business card, and hands it to Martin. "If you think of anything that can be useful between now and the next time we meet, feel free to call."

Martin looks so relieved that Clint thinks he may faint.

"Yes, of course, if I think of anything that can help, I'll call."

Clint pulls a small notepad from his shirt pocket and makes a notation with Martin's name and address. Without looking up, he asks for Martin's phone number, which Martin provides without hesitation. Martin hopes it will stave off any further intrusion on his property.

He adds, "And Monday is great. I'm happy to meet you in town. Maybe at the marshal's office or the courthouse? You name the time, and I'll be there."

Clint nods. "Great. The phone number you gave me, is that here?"

"Yes, sir, it is. Like I said, just call me, and I will meet you anywhere."

Clint shakes Martin's hand, turns, and heads back to his car. He closes the car door, cranks the motor, and backs out of the driveway.

Once they are far enough away, Clint stops the car and turns to Jerry.

"Okay, so, you want to explain to me just what the hell that was?"

Without hesitation, Jerry answers, "Did you happen to notice the baseball cap hanging from a broken tree branch near his front door? It clearly says 'Shreveport Captains' on the front panel. Not to mention the odd tint to it."

Clint snaps to attention in the car seat. "What? How did I miss that? I wondered why you cut things off so abruptly. There is no Channel 12 interview, is there?"

"Nope. But we need to get our hands on that cap. I'll bet the initials *T* and *J* are written in blue ink on the inside. You know that weirdo is involved. You saw how he freaked out when you said we would get a warrant and toss his lab. Dollars to donuts, Martin knows who killed Timmy, and I bet somehow that murderer from Cincinnati is, or was, involved too. I bet he also knows what's happening with the animal bones. All clues lead to Martin Landry. I say it's time we turn up the heat and make him sweat."

Clint contemplates Jerry's comments for a few minutes. He shifts the car into gear and says, "I think you're correct. He either is a direct link to the killer, or—"

"Or he is the killer," Jerry finishes.

"And if he is, then this case just got bumped up to bizarro world status. I think it might be time to brief Andrew on what we've found."

"Agreed."

"Wait a minute. Before we bother Andrew, can you call in a favor and ask to look at the tax records today? I'd like to know where Martin's property line begins and ends since we found those other items of Timmy's and the personal effects of that guy wanted out of Cincinnati. I want to be certain we shouldn't be focusing our attention on someone else."

"Don't even need to call. I have keys to all the city offices, so we can look it up ourselves. Of course, I'll let the clerk know what we're doing, within reason, maybe withhold the exact nature of what we're looking for—don't want her calling the news media too."

"Awesome." Clint turns off Parish Road 116 onto Dorcheat towards Minden. "Tax office, here we come."

18

Listening to Clint and Jerry relate all the new developments, Andrew is impressed. "And you say this Martin Landry fellow's lab was built to withstand a nuclear explosion?"

"Yes. I know it all sounds pretty bizarre, but it's true. We thought we'd come to you before we made any other moves."

"Is Mr. Landry still there? He hasn't gotten spooked and left the state, has he?"

Jerry shakes his head. "I've had a couple of my guys in full ghillie suits up on the dam since yesterday. They rotate shifts, and from what they report, he spends a lot of time outside, crying."

"You don't say." Turning towards Clint, he asks, "Does that say anything to you?"

"That he feels very guilty. I say either he's the murderer, or he has important information about the crimes. Who knows, maybe it's something about his missing son too. And, honestly, with what you described a couple of days ago and what your chief deputy told me, Timmy's murder does seem to fit the pattern the FBI was working last year over in Texas. Somehow, they're all connected, and Martin Landry is the common link. Sounds like probable cause for a warrant, don't you think?"

Andrew chews his bottom lip for a second, thinking over Clint and Jerry's evidence. He asks Clint, "Does your radiophone work out here?"

"It does."

"Mind if I make a quick call?"

"Of course not. Though we have what's called a continuous tone-controlled squelch system, so every word still goes through our tower repeater. Whatever you say can be heard by our dispatch center, and maybe anyone with a scanner tuned to that frequency."

"Gotcha, yeah, I know CTCSS is no guarantee of privacy. Unfortunately, we've been bitten by that issue before," Andrew says, following Clint to his car.

Andrew takes the handset from Clint and punches in the numbers. The phone rings three times before a man picks up. "Hello?"

"Morning, Mitch, this is Andrew."

"Hey, boss, what's up?"

"I'm using a radiophone, so be careful with your answers."

"Roger that," Mitch says with a tentative tone.

"I need you out here. I'll have Jerry, the Minden city marshal, call you from a landline to give you my location. When you come, bring Mark Conway too. I think this is about to get complicated, and I'm going to have Mark take my family back home."

All three men hear Mitch laughing on the other line.

"Boss, I thought you were on vacation for a week. If this is how you do vacations, I don't see how you've stayed married as long as you have."

"There's lots of things we're not telling my wife.

Clint and Jerry chuckle, and Mitch laughs again and replies, "Alright, well, let me start working on this. I'll call Mark and get him moving forward as well. Give me a day, and I'll be there. Have the marshal call me whenever is convenient for him."

"Thank you, Mitch. I'm pretty sure this one will peg on your 'weird' scale."

"Awesome," he replies just before Andrew disconnects.

"Okay, that is in motion. Jerry, since you're the city marshal, you're inside Minden courts every day. I'm guessing you have a decent relationship with the district attorney?"

"I do."

"Do you have a favorite judge? One who, if we go to him with the evidence as it stands currently, will issue a search warrant for Martin's place?"

"I have someone in mind."

"Great. Get with your DA and put together a search warrant. Make sure the cap is in it."

Jerry nods slowly.

"If your judge is any good, what you have now should be sufficient to get us access to the bayou as well as the house. The cap sells it for me, especially if you can establish that it did belong to the deceased once you can examine it. If it is missing when you return to the residence, then clearly Martin is trying to obstruct the investigation. Of course, that's a crime too. Martin is hiding something, either in the bayou or in the lab."

"Or in both," Jerry offers.

"I agree. There is still evidence to be found, so let's find it. You guys go to work on securing that warrant."

Clint and Jerry nod as Clint replies, "Thank you, Andrew. Appreciate your time. We'll get outta your hair and be back in touch when we're ready."

"Great. Be safe, guys. Remember, if Mr. Landry is connected somehow, then he is a very dangerous person. Don't let your guard down for a second if you run across him again."

"Roger that. See you when we've got all our ducks in a row," Clint says, shutting the car door.

Andrew watches as they drive away. Turning, he sees Colin approaching.

"They need your help, don't they, Dad?"

"Well, son, a lot of police work is about cooperation. Those two men are concerned about something pretty serious, and I'll never turn another law enforcement officer away if they need my help. Remember that when you're my age!"

"I will. Promise. Though, when I'm your age, I hope we have flying cars and can live on the moon." Changing the subject, Colin blurts out, "So, we are going fishing, right?"

Andrew laughs. "Flying cars? You've been reading those science fiction books again, haven't you?" He doesn't wait for an answer and instead says with some infectious enthusiasm, "There's fish still in the lake! Time for us to go get them, unless they've already invented fish rockets and have left Earth for a planet that is all water with no human fishermen." He steers Colin back towards the trailer.

Colin is intrigued. *All water and no humans? Is that possible?*

19

C lint and Jerry are silent as the Webster Parish district attorney relates the details of their request for a search warrant to the chief district judge, Paul Hardison.

"And that is why we request that you issue a search warrant for Mr. Landry's property. You will notice that our request for a search warrant includes the bayou behind his residence. Yesterday, Marshal Thomson and Captain Ward, in conjunction with a search party comprised of Webster deputies and KCS Rail Police, recovered personal effects on Mr. Landry's property that belonged to Mr. Timothy Johnson, the homicide victim whose remains were discovered last week. They also discovered the remains and effects of a murder suspect from Cincinnati in the same woods. Therefore, we believe Mr. Landry and his residence/business may harbor materials related to the disappearance and murders of both victims or evidence of his involvement or complicity in the crimes."

Judge Hardison takes his time reading the warrant. When he finishes, he sits back and looks over his reading glasses at Clint.

"Captain Ward, why were you looking at Mr. Landry's property in the first place? On a Saturday, I might add, without a search warrant, his permission, or anyone from the sheriff's homicide branch?"

"Your Honor, this case is different than most homicide cases we get. I thought it needed a little bit of extra attention, which is why I engaged the cooperation of the city marshal to assist with canvassing and the search for any evidence related to Mr. Johnson's murder. We did not know Mr. Landry owned the land where we found the items listed in the warrant until we searched the tax records. It is heavily wooded with no signs regarding trespassing, ownership, or habitation.

"We were searching for items described as missing from her son's personal effects by the mother of the deceased. The marshal and I thought we'd take a few minutes and walk the rail line, since its proximity to where Mr. Johnson's vehicle was left made it a likely place for the killer to discard anything related to or connected to the crime. In the course of our search, we located Mr. Johnson's tennis shoes on the bank of the small tributary bayou that originates in the tailwater bayou behind Mr. Landry's home."

Jerry interjects, "I think I should add that where we found the shoes very close to where we found his abandoned vehicle. On a hunch that the killer might have used the water to mask or hide his travels, we then followed that little bayou a short distance into the woods and found the other two items in plain sight, as well as the remains of the wanted fugitive from Cincinnati."

Clint finishes with "And concerning the sheriff's homicide detective: I had asked the marshal to help me follow up on some hunches, and when we found the new evidence, I immediately contacted the sheriff's office. So, the detective is completely aware of what we've found, our suspicions, and this warrant."

Hardison shakes his head approvingly, sits back, and considers another question.

"Now, the baseball cap you list. Marshal Thomson, you say it hangs on a broken tree limb, near Mr. Landry's front door?"

"Yes sir. When I spoke with the deceased man's mother, she told me that Mr. Johnson had a habit of writing his initials in blue ink on his clothes and shoes, as described in the warrant. When we recovered Mr. Johnson's shoes, they had his initials written in blue ink, so it stands to reason that if the cap is his, his initials will be found on the inside of the cap. When we left Mr. Landry's, the cap was in plain view, so it's critical that the cap is included in the warrant. Once we have it in hand, we should be able to determine if it is Mr. Johnson's."

"And if, in blue ink, the initials *T* and *J* are written on the inside of the cap, then you believe that the cap belonged to the murder victim?"

"Yes. All we have to do is turn it over and check. Then, once we take possession of it, I hope to get the cap to the state forensic section in Bossier so they can check for other trace evidence and match the initials to those on his other property. If we can prove it was Mr. Johnson's, then we'll be coming back to you to secure a warrant to arrest Mr. Landry, not just one to search his home and property."

The judge nods. "I see that you will be asking the new US marshal from over in Shreveport, Andrew McLean, to participate. What is his stake in this issue?"

"Well, Your Honor—"

Judge Hardison holds up one hand. "Why don't we drop the formalities, Captain. Just call me Paul."

Clint shrugs. "I'll try. Jerry and I met the marshal a few days ago. He and his family are over at the Beaver Dam Campground on Upper Caney Lake. When we related some of the non-public details of the case to him, the marshal recounted his work with the FBI on two similar cases in Texas last year that might have involved a fugitive serial killer. He believes there is a pattern in the offenses, and we think he is correct. We thought his expertise would be helpful—plus, if there is a federal component to this investigation, we'd rather have his assistance than the FBI's."

Hardison looks over at the district attorney, who half shrugs and eventually nods in agreement. Satisfied, he pulls out his favorite ink pen and signs the original warrant and three copies. He looks up and hands one to the DA and the other three to Clint.

"Alright, gentlemen, I do believe you've enough probable cause for this warrant. The fact that you found the personal items on his property is enough for me. But bear in mind, if, through the course of your investigation, you believe you've discovered more than is covered in this warrant, come back so that we can amend it or issue a new one that covers any new evidence related to any other crime."

"Thank you, sir. We'll keep you posted on what we find."

As Clint and Jerry turn to leave, Hardison once again holds out one hand, palm up. "You boys stay put." Looking at the DA, he says, "Debbie, I need to have a personal conversation with the captain and the marshal. Sorry to do this. I'll catch up with you before court resumes this afternoon."

The DA nods, collects a file she propped against a chair, and leaves, shutting the door behind her. Both men are intrigued. Hardison stands and goes over to a cabinet on the wall close to his desk and pulls open a door, revealing an impressive collection of scotches, bourbons, and three mason jars that hold a clear liquid.

Moonshine? Here in the judge's chambers? Clint wonders.

Without hesitation, Hardison takes down a glass and a half-empty mason jar. He shakes the mason jar with practiced expertise, and as the bubbles subside, a satisfied look crosses his face. Unscrewing the lid, he pours himself two fingers. He looks over his shoulder at Clint and Jerry and takes down two more glasses and pours. He hands Clint and Jerry their own and takes a sip as he sits. They take tentative sips because now they have no idea what to expect.

Guess we're having a liquid lunch, Clint thinks as he takes another sip.

"Men, my first point is that the bayous, creeks, and springs around here make some of the best shine in the world. If someone is using them to hide their criminal activities, especially to perpetrate murders in my jurisdiction, then that is something I take very personally."

Taking another sip, Clint realizes that this isn't just smooth; it may be the smoothest moonshine he's ever tasted. Hardison sees Clint's reaction and smiles.

"Right, Captain? Pretty smooth and amazing shine. Anyway, I wanted to talk with you two privately because this Landry issue is somewhat of a personal matter for me, but it doesn't rise to the level where I should have recused myself from signing your warrant. You see, Mr. Landry is not entirely unknown around here—because of his kidnapped son, Oscar. I also know of the family involved."

Clint and Jerry raise their eyebrows.

"Politically speaking, that is. That's how I know the family."

"Sir?" both ask, almost in unison.

"While I have never had any dealings with Mr. Landry or his ex-wife, I do know her ties go back to an extended and well-connected family over in Shreveport."

With a sinking feeling in his gut, and curious about the look on Hardison's face, Clint has to ask. "Which family?"

"The Lamberts."

Clint exhales and tries not to appear shocked. "When you said 'family,' I thought you meant her immediate family might be rich, or political, or powerful, but not all three."

Jerry is surprised too. "The actual Lamberts? How is it we never knew this when we were searching for that kidnapped boy?"

"I heard Mr. Lambert sent someone to convince the local media that it was a bad idea to anger the family with specious coverage or inaccurate reporting regarding the boy's disappearance. After the family decided the FBI didn't pay them enough attention because of their notoriety, they sent their own investigators—mostly retired spooks and fibbies, who did a significant amount of sleuthing around to figure out what happened. Their main area of inquiry was who in the world was stupid enough to snatch John Lambert's only grandchild."

"They ever come up with anything?" Clint asks.

"Not a thing. The investigators shook the trees in all sixty-four Louisiana parishes and still came up empty-handed. They even contacted the governor through a back-channel intermediary to see if he would contact some of his more infamous friends for assistance or information, which he was happy to do. I heard they came up empty on that as well.

"Now, I tell you all this because if you find anything in Mr. Landry's house that relates back to his son's disappearance, then that's gonna be like kicking a big ole hornet's nest on steroids, so you should be prepared. They are the richest Irish Catholics in Louisiana. Outside the southern Louisiana Cajun mob, they are also the most powerful family with the best political connections. Everyone knows they're tied in with the Irish families in Chicago, Boston, Jersey, and New York and even overseas with the IRA. I am sure you both are aware, no one messes with them and emerges unscathed."

Clint nods and squints. He recalls a news story about the Lamberts and tries to remember what it was. Then, it hits him. "Wait, aren't they lobbying the legislature and governor? Trying to get approvals for riverboat gambling on the Mississippi?"

Hardison nods. "Yes. And trust me, they'll get it. I would not be surprised if they get casinos on the Louisiana *and* Mississippi sides of the river. They'll eventually get permission for boats over on the Red River in Bossier and Shreveport too. Just wait and see."

"Seriously?"

"Yes. Now, some background on Mr. Landry. As I understand it, when Lambert's daughter met Mr. Landry—who, by the way, has a bona fide, first-family Cajun heritage—and started dating him, he was a second-year resident at a teaching hospital in New Orleans. Landry had a brilliant career at Tulane as a student and an equally brilliant career ahead of him as a physician. They were initially pleased that she might marry a successful doctor. Then, during his residency, he went a little sideways and started to gravitate towards scientific research and not the practice of medicine. He latched onto bizarre theories of earth science, especially those that involved human mutation and survival after a nuclear war.

"He believes, by the way, that all life on Earth came from outer space. Ancient alien technologies, and other nonsense. He became embroiled in a scandal of some kind for his experimentation with radioactive isotopes he had no reason to possess. That got his license revoked by the medical licensing board. The Lamberts were mortified. During all this, Patricia, the only daughter of John Lambert, got pregnant and married Mr.

Landry. It was almost more than the Lambert family could take.

"By all accounts, they had a stormy relationship and divorced soon after their son, Oscar, was born. The Lambert family filed injunctions in every court possible in the state against Mr. Landry. These were designed to head off the mere possibility that he might speak publicly regarding family business practices to which he'd been exposed. However, even in their anger at him, they still felt obliged to take care of their grandson, so in an attempt to entice Mr. Landry to play nice, they offered him a substantial sum of money, more than a few million dollars, to be used to purchase, build, and maintain a residence where Oscar, the grandchild and sole family heir, could safely visit and live during court-ordered visitation."

"Wow" is Jerry's only reaction.

Clint exhales as he speaks. "More than a million bucks?"

"Several. And that's a drop in the bucket for the Lamberts. Honestly, I bet it was some money they found in a couch while the maids were cleaning their house. I was surprised that Landry didn't disappear during the divorce proceedings; instead, they gave him enough money to never work again. A lot of people say it was Patricia's drug use and constantly stepping out on Martin that led to the divorce. Just another black eye the family wanted to sweep under the rug.

"To say I was doubly surprised he didn't become gator bait after the kid got kidnapped would be an understatement. I guess they all believed him, given the injuries he appeared to suffer in the attack, the mess the kidnappers made of his house, and the fact that the child was connected to a very prominent and wealthy family. It has always bothered me that we never heard a peep about the kid again and never a ransom demand. John Lambert, the family patriarch, has said as much many times. When Oscar vanished, it crushed Mr. Lambert, and I think it made him meaner. Some of us believe that with his only hope to carry on the Lambert name gone, he had no reason left to be a better person.

"Anyway, this warrant gives you entrance to Mr. Landry's residence, where he conducts whatever it is he does as a business. I suggest you keep your eyes open. And if you come across any new evidence that you believe could be related to Oscar's disappearance, you should think before you act. As soon as this warrant was filed in the DA's office, someone there called John Lambert to tell him that we're looking at Martin and that we think something odd is going on out there. So, be careful, be thorough, and be smart about what you do."

Hardison glances up at a wall clock next to the wet bar and, with a tilt of his glass, downs what remains of his drink and grabs several file folders. "Now, if you gentlemen don't mind, court resumes in about an hour, and I guess I should at least pretend to review my afternoon caseload."

Clint and Jerry wonder what to do with their empty glasses.

Without looking up from the manila folder he's just opened, Hardison says, "Just put your glasses on the liquor cabinet shelf. I'll have my secretary clean up after I go to court. Good day, Captain, Marshal."

"Thank you, sir. We will certainly keep you informed on what we find."

"You do that," they hear as the door closes behind them.

20

"Thought you might need these," Andrew's chief deputy, Mitch, says, handing over a US Marshals raid jacket, a ballistic vest, a gun belt, and all the accessories. "I assumed you'd have your service-issued sidearm, but even if you didn't, I brought spares."

"You assumed correctly. And thanks."

"Just practicing my mind reading."

Andrew smiles as he dons all his gear.

"What about your family?" Mitch asks.

"Well, Margery knows this is the job I signed up for. Colin was having a great time fishing and of course wanted to stay and watch. I told him we'd go fishing later this summer and didn't address exactly what we were doing today."

His voice trails off as he listens to Jerry talking with one of his deputy marshals by police radio. Jerry comes to Andrew with a situation report.

"My guy says Martin is outside again, looking at the bayou. He can't see if the cap is still on the tree."

"Great. Okay now, everyone, gather around."

The group quiets and turns to face Andrew, Clint, and Jerry.

"I'm passing around an enlarged DMV photo of our subject, Martin Landry. We understand he is outside his lab, so we're going in hot, given he will see, and hear, us coming. No sirens, though. Let's at least surprise him when we roll into the driveway. Webster SWAT, you will have your breach ram ready, just in case he beats us into the house, locks us out, and we have to ram the door. State, you are primary, so he is all yours once we serve him the warrant. You can choose to interview him there, or we can take him into town.

"Keep in mind, our search warrant only covers items that may be associated with the murder of Timmy Johnson. However, we will also be searching for anything related to his missing minor child, Oscar. Here, please pass this around," he says to Clint, who hands out color eight-by-tens of Oscar. "I'm passing around a photo of the missing child, who was reported kidnapped last year. Take a look at it and commit it to memory. We find anything related to the kid, we stop to determine if it's outside the scope of our warrant. Webster dive team, you guys can launch your airboat from behind his house. You are going to drag the bayou, specifically looking for anything related to the homicide. Questions?"

"Yeah, not a question, more a point of fact. We understand that his place is built out of reinforced concrete, so if our ram doesn't break his door, we could blow it, but that might damage any evidence. Thoughts or suggestions?" the SWAT commander asks.

Andrew looks at Clint and Jerry. "You guys have been there. Anything to add?"

"The door looks to be steel. Not wood. However," Clint says, looking over at the heavy-duty-tow-truck-turned-SWAT-vehicle, "it looks like you guys have a winch on that truck. I bet you could pull it off its hinges if needed."

Jerry looks at a new device attached to the side of the SWAT vehicle. "And if you have to use that battering ram, or whatever it is, it looks like that will not be an issue. Does that help?"

The Webster SWAT commander smiles and pats the newly installed ram. "Sure does. We can use my new baby here to ram it into next week. Been waiting for the right opportunity to try her out."

Andrew smiles at the commander's enthusiasm but senses that Jerry has more to say.

"Is there something else, Jerry?"

"Well, I have a buddy who sells medical research equipment. He told me once last year that he sold Martin the equipment for a negative-pressure room."

Many in the group look concerned. Webster sheriff Homer Hancock shakes his head, looks a bit confused, and asks, "Negative-pressure room? Why would he need one of those?"

Jerry shrugs.

Andrew interjects, "From what I know, negative rooms are used as an isolation technique in hospitals and medical centers to prevent cross-contamination from room to room."

From the back, someone asks, "You mean, like, in a laboratory setting where they fool around with stuff like viruses and germ warfare?"

Andrew nods. "Yes. Normally, it will include a ventilation system that generates negative pressure, which means the pressure in the room will be lower than in surrounding rooms. This allows air to flow into the isolation room but not escape from the room, as air will naturally flow from areas with higher pressure to areas with lower pressure—"

"Oh, I get it, to prevent contaminated air from escaping the room but to allow the person inside not to suffocate," the sheriff interrupts.

Andrew nods again. "Yes. Hospitals use this technique to isolate patients with airborne contagious diseases. Research scientists use it to study diseases, both those we've already cured and those that have no known cure, such as that hemorrhagic fever over in Africa and, of course, as you said a minute ago, germ warfare."

Sheriff Hancock exhales heavily and turns to the assembled men.

"Alright, this new information doesn't change how we approach the lab. What does change is how we might conduct the search once we're inside. So, if we have to breach the door, no one is to enter until it's deemed safe, understand?"

A chorus of yessirs satisfies the sheriff, and he turns back to Andrew and indicates he can resume the pre-raid briefing.

"Look, we don't know what we'll find. I want everyone here to keep your head on a swivel and your wits about you." He points at two rookie deputies. "You two will be on access control. You are to block 116 east and west at least one hundred yards on either side of the raid location and deny access to anyone but law enforcement. Luckily, the media hasn't shown up, but if they do, I expect they'll want a statement from me." He puts one hand on Andrew's shoulder and says, "I am happy to talk to them if I have to, but I'll also be happier if they never show up."

Everyone laughs at that remark. Sheriff Hancock finishes with, "Alright, Marshal, they're all yours."

Andrew smiles, dons a baseball cap with the US Marshals logo, and says, "Okay, everyone, let's go. As the sheriff said, be safe, watch out for this guy—no telling what he might do or be capable of doing. I would particularly be aware of your surroundings outside the residence. Mr. Landry may have created some unknown defensive traps, so be forewarned. The house is a total unknown. As we approach the site, the sheriff will take point. I'll fall in line behind him. Webster SWAT, in line behind me, and set up as close to the house as you might need to. State Police, behind Webster but deploy immediately with your airboat to the rear of the residence."

Seeing every head nod, Andrew says, "Great. Let's hit it."

With Clint and Jerry in the back and Sheriff Hancock riding shotgun, Andrew hits the gas on his government-issued Plymouth Satellite, and the 426-cubic-inch V8 roars. As he accelerates, Clint and Jerry are pushed back against the seat. The car swerves slightly when it transitions from the gravel in the Beaver Cheeks parking lot to the asphalt roadway.

"Now, that's how the motor of a police car should sound," Clint says approvingly.

The sheriff turns partly around and addresses Jerry. "Say, can you raise your man on the radio? Find out if Martin is still in the backyard."

Jerry keys his portable radio. "Robert, this is Jerry. Is the subject still outside?"

The radio squawks to life. "Ten-four. The subject has not moved."

"Copy that. Be advised, we are two minutes out. Repeat: we are two minutes out."

"Ten-four. No change in the subject. He is outside near the bayou, sitting in the grass. No weapons visible."

"Ten-four. When you see us arrive, wait a few minutes to make sure he doesn't try to escape up the dam. Once we detain him, come on down and join the party."

"You got it, boss. Personally, I hope he runs. Been too long since I got in a scrap."

21

Two minutes later, still sitting on the grass behind his laboratory, Martin is startled to hear what sounds like a convoy of trucks and cars. He wonders if it might be workers going to the church camp just up the road. His heart jumps when it sounds like all the vehicles are turning in to his driveway. Standing, he sprints around his lab and is almost run over by the Webster sheriff's dive team in a pickup truck, pulling an airboat on a trailer. He jumps back to avoid getting hit, then breaks into a full-out run towards the open side door of his lab.

"There he is! Don't let him get inside!" Andrew slams his feet on the brake pedal and skids to a halt in the dirt. He jumps out, yelling for Martin to stop. Every other vehicle empties as well. Deputies, marshals, and troopers vector towards Martin to intercept him. Sheriff Hancock, Clint, and Jerry follow Andrew, all yelling for Martin to stop running.

"Martin Landry, freeze! Stop! Don't make this worse than it has to be! We just want to talk! *Stop*! Do *not* go inside!"

Martin ignores the crowd of screaming law enforcement officers and makes it into the building just ahead of Andrew.

"Dammit!" Andrew yells as he slams his hand on the steel door. He hears Martin engage a locking mechanism and he swears again. Re-holstering his pistol, he motions for the Webster SWAT team to set up on the front door as the dive team prepares to put their boat in the water behind the lab. "That fellow is fast. He moved like he was expecting us. I heard him setting some sort of locking device on the steel door. I guess when he built this place he knew one day it would need to withstand an assault from outside."

"Yeah, and now even more about Martin Landry doesn't add up," Jerry says over Andrew's shoulder.

"Sheriff, should we go ahead and start?" the SWAT lieutenant asks from behind cover.

Andrew nods and looks at the sheriff, who replies, "Go ahead. Verbal commands first; then, if he doesn't comply, let's talk about a plan to ram it or rip the door off its hinges."

Over the loudspeaker attached to the SWAT vehicle, the commander announces, "Martin Landry, this is the Webster Parish Sheriff's Office. We have a warrant to search the building. Come out with your hands up and in plain view. Martin Landry, this is the Webster Parish Sheriff's Office. We have a warrant to search the building. Come out with your hands up! We're not going away, Martin. Come out with your hands up!"

The commander repeats the phrase several times without success. He shifts his gaze over to Sheriff Hancock, who rotates one hand in a circular motion.

As the SWAT commander repeats the commands for Martin to exit the building, two deputies low crawl to the front door while a sniper covers them. One sits upright with his back to the concrete structure and keys his radio.

"I don't see anywhere for us to hook onto the door. I think it's one piece of steel. There is no external structure to it. I believe we'll have to ram it to breach."

Behind the SWAT vehicle, Andrew, Clint, Jerry, and the sheriff watch as another deputy darts up to the tree and secures the baseball cap. He brings it back and hands it to the sheriff, who makes eye contact with Clint and Jerry and flips it upside down. In runny, blue ink, the initials *T* and *J* are easily read.

Jerry shakes his head. "Oh man, that's Timmy's cap." He looks towards the lab where Martin is barricaded. "I knew this guy was involved somehow!"

Sheriff Hancock scratches at the red tint on the lettering. "What is this?" he asks as they all hear the airboat come to life behind the lab.

"We don't know yet. Timmy's bones had the same tint to them, remember? So did his clothes."

"Well, this seals it for me. You found Timmy's tennis shoes on the tracks, his jewelry, and now his baseball cap on Martin's property. I'm convinced." Turning to the SWAT commander, he yells, "Prepare your men! Permission to breach the door!"

The SWAT commander smiles. He loves his job so much right now that he can't stand it. While another officer continues imploring Martin to come out, the commander turns a large hand crank to extend the new battering ram. He locks it into place, goes to the vehicle's front, and flips up a steel-reinforced bar that helps support the added weight, then kisses his fingers and places them on the ram lovingly. His ram is thirty feet of heavyweight drill pipe straight from the oil fields. The typically hollow pipe is filled with concrete and rebar. A large, flat plate welded to the end bears a painted yellow smiley-face, and the commander can't wait to use it in the real world.

He turns to the deputy giving verbal commands. "Give me the mike."

With the public address microphone in hand, the commander stands and looks over the open front door of the SWAT vehicle.

"Martin Landry, this is SWAT team commander for the Webster Sheriff's Office. If you look outside, you will see I have a ram affixed to my SWAT vehicle. If you do not come out, I will be ramming your door. I don't care how strong you think your door is; it will not survive! If you know what is good for you, surrender now! Come out with your hands up! I will count to ten. When I reach ten, your door will no longer exist. It doesn't matter what countermeasures you have in place; they will not prevent us from destroying it. If you love your house as much as I have heard, you'll come out with your hands in the air!"

He repeats the entire phrase three times and shrugs when he sees the sheriff laughing about his last sentence. "Why not rattle him a bit?" the commander quips.

"Hey, works for me. It looks like you didn't convince him, so do your thing."

While the commander counts back from ten, Andrew sees Martin briefly in the window. "He's at the window!"

The SWAT vehicle roars to life, and the driver guns the motor several ear-splitting times. The sheriff leans close and yells to Andrew, Clint, and Jerry, "We got the motor from one of those dirt-track racers over on Hilltop raceway off of 80! Makes a hell of a lot of noise, doesn't it? We think maybe it will scare people into surrendering!"

"I'd surrender for sure if I heard that monster coming towards me," Jerry yells.

Lurching forward and back several times, the vehicle repositions so that the ram is fifty feet or so away and aimed directly at Martin's steel front door. He looks at Sheriff Hancock, who nods his approval and gives a thumbs-up.

The heavy vehicle jumps towards the door with surprising agility. The motor screams and blasts fire from the exhaust system. It gains momentum with every foot it covers.

With the vehicle ten feet from the building, the door flies open, and Martin appears, hands up, yelling, though no one can hear him over the roaring engine. Andrew thinks he sees Martin's lips saying, "Please! I surrender! I surrender!"

To avoid killing Martin with the steel plate and battering ram, the driver stomps on the brakes and turns the wheels slightly to the left. The SWAT vehicle skids to a stop. Ten feet of concrete-and-rebar-filled oil pipe just miss Martin. Deputies swarm and take him to the ground, then yank him upright and march towards Andrew, Clint, Jerry, and the sheriff.

"Wise move," Sheriff Hancock says. "Captain, want to read the warrant to Mr. Landry? And his rights, I guess?" he adds with some hesitation.

While Clint reads the warrant to Martin, the SWAT vehicle backs up. Andrew stands at the front door and peers inside. The cool air leaving the building makes him shiver for a moment.

"Alright. SWAT, great job! Sorry you didn't get to ram the door, but I'm sure some drug dealers are going to meet your ram soon enough. To me, your actions are what led him to surrender. Thank you! I don't know what else there is for you to do here, so if you want to go ten-eight, ten-nineteen—with the sheriff's permission, of course—that is fine with me. The troopers in the boat behind the lab are going to be busy for a while dragging the bayou."

Calling two troopers over, he orders them to guard the door but not to go inside. Turning to Martin, he says, "Mr. Landry, you are being detained. You are not under arrest. Did you understand the terms of the warrant the captain read to you just now, as well as your Miranda rights?"

"Yes, of course I did. I'm not an idiot."

"Good. Captain? You want him hooked front or back?"

"Front is fine, for now," Clint responds. With a satisfied nod, a nearby deputy pulls handcuffs from his gun belt and clicks them into place around Martin's wrists. As this happens, the look of shock in Martin's eyes is evident.

"What the hell is this? I can't believe you guys were going to break down my door with some kind of medieval battering ram. All you hick cops are the same. Big toys, little brains."

Out behind Martin's lab, the sheriff's dive team is busy with a grappling hook. One deputy stands on the boat's bow and tosses the hook into the water while another is on the lookout with a long rifle in hand, ready to dispatch any gator they may hook by accident.

Below them, the newcomer is silent and curious. All this activity is a new thing, and it is unsure how to proceed or if it should proceed at all. It is spread out thinly, with its body covering the bottom at the deepest spot in the bayou. The newcomer rests here frequently, far away from the large, yellow, unblinking eye in the sky and its harmful rays. It takes a meal every now and then as crawfish and other aquatic things foolishly wander within reach.

Then, there is a disturbance above it, towards the surface. Though the water is quite turbid, it senses movement, accompanied by odd noises as something is dropped into the water and dragged across the bottom. It moves to avoid the treacherous thing, correctly assessing their motives for such behavior, and watches as the process is repeated over and over. It believes the one who captured it may be responsible, and it remains still, content in the belief that one day it will be free. Then, it will remove the things that have insulted it and hurt this place.

Not far away on dry ground, Andrew addresses Martin.

"Mr. Landry, in my experience, innocent men do not run when they see the police. They especially don't run into concrete bunkers and lock the doors, preventing entrance by the police. Any other smart comments to make?"

Martin shrugs. "I don't even know why you're here. Why are you bothering me? You can't go inside my lab without my permission anyway. I know the law!

"Oh, so, I guess you're as good a lawyer as you were a medical doctor?" Jerry asks from behind Martin, who turns and sneers at him before he's jerked back around by two deputies. "Did you not hear what my colleague read to you? We found items, personal effects belonging to a homicide victim, on your property. Do you see the baseball cap the sheriff is holding right now? That belonged to Timmy Johnson. You may recall we asked you about him.

"Just so you understand why we're all here and why you're in handcuffs, we now think that you are involved somehow in the murder of Mr. Johnson. Sounds like you didn't pay attention when the captain read the warrant. It not only permits us to search your lab, but it also orders us to search your lab. You can't stop us, even if you tried. If you want to talk now, we'll listen. If you want to invoke your right to a lawyer, well then, I hear Mr. Lambert might have someone who can represent you."

At the mention of John Lambert, Martin's bravado melts away. He slumps, and only the fact that two deputies are still holding him prevents him from falling face-first to the ground. Martin begins to speak in a rapid-fire but weak voice.

"Please. No. Don't call Mr. Lambert. He sent the guys who beat me when Oscar got—I mean, went, uh, missing. I think they would have killed me, except it started raining, and Oscar showed up as I escaped to the lab. He killed them, and I had to destroy their clothes and car. I didn't understand the connection to thunder, lightning, and rain at that point because everything was just so . . . I, just, I . . ."

His voice trails off as he hears noises from behind the lab. He cranes his head and torques his body. It's easy to see the airboat as it does a slow orbit around a large cypress tree, just about where he believes Oscar rests on the bottom, waiting. A man in a wetsuit is throwing a large grappling hook into the water. This is more than Martin can take. He turns and addresses Sheriff Hancock and Andrew in a voice that increases in emotion with every word.

"You have to tell them to get out of the water! There isn't anything in there, trust me! But you have to get them off the water now!"

Clint is confused. "What did you just say about your son, Oscar? What did you mean when you said that Oscar appeared when someone Mr. Lambert sent to assault you was here?"

Now Martin looks confused for a moment. He blinks and shakes his head a few times. "Nothing. I haven't said a word about Oscar or seen him since it happened. Really," he adds with very little believability.

A familiar noise catches his attention. Glancing skyward, his worst fears are confirmed. On the horizon, the dark clouds of a summer storm brew. He has to get these people off his property before Oscar shows up and kills everyone. *How do I get them to leave?* In his desperation, Martin hits on a course of action. He lies. He knows they'll have to release him eventually, so he figures a big lie is worth a try.

"There is a bomb in my lab. I activated it when I ran to my lab. If we don't leave, we're all going to die."

"What the hell did you just say?" Clint asks, stepping within inches of Martin's face. "Repeat that."

Martin summons as much courage as possible to sell the lie, stands straight, and replies, "I said I have a bomb in my lab, set to go off, and I cannot stop it. I did it so that no one could get my research if something like this ever happened to me. There is a trip switch on both doors. It's like the doomsday bombs America and Russia have set to kill anyone who survives the coming nuclear war. We must leave, or else we're all dead. When I saw you trying to get into the lab, I set the bomb to explode in desperation. I cannot stop it."

"Think he's telling the truth?" the sheriff asks.

Andrew shrugs and directs a question towards Martin.

"So, when did you hit the switch? Is it on a timer? Can't you shut it off?"

"I built it such that anything inside would be destroyed, and it can't be disarmed. It is set to go off and incinerate everything within a hundred yards or so." He leans his body towards the large shipping container next to the lab and continues, "It's in that shipping container over there."

"Yeah, cuz that's what all innocent people do," Jerry mutters.

Sheriff Hancock, Andrew, Clint, and Jerry all stare at the large, metal shipping container attached to the side of the concrete building. Every other cop in the front yard follows suit. Now they're all wondering what inside has the sheriff and the fed so concerned.

"Before I stepped outside to prevent your man from ramming my front door, I checked to make sure it was on. It is. At the moment, we have less than fifteen minutes to clear out. I set it that way so no one would have time to disarm it if something happened to me."

Andrew turns to the sheriff and says, "Let's assume he has the skills and motive. I'd err on the side of survival to fight another day. So, why not set a watch on the house—say, from where Jerry had one of his men on the top of the dam—and then clear everyone else out? Just to be sure."

The sheriff nods and reaches into a shirt pocket, retrieving a police whistle hanging on a silver chain. He gives it three short blasts, and all movement stops.

"Listen up, everyone. This is an emergency evacuation. The building is rigged with explosives that are set to go off very soon! Wrap everything up and get out of here, chop, chop. Hustle up. This ain't a drill; this is real world! Everyone can rally at Beaver Cheeks. We're taking the prisoner to my lockup."

Jerry calls out to his deputy, who, after trekking from the top of the dam down to Martin's lab, has finally arrived at the edge of the property. "Saddle up. We believe there is a bomb in the building. Get back up the dam but farther away from where you were, maybe prone out just over the edge so you can see what happens when the building explodes. Stay on the radio. You'll be in a good spot to provide us real-time updates!"

The deputy waves his acknowledgment, turns on his heel, and makes his way back to the trail he blazed from the top of the dam.

Distant thunder travels across the heavens as the airboat operator makes a beeline for the shore and its trailer, which still sits low in the water. He revs the motor, and with one motion, the boat is out and onto the trailer, with water, dirt, and slimy green grass trailing behind it. The operator stays put as they pull around the lab and onto the surface street, where he jumps down and helps secure the airboat to the trailer.

Twelve feet below the surface of the bayou, the newcomer is curious. The thing above it that had been loud and ugly is no longer there. The disturbed bayou begins to settle, and peace returns for a moment. Then, the newcomer senses another type of vibration. This vibration brings a measure of excitement even as it agitates the newcomer's genetic memory. Soon, perhaps, when the magic falls from the sky, it can rise from the bottom and feed.

Every vehicle but two are moving when Sheriff Hancock looks at Andrew and asks, "You want to keep him or want me to take him in for questioning?"

Andrew looks over at Clint, who steps into the conversation. "Well, Sheriff, if you don't mind, I'd like to interrogate him back at your office in Minden, if that's okay with you. There are some serious issues to discuss regarding several odd occurrences, including the murder of Timmy Johnson. As you know, Mr. Landry here is the link."

"Sounds like a plan. I'll see you back at the sheriff's office. I'd like a copy of your report on the raid here, as soon as you get it written and submitted."

"Yes sir, happy to provide you with one when it's ready."

Lightning illuminates the panorama, followed by a deep, rolling thunder.

Now beside himself, Martin screams, "*WE HAVE TO LEAVE NOW*!!! You don't understand. We have to go. Please, stop talking and leave!!"

Jerry shoves Martin into the back seat of Andrew's car and slides in beside him while Clint takes the passenger seat. Andrew guns the engine and spins his car in a tight circle as fat raindrops start plopping onto the windshield.

From the back seat, they all hear Martin whimpering. "Oh my God, please, hurry. Hurry! He will come, and I can't stop him. I tried to tell Timmy that. I could have stopped and picked him up, but Oscar was right behind me. It was him or me, and I'm way more important that Timmy."

Clint looks over at Andrew.

"What are you talking about?" Andrew demands.

"Oscar!" Martin yells. "He's in the bayou!"

"You saw Timmy Johnson the night he was killed?" Clint asks, incredulous.

"Of course I did! I saw him on the side of the road, but I didn't know his car was broken down. I yelled at him that he had to get back in his car and get out because Oscar was right behind me." He begins to weep softly and finishes with "And I can't stop him from killing."

The newcomer rises from the deep, breaks the bayou's surface, and raises both arms wide, taking in every drop of rain. Then, in the distance, it spots something. It begins to move as a resounding clap of thunder reverberates over the landscape.

Andrew stops the car a few hundred feet from the house, despite the imminent alleged explosion. Heavy rain overwhelms the windshield wipers.

Andrew turns slightly and fixes his eyes on Martin.

"You said your son, Oscar, who has been missing for more than a year, is in the bayou? What do you mean by that?"

Martin jerks his head around, terror radiating from his eyes. "Why have you stopped? He can run faster than you can imagine; he'll catch us, I know it! I saw him do it the night he killed Timmy!"

"What the hell did you just say?" Jerry asks, now inches away from Martin in the back seat.

Martin tries to calm down. He wants to come clean, to spit out the truth, but he knows that in the rain, Oscar comes without warning. "We have to go! I'll tell you everything, but we'll all die if we stay here! Please. You have to put the car in drive and get out of here. I promise to be completely truthful with you, but we must leave now. Take me with you, please, but we have to get as far away from here as possible!"

"So, no bomb in your lab?" Clint asks with a smirk, shaking his head.

Martin bounces several times in the back seat out of pure frustration. "Of course not! What's in the bayou behind my lab is much worse than any bomb! The thing in the bayou is the end of all life on Earth if it gets out! I've done what I can to stop or slow it, but if he can mutate any further—if he doesn't need to stay in the water—we'll all die!"

"I think he's having a nervous breakdown of some kind, possibly psychotic in nature . . . but maybe we should put more distance between the lab and us, just to be sure," Clint offers to Andrew, who nods in agreement. "He could also be lying to get us to return and get killed by the blast."

Jerry keys the radio. "Bill, you there?"

His deputy answers, "Yeah, I'm here, but I'm getting soaked to the skin! Still working my way back to the car. Had to stop for a minute, dropped my backpack."

Martin is horrified.

"You *left someone there*? Oh my God, how could you . . ." Martin looks off as if to peer through the cascade of rain pounding the window. "Of course, you didn't know about Oscar. You have to tell that man to get away as fast as possible."

Jerry looks at Martin and keys the radio.

"Bill, this is Jerry. I need you to step it up and get out of the area. Copy?"

"Copy, boss, but it'd be easier if you'd stop calling me or if you'd turn around and come get me," he replies.

Behind Andrew, Martin screams, "NO! You can't go back! I know Oscar is out now. He's probably watching us right now, trying to figure out what we're doing and how to get to us!"

Clint mutters just loud enough for Andrew to hear him, "He's completely insane."

Looking directly at Martin, Jerry keys his radio once again.

"Bill, this is Jerry. Twenty-two the mission. Martin says the bomb was a hoax. Repeat. There is no bomb. Get to your car ASAP and come back to the office." Looking at Martin, he asks, "Satisfied?" as Andrew floors the big car's engine.

The yellow eye blinks once, then again, as sadness overwhelms the newcomer. Standing at the edge of Martin's property, about forty feet to the rear of where Andrew's car was stopped, it knows that now there will be no meal. As the big metal thing with the sustenance accelerates away and out of reach, a noise in the distance captures the newcomer's attention. It turns.

Perhaps this hunt will be more successful.

"Dammit," yells Bill. He needs to get up the dam to his car and dry clothes. But he makes one critical misstep and tumbles through the tall grass and rocks, back to where the flat land begins its upslope. Now it isn't possible to climb back up in the heavy rain. He slips and slides but can't get traction. He curses everyone who left him alone at Martin's lab. "Man, I'm gonna get soaked to the skin. This is ridiculous. I hate you guys!" he screams to the heavens.

He reaches down for his radio, but it isn't there. Looking up, he sees it embedded in the mud twenty feet above his head. "Dammit, Jerry is gonna have my butt for that." He doesn't even try to climb back up to retrieve it. Instead, out of the corner of his eye, he sees that the back door to Martin's lab is still open and the lights inside are on.

Awesome. Maybe they left someone here for scene security.

Lightning strikes a tree in the forest about a hundred yards away, and it explodes, throwing shards of smoking bark in every direction. The thunder is immediate and rocks the ground underneath his feet.

"Mother Nature is in a nasty mood. That is just perfect. I'm gonna get fried by lightning or drown in this frog strangler." He has to get out of this rain, wait for it to stop. *Maybe whoever is inside can raise someone on their radio.* "And maybe weepy scientist boy has a coffee maker inside. I'll just make those ding-a-lings come back and get me."

He gathers his rifle and binoculars to his chest, bends down, and breaks into a fast trot towards the open door. Avoiding a large puddle, he slips and falls hard, banging his head. As he regains his composure, he sees someone standing at his feet. He laughs as the rain hitting his face obscures his vision. He thinks maybe it's Jerry, or the deputy they must have left inside the lab, so he yells, "You came back for me! Man, I need a drink. I can't believe you guys tried to make me climb back up the hill!"

When he rubs the rain out of his eyes, he comes to understand that what stands at his feet is not a person. It's not human at all. He's not sure what it is, but it looks angry, and the large, yellow eye bores a hole into his soul as odd-looking arms appear. Bill instantly realizes this is a life-and-death situation. Still on his back, he pulls his pistol and fires until the slide racks open. Lightning strikes another tree, and the noise is far more deafening than the gunshots. It distracts whatever is at his feet, though now it looks even angrier.

The thing absorbs all fifteen hollow-point .45 ACP rounds without dropping. Bill reaches for another magazine, discarding the empty one in the mud. On his elbows, he crab-walks backward, seating the magazine against his thigh and closing the slide with a quick reflex born out of muscle memory. The thing keeps pace with him. He stops and flattens out, making sure not to shoot his own feet, and fires another barrage of rounds into the red mass. He repeats the procedure one more time. Now stationary, he realizes he's been aiming at the wrong spot. With his last magazine seated, he fires the first two rounds directly at the yellow eye.

The huge, walking mud puddle makes no sound but reacts as if the bullets have hit essential organs. Bill smiles grimly, knowing he's finally found the right spot to shoot, and he methodically empties the entire magazine into the huge, yellow eye. When the slide racks open, he is out of bullets, so he throws his gun at the thing, and the weapon disappears.

Still recovering from the bullets, the eye almost vanishes. Bill watches in horror as a new eye appears and absorbs the injured one. He notes this new eye looks much angrier than the first one. He struggles to understand how the bullets and the gun went right through the thing.

"What are you?" he screams as a large hand unfolds from the body and surrounds his face, effectively drowning out his cries.

A red tendril snakes down his throat, and the newcomer begins to feed.

22

In despair, Martin assesses the sparse, dimly lit room. He jerks his hands slightly, testing the strength of his handcuffs, now attached to a steel ring welded into the middle of the table in front of him.

"Hey! Is anyone there? Can I have a glass of water? A 7 Up would be great!"

Behind the one-way glass, Clint chuckles.

"Hey, Jerry, is there 7 Up in that Coke machine out in the lobby?"

"I don't know. But let me check," Jerry replies. As he leaves the room, he reaches into his front pocket and jingles some coins.

Clint turns to Andrew. "Well, Andrew, do you want to talk to him, or do you want me to take a crack at him? We have quite a lot to go over. I'd like to start with whatever it was he was babbling about in the car."

Andrew, silent since they marched Martin into the sheriff's department through the secure sally port, clearly has something on his mind. When Jerry returns with a can of 7 Up and a Dr. Pepper, he voices his concern.

"Jerry, have you had contact with your man on the dam?"

"Come to think of it, no. When I told him to twenty-two his mission, I don't recall his response. I figured he'd return to the office." Jerry looks outside and sees that the summer thunderstorm has released its fury and moved on. He shares Andrew's look of concern and grabs his radio.

"It's not certain my radio will work all the way out there, but it might." Pushing the transmit button, Jerry speaks into the microphone. "Bill, this is Jerry. Got your ears on? Bill, this is Jerry, come in. Marshal One to Marshal Five, come in."

No response. Jerry tries one more time, then switches frequencies and raises the Webster dispatch center.

"Dispatch, this is Marshal One."

"Marshal One, dispatch. Go ahead. What do you need, sir?" the dispatcher asks.

"I need you to send a scout car to the Landry lab over off Parish Road 116 immediately. That is the scene of the raid from this afternoon. I have a deputy marshal there who is not in radio contact. Check his welfare. His name is Bill. He was supposed to be observing the building from the dam on Lower Caney Lake."

"Copy, Marshal. Sending a scout car. Will advise."

Jerry looks a little calmer. "Maybe he accidentally turned off his radio, or it got flooded out in the rain."

Clint has another idea. He enters the interrogation room, shutting the door securely behind him, and stands in front of Martin so that Jerry cannot see Martin's reaction. His voice is terse when he asks the only question he cares about at the moment.

"Why hasn't the deputy we left at your lab returned to the office or answered our calls on the radio?"

Martin blanches and jerks back, and the handcuffs bite into his wrists, leaving angry, red marks on his skin. Then, shaking his head, he dips in the chair and shrinks. "He's dead. There's no way he's alive if Oscar found him."

Clint is stunned into silence.

Behind the one-way glass, Jerry drops his drink and rushes past Andrew's attempt to stop him and into the interrogation room. He shoves Clint out of the way and grabs Martin by the throat, lifting him as far as the restraints will allow.

"What the hell are you saying? What do you mean my man is dead and that your dead son killed him?" he bellows.

Clint works to remove Jerry's hands from Martin's throat just as three deputies rush into the room, believing the prisoner has started a fight. Seeing Martin still in restraints, they relax somewhat. Martin tries to stand, so two of them push him down with a loud *thunk*. The deputies mill about, uncertain what to do next, and Martin begins to weep. Jerry reaches for him once again, only to be stopped by Clint and Andrew.

Once Jerry settles down and the deputies have left the four men alone, Martin spews out a story that Clint, Jerry, and Andrew find hard to understand through his sobbing.

"Oscar's not dead. Well, he may be dead, but I think part of him still lives inside whatever he's become. I can't stop what Oscar does. I've been trying for more than a year to understand it. At first, I thought I could communicate with it. Trust me, I have tried. That's why I was outside at the bayou when your men arrived. I've been feeding him animals that I catch on the theory that it might stop him from eating people.

"I don't even know where it's from, you know—the origin of what emerged after picking up that meteorite from my bayou. I thought it must be some military experiment and that they'd come looking for it one day. I eventually came to realize that whatever it was, before it killed and consumed Oscar, it must have been from some other place, and no one knew it was even here."

Martin stops speaking and sits back, spent, and relieved to have finally told someone the truth.

Clint, Jerry, and Andrew stand in silence. All three have conducted hundreds of interrogations in their careers and recognize the ring of truth when a criminal comes clean. They exchange perplexed glances, each wondering if they heard Martin correctly. Finally, Clint opens his mouth to ask a question—only to be interrupted by a persistent knock on the metal door.

Whoever is knocking doesn't wait for a "Come in." They turn and are surprised to see the sheriff, followed by more deputies.

"Jerry, you need to come with me," Sheriff Hancock says softly.

"Sheriff, we're kind of in the middle of something here," he responds.

He turns to Clint and says, "Clint, Andrew, grab Jerry and follow me."

Clint takes Jerry by the arm and leads him out of the interrogation room. Andrew follows, looking over his shoulder at Martin, who appears to know precisely why the sheriff is there. Martin buries his head and begins blubbering over and over, "I'm sorry, I'm so very sorry. It's not my fault."

The sheriff leads them into another room and without preamble states, "Jerry, your man is gone."

Jerry whirls back towards Martin's room, but Andrew and Clint stop him.

With one hand on Jerry's shoulder, Clint asks, "What are you saying, Sheriff? What do you mean he's gone?"

Sheriff Hancock's look of exasperation says as much as his words. "His gear is there. His gun is there, it's clear he was firing at something because there are four empty mags, and the slide on his forty-five is locked open. His clothes are there, with every other piece of his equipment. Everything is covered in some slimy red coloring that we've encountered before."

Jerry sits down hard in a chair and asks the question he doesn't want to ask.

"Bones?"

"Yes. Bones. They are in a direct line from his gear to the bayou behind Martin's lab. Whatever did this to your man must be using the bayou to mask its approach and retreat. I can't even believe I'm saying this, but I think something in the bayou is killing people and animals. Whatever you guys can get out of Martin, step it up. I'm going to quarantine the entire area around Martin's lab. I've already started the conversation with the Park Service about closing the Caney Lake recreation area and the Kisatchie National Forest hiking trails until we get a handle on this. I may need to call the feds in to help."

"I can't believe it. We should have gone back for him. What will I tell his mother?" Jerry wonders aloud, the anger building along with his bewilderment and sense of loss.

"What did Martin say before I pulled you out of the room?" the sheriff inquires. "Anything useful, given he's here and another murder just occurred?"

Everyone looks at Andrew, who shakes his head.

"I don't know, Sheriff. He wants to talk. In fact, after we got him the soda, he couldn't wait to start talking. But what he says sounds like the rantings of a total lunatic. He's kind of all over the map. I say we let him stew for a while, make him believe that we are unsure of our next move, and then I'll go back in and try a different tactic."

Turning to Jerry, he says, "Look, I don't think it's a good idea for you to question him. We're facing an event that has transitioned from a law enforcement issue to a personal issue for you, and I think you need to stay on the other side of the glass. Just my opinion, but I believe it's a valid one."

The public address system clicks to life, and everyone hears, "Sheriff, this is the front desk. A reporter with Channel 3, Diane Chase, is in the lobby. She wants an interview about Martin Landry's arrest and the raid on his laboratory. She also wants a statement or interview with you and the captain."

"Dammit," Sheriff Hancock mutters. "How did she find out about this?"

"Well, Sheriff, I hate to say it, but someone must be calling the media and feeding them details about this case."

Jerry adds, "Ms. Chase showed up after we found evidence on Landry's property. I imagine that she knows more than we suspect."

"I'll go speak to her if that's what you want. But—"

The sheriff is interrupted by Martin yelling from the other room.

"Hello! Anyone? Marshal? Sheriff? Has the rain stopped? If so, can we go back to my lab? There's no bomb. I was lying, but I need to show you proof of what I've told you. It should explain everything! Hello?"

Jerry exhales heavily and almost stands but thinks better of it.

Clint looks at Andrew and the sheriff. "He says he has proof of some kind that he wants to show us. Maybe we should go ahead and take him back to the lab, see what he has."

Andrew has been in situations like this before and offers a comment.

"Sheriff, can your forensic people work the scene? In my experience, taking a killer or a witness back to the scene of a crime can yield valuable information."

"I sent my deputies there just before I interrupted your interrogation." He turns to Jerry. "I'm sorry for your loss, Jerry. I agree with Andrew. If you take him back to the lab, maybe Martin can shed some light on what's been happening, especially if you can get him to describe how and why he's either been killing people or working with someone who is. I still don't understand what got Jerry's man, but it has to be connected to Martin somehow, even though he's been in our custody. While you guys do that, how about I keep Ms. Chase occupied so that she can't follow you and insert herself into the investigation any further? I bet I can keep her busy chasing her tail for a couple of hours."

"Thank you, Sheriff. We'll keep you posted," Andrew says as he leaves the room. Entering the interrogation room, he uncuffs Martin from the metal table, gruffly says, "Stand up," and cuffs his hands behind his back. "Okay. We're going on a little expedition, as you requested."

Recognition lights up Martin's eyes. "My lab? Has the rain stopped?"

"Yes. But there's been another murder. One of Marshal Thomson's men."

Martin puffs up his chest and spits out, "That's on you guys. I told you not to leave anyone there. If Oscar got another man, it has nothing to do with me."

Andrew steps close and with one hand tightly grasps the metal connection between the left and right handcuffs. He yanks Martin's wrists up and then down, forcing Martin to bend at the waist, his head hitting the metal table just hard enough not to break the skin. He emits a tiny scream of pain. Teeth clenched, Andrew bends down and places his mouth right next to Martin's left ear.

"Yes, it does, you little worm. It has everything to do with you. Show some damn respect for the life of a man who swore to uphold the law and help his fellow man." Andrew jerks Martin upright and continues,

"While you're at it, you better be thinking of a new fantasy story to tell us once we get back to your lab because the bomb in your lab and the monster-in-the-bayou stories you've tried on us won't cut it."

Releasing his grip, Andrew pushes him towards the door as he mutters loud enough for Martin to hear, "Personally, I think you're full of shit. Maybe I'll feed you to the alligators."

As they march down the hall towards the sally port and Andrew's car, Jerry accepts condolences from everyone they pass. He shakes his head and fights back the tears each time.

Jerry overheard Andrew's brief but forceful rebuke of Martin and appreciates how he approached the issue. He also saw the look in Martin's eyes, and it wasn't defiance. It was belief. Belief and pure, raw fear. Whatever is in the bayou, Martin is frightened to death of it, and he truly believes what he says.

23

Andrew, Clint, Jerry, and Martin arrive at Martin's lab two hours before dark. Andrew shuts off the engine and sits without moving for a few minutes. Clint and Jerry remain still as well. Martin shifts uncomfortably in the seat next to Jerry.

The forensic team of deputies is focused on the ground about twenty feet from the edge of Martin's lab. More than fifty yellow and orange triangles mark the ground, each with a number written to denote that individual piece of evidence. The markers are scattered from a site near the foot of the dam to the edge of the bayou.

Clint says what they're all thinking.

"Expended rounds. At least he tried."

One deputy wipes away sweat, bows his head, and says a quick prayer over an empty uniform lying in a large mud puddle. Andrew, Clint, and Jerry understand. *We lost one of our own.*

The side door to the lab is still open. Andrew looks at Jerry and gently offers, "Jerry, if you need to sit this one out, I encourage you to do exactly that. Clint and I can handle Martin."

Jerry takes a measured breath and squeezes the door handle as his heart rate accelerates. "I need to understand what happened, and I believe Martin is the best way to accomplish that." He leans forward and pats Andrew's shoulder in a show of comradeship. "But you're a good man for offering me a way out."

Andrew nods, and they all exit the car. Jerry grabs the chain connecting Martin's handcuffs behind his back and drags him out of the car. When they get to the front door, Andrew pulls Martin in close.

"Alright, Martin, this is your only chance at full disclosure. Bear in mind, the Miranda warning Clint read you is still in play, so anything you say can and will be used against you. I strongly encourage you to be completely truthful. I would also remind you that Louisiana is a death-penalty state. After your conviction for killing Mr. Johnson, you'll be sent to Angola, where if Mr. Lambert doesn't pay someone to kill you, the state will happily strap you to the electric chair and fry you like a piece of bacon."

Martin doesn't react for a moment. Then he blurts out, "But I didn't kill Timmy; I've told you that! How can they convict me for something I haven't done?"

"As I said, this is your one opportunity to come clean. The three of us will listen to anything you have to say. But you better be telling the truth." Taking Martin by the shoulders, Andrew twists him 180 degrees to face the evidence markers that populate his side yard. "See those? Each one represents evidence related to the murder of a cop. That cop was one of Jerry's men. Now, Jerry's of a mind to feed you to the alligators. Frankly, I'm on his side. If I were you, I'd start talking and quick."

There is silence for a few seconds as Martin considers his options. Finally, he dips his head and nods. He knows in his heart that his time has come.

Andrew is distracted when one of the forensic deputies looks up and catches his eye.

"Are you guys finished?" he calls out as they begin to remove their evidence markers and put up their gear.

"Yeah, going to be dark soon, not much more we can do here. Are you guys staying? Want us to leave the lights?" one deputy asks, referring to the large commercial lights they've been using to search for evidence. Clint notes that the lights have already been disassembled.

"No. But thank you. We'll only be here for a short time, and if it gets too dark, we'll just go inside the lab. Appreciate everything you guys have done."

"Ten-four. Y'all be safe," the last deputy says as he throws his gear into the back of a large, brown pickup truck.

With no one mingling around, and the huge lights off, the bayou begins to settle down. The tree frogs start singing again, as do the cicadas. Surrounded by this symphony, Martin realizes his wrists hurt.

"Hey, can you loosen these, or take the cuffs off, or put them in front? They're cutting off the circulation in my hands. Please? I promise this isn't a ruse to fool you guys. Please? They are very painful."

Andrew considers Martin's request. Looking at Clint and Jerry, all three shrug and nod in general agreement. Jerry fishes a handcuff key from a front pocket and uncuffs Martin. He then puts his hands on Martin's shoulders and roughly spins him back around to face Clint, who utilizes an old cop trick and runs the cuffs behind Martin's leather belt, further restricting any movement he might have been planning.

"There. Is that better?" Clint says.

Andrew and Jerry discern a tone of mockery in his voice.

"Thank you," Martin replies. "If you will just listen to me, I want to tell you how this came to happen. First, let me say that there are no traps inside my lab, no bombs, nothing remotely dangerous, except for what is inside my freezer on the other side of the negative-pressure door."

"So, the rumors are true? You have a negative-pressure room in there?" Clint asks.

Martin nods. "Yes. It was the only thing I could think of to contain it, whatever it is, other than building everything out of concrete and sealing it tightly, which is what I did. I have what's left of the original creature I discovered in the freezer. Every now and then, I remove it for a few moments, just long enough to shave off small pieces for examination and experimentation. Those small pieces never attain full life force, I guess you'd call it. They are fragile and susceptible to any number of things that humans would just wash off with some Dawn dish soap and hot water."

"Are you still on the 'it came from space' kick? Seriously? I told you to be truthful and stop with the BS," Andrew says with some exasperation.

Martin knows what he must do—the one thing he's always known he'd have to do one day to pay for the mistakes of his misbegotten life. The cuffs clink as he moves his wrists to get their attention and points inside his lab.

"Once you get inside, you will find a fully intact human skeleton hanging from a wall inside the negative-pressure room. That skeleton was once my son, Oscar."

This admission is so incredible that it takes all three lawmen completely by surprise, and for a few heartbeats, they remain silent.

"What the hell are you talking about?" Clint finally asks.

"All the bones you've found—Timmy's, the various animals, the marshal from this afternoon—are all that's left of whatever Oscar consumes."

"'Oscar consumes'? Martin, have you completely lost your mind? You're making no sense at all!" Clint moves as if to force Martin inside his lab. Martin resists and waves his cuffed hands to stop all forward movement.

"Wait! Wait, I know it's not Oscar, I know that, but I just call him—call it—that. I don't exactly know what it is. It was inside a meteorite that crashed into the bayou behind my home more than a year ago. I know it's not Oscar. He—well, it—hasn't been Oscar since the accident."

"What in the world are you babbling on about?"

Martin nods towards the water. "It's out there, somewhere. I believe it rests on the bottom of the bayou in its deepest spot, spread out where sunlight can't reach it easily."

"Sunlight?" Jerry asks.

"I've experimented on pieces of the original many times. Sunlight seems to be deadly to it. Maybe it's how our light is filtered through the atmosphere, the wavelength or spectrum. Perhaps it's some other factor. I just know it's out there, in the bayou. I believe the only reason it rises off the bottom is to feed."

"Rises off the bottom?"

Hearing a familiar sound, Martin looks up at the sky. The time has come for all the truth to be revealed. "Listen to me. Do you hear that thunder in the distance? It's like ringing the dinner bell for what lives in my bayou."

Martin's body language and tone of voice almost make Andrew believe. "Martin, tell us, what exactly lives in your bayou?" he finally asks, his voice flat. Another low rumble of thunder passes through the trees, and the wind picks up.

"I know I need to tell you everything, but for our safety, we need to either leave or get inside my lab and pressure lock the doors."

"Will we be protected inside?" Andrew asks, his cop intuition now ramped up to eleven on a ten-point scale.

"Yes. How do you think I've survived all this time? When I manufactured the building, I made sure it was completely sealed. There are no open access points. From what I have seen, it can't squeeze through things and retain its abilities. But just to be sure, I built the HVAC system underground. It delivers heat or cool air in a sealed conduit. Nothing can get inside the lab once I lock the doors and enter the negative-pressure room.

"Oh, trust me, my monster has tried to get in, but it's never been successful. I've spent many rainy nights watching it try. I guess it can sense me when I'm inside, but I've always been safe there. There is something in the thunder that angers it. I have done hundreds of hours' worth of research using sonic and auditory measures on the pieces I've shaved off the larger parts I have in the freezer, and the low-frequency wave produced by thunder is an activator for a very primal response. I liken it to a child who was scared by a storm or thunder as a kid; that child will fear thunder or loud noises as an adult."

Jerry responds first. "So, you say that the thing that has been killing people crashed to Earth, in a rock from space, and you have parts of it in your freezer? Oh, and it ate your son, Oscar? Then you told the FBI and every other cop involved that mobsters kidnapped your son?"

Martin opens his mouth to respond, but Jerry holds up both hands. "And this thing now lives in your bayou and is currently chewing its way through Webster Parish? Is that what we're supposed to believe? Oh, and it also hates thunderstorms?"

"I know it sounds crazy, but if you wait here and watch, you'll see what I mean. Just wait for the storm to approach. When it starts to rain, Oscar comes out. I am not lying when I say that if he comes out of the bayou, we will be in grave danger every minute we stay outside my lab. He's incredibly fast and getting faster every time I see him."

As he finishes, lightning flashes across the sky, prompting what he says next.

"The storm is coming our direction. We have to get inside or leave. If you want to see what Oscar looks like now, you can wait out here for the storm to start, and he'll appear out of the water. I've seen him do it many times. Or we can get into the safety of my lab, and you can observe him through the bulletproof glass, though that is just as scary because he tries and tries to get inside. I guess if he ever does, I'm dead. It's up to you."

Martin sees Clint's hand move down to his holstered weapon as another flash with accompanying thunder occurs.

"Don't bother. I finally figured out that I could kill the small ones using a combination of chemicals like simple creosote or through exposure to extreme heat. Cold temperatures and freezing triggers hibernation of some sort, like bears in the wild. I've never tried it, but judging from the expended ammo from your deputy, I'm sure bullets and projectile weapons won't stop them either." Martin pauses for a moment, then continues, "The eye might be vulnerable, but I never got the nerve to try because if it ever caught me, well, I'd be dead."

Clint and Jerry share a look. *That explains the report about Martin standing outside near the vat of creosote mixture.*

"Why do you think the eye is vulnerable? Wait, *the* eye? It doesn't have two?"

"No. The original creature had no eyes. I don't know how the first one saw prey. My theory is that it senses prey somehow. I have seen the small ones hit meals with what looks like a tendril from an octopus, without the suckers, with one-hundred-percent accuracy,"

"Never miss?"

"Never. Soon after it ate—well, absorbed, or whatever you want to call what it did to Oscar—both eyes were still functional, at least when it turned and looked at me before it retreated into the bayou. The next time I saw it, there was only one eye. I don't know what kind of mutation happened, but human eyes are very complex structures. They have at least forty individual subsystems. Maybe it can't replicate all the structures for two eyes. I have wondered, if the eye got injured, whether it would just mutate to fix the injury. I could never bring myself to try it. I mean, that is my Oscar, no matter what he has become. Inside the monster in my bayou is Oscar."

The next flash illuminates big raindrops falling. Tiny puffs of dirt resembling miniature nuclear clouds fill the ground with each impact.

"Well, since we're not inside, I guess you've decided to see him. Fine. But remember, when he shows and sees you, you have to move immediately. Get inside and lock the door. It is alive, but it isn't a living organism like we understand them. I do believe that somehow, it is a sentient life-form. It knows when I'm trying to feed it or just trying to observe it. But you have to remember that it is not from our world. I don't know if this is the only one. I guess more could be here, snatching people and animals at random. I've tried to investigate that, but sadly our technology isn't advanced enough for a thorough, reliable, and anonymous search. Anyway, remember all of this, okay?"

Clint and Jerry look confused. Martin, facing the bayou, shakes his head and says, "Pay attention."

He looks at Andrew. "The marshal gets it; I can see it in his eyes. Anyway, when you get inside and shut the door, make sure to utilize the locking mechanism. Then, get into the negative-pressure chamber. Press the red button by the door to engage the pumps. Whenever the rain stops, press it again and open the door. But you have to wait for the rain to stop. If it's dark and not raining, you can move around.

If it's raining, do not go outside, especially if there is thunder. One more thing: inside, you will find a commercial-grade video camera and recorder. I have left most of what I just told you on video. You should watch it a few times and then use the information as you see fit."

Andrew believes he understands the tone of Martin's instructions. Clint and Jerry see Andrew relax, so they do the same. The weather moves in with a vengeance. Large raindrops assault the aluminum awning over the back door. Even over this noise, they hear Martin's labored breathing.

"Hey, Martin, are you going to be okay?" Clint inquires. With no response, he taps Martin on the shoulders and asks again, "Martin! Are you okay?"

This startles Martin, who turns slightly and shakes his head. "No, Captain, and I'll never be okay ever again." He breaks away from Andrew, Clint, and Jerry and bolts directly towards the bayou.

Clint and Jerry start after him, but Andrew yells, "Wait!" Both men come to a stop and return to the shelter of the awning.

"What gives?" Jerry asks, clearly not happy.

"He's not going to get away from us. I want to see what he's got up his handcuffed sleeve. Let this play out, okay? Make you a deal; if he gets out of the cuffs, or tries to escape into the woods, just shoot him somewhere that'll hurt but not kill him."

Jerry draws his weapon, thumbs off the safety, and holds it down by his side. "I can live with that."

With an agreement in place, Andrew, Clint, and Jerry watch Martin make his way to the edge of the bayou. His soaked clothes cling to his skin. Hyperventilating, his shoulders heave upwards with every breath. Martin begins to yell.

"What is he doing? Is he really standing there yelling his dead son's name?"

Martin turns and smiles. He backs up about five feet and, though still cuffed, tries to point towards the water.

"There! Do you believe me now?"

Rising out of the bayou, the newcomer is filled with pure joy. The time it has waited for has finally come. Lightning flashes, and as the newcomer moves, it revels in the magic that falls from the sky. The thunder dredges up billion-year-old memories of hunger and anger. Once again, the anger is no match for the hunger. It knows that this meal will be the most satisfying one it has had in a very long time.

The three men don't see what Martin is pointing at until the area is lit momentarily by a series of lightning strikes, followed by thunder so loud they feel it in every bone in their bodies.

What they see is so incomprehensible that each man is shocked into silence.

They watch as the creature moves quickly, stopping mere feet away from Martin at the bayou's edge.

"What the living hell is that?" Jerry brings the .45 up and centers his front sight on the thing standing in front of Martin.

"I don't believe it," Clint says, also reaching for his sidearm. He instinctively shifts into the modified Weaver stance.

Andrew's sidearm stays holstered. He wants to see what happens next. "Boys, if you fire, remember Martin thinks the eye is vulnerable. Aim high for the eye!"

"Gotcha!" they say in unison.

They stand transfixed as Martin turns towards Oscar for the last time. The newcomer, now more than six feet tall and four feet across, hasn't moved. Instead, it is focused solely on Martin. The large, yellow eye disappears for a second, then reappears. The next flash of lightning shows it has moved closer to Martin, who is still yelling though he is inches away from the thing about to end his life.

"Did it just blink?" Jerry asks.

"I think so," Andrew replies as he shakes his head. They can hear Martin's voice through the rain and wind. He has backed up and yells, straining to be heard over the rainfall.

"Son, what happened to you is my fault. I hope there is some of you left inside this thing that can understand what I say." He turns slightly and points towards Andrew, Clint, and Jerry. "Those men back there don't know you, but I do. I know you are still my little man. Whatever has happened to you, I can try to fix it if you just let me try!"

The eye changes shape several times as an arm slowly appears and begins to wrap around Martin. They watch as the thing that holds Martin, who squirms and screams in agony, stops and with astonishing speed turns its attention towards them. Each flash of lightning transmits the anger and determination in the yellow eye.

"Oh shit! Is it looking at us?" Clint asks. He shivers at the realization.

"Yeah, it's like it sees us and is deciding what to do next. Right?"

"Agreed," Andrew says.

Before Clint can reply, the eye blinks, and they see its focus return to Martin. A mouth appears.

Through the screams, they barely make out his final instructions.

"In my lab are my notes." They hear his voice more clearly as the rain lets up a bit. "You have to watch the videotape in my lab! Lots of information there about it! You must go inside. You have to—*gguurrrgggg*."

Martin stops yelling instructions and begins a horrific death scream as tendrils enter his ears, nose, and mouth. Martin's body pulses once, twice, then his elbows fly out by his side, his wrists broken but still attached to the handcuffs.

All three men stop breathing as strobe lights from the heavens reveal every second of Martin Landry's gruesome death. Martin's feet leave the ground, and his entire body disappears headfirst into something that resembles a large, muddy mouth.

The newcomer sits back for a moment as if satisfied. Then, with a predatory speed that takes Andrew, Clint, and Jerry by surprise, it returns its attention to them.

"Okay, guys, this is where we shoot better than you ever have, and then retreat. *Aim for the eye*! Fire!" Andrew yells as he draws and centers the front sight of his .45 on the yellow eye. All three men empty their magazines towards the brown thing that just ate Martin.

Their aim is perfect, hitting its eye with virtually every round. It changes shape, absorbing the gunfire. However, the impacts cause it pain; it rocks back every time the eye is penetrated. The arms flail, but it makes no sound.

Though it feels some measure of happiness, having dealt with the creature that tortured it for so long, fury builds. Now it must deal with the three things near the torture place. It leans forward and dashes across the wet ground.

Andrew grabs Clint and Jerry and shoves them roughly inside the lab. Slamming the heavy metal door shut, he slides a crossbar in place. The seal is as tight as any he's ever seen. The negative-pressure chamber beckons, and one second later, all three men are inside. Clint shuts the door while Andrew hits the red button with the palm of his hand.

"Look at that," Jerry mutters. Andrew and Clint turn and see the ugly yellow eye through the bulletproof window facing the bayou.

"Reload," Clint says, his gaze fixed on the eye.

As the rain falls, each flash of lightning shows the yellow eye at a different window around the laboratory. They watch in horrified fascination as the eyes changes shape each time the eye appears.

More than an hour later, the storm winds down, and the eye finally disappears.

"Am I the only one going insane here?" Jerry wonders aloud.

"No," Clint answers. "Wish I could thank Martin for building such a fortress."

"Well, he said this was a safe place. I guess whatever that is can't get around the seals and other countermeasures he's built. We might be here for a while," Andrew responds. "Plus, I bet if it could . . . even though it just—I can't believe I'm even saying this—ate Martin . . . If it could get to us, I think it would have already done so."

Clint looks at a clock on the wall and confirms the time by checking his diver's watch. Though still raining, the storm has spent its energy and is moving away.

"If we're going to be here all night, maybe we should occupy ourselves by trying to find the notes and videotapes Martin was yelling about just before he—"

"Before he what?" Jerry interrupts, shaking his head. "No one on God's green earth is ever going to believe what we just saw. Hell, I saw it, and I don't believe it."

Andrew chimes in. "Yeah, I, uh, I guess I owe Martin an apology. He does have some kind of man-eating space alien out in his bayou."

Clint turns to Andrew and asks, "How is this even possible? Should we call the military? They've got to have something that can kill whatever that thing is, right?" Clint stops speaking, and a look crosses his face. "I mean, can something like that even be killed?"

"I don't know about the military. What happens if they decide the only way to kill it is to nuke it? Do you want them to nuke the Ark-La-Tex? I sure don't. Didn't Martin say he'd been able to kill the small ones with a mixture of chemicals? I bet we can do the same with the big one. We just need to know what to use!"

"He mentioned creosote and extreme heat," Clint says as he thumbs through a notepad on the metal desk in the corner. "But I don't know how we're ever going to beat that thing with creosote or extreme heat."

All three men glance over at the window, expecting it to reappear. Jerry shivers, and Clint wonders if they're actually dead and have gone to a weird cop purgatory filled with every nightmare from his childhood.

"Hey, look at this. It must be the setup Martin mentioned," Jerry says, pointing at a commercial-grade, Sony U-Matic three-quarter-inch video cassette recorder/player. It is attached to a broadcast-grade Sony camera connected to a large Magnavox color television pushed up against the wall. A tape is in the machine, and Clint shrugs and pushes the button labeled *Rewind*. When it finishes rewinding, he looks at Andrew and Jerry.

Andrew nods. "I think you push the play button. Just don't touch that red button that says *Record*. Let's see what Martin thought important enough that he had to spend fifty-thousand dollars on a personal television studio."

Jerry nods and pushes play.

The machine makes a metallic winding noise as servos spin the magnetic heads. The television comes to life, and they see the negative-pressure room on the screen. The camera focuses on the farthest item on a nearby desk, racks out of focus, back into focus, and slowly zooms out. Finally, the image settles on a chair against the wall, where Clint currently sits. They hear Martin's voice saying, "Mike test, mike test, one, two three." Martin comes into view and takes a seat in front of the camera. He smiles and clears his throat.

"If you're watching this, I promise what I have to say is gonna blow your socks off."

24

"As you probably already know, my name is Martin Landry. What follows is my official record of the animal; well, I'm not sure it's an animal. I guess I should call it the unknown organism I discovered in a meteorite. It crashed into the earth just behind my laboratory, on 13 July 1973. I've gone over and over in my mind what I would say here, but this will end up more like a scientific stream of consciousness than a scripted speech.

"First, if you see this, I guess I must be dead, or someone figured it out, and I'm in the custody of the military. If I am dead, I hope I had the opportunity to tell someone about this tape before I died. You need to watch this entire tape and then give it to whomever you think needs to see it. But don't watch it and then try to leave my lab if it's a rainy night. I'll get to why in just a few minutes. Anyway, whoever you are, you must listen closely. By the way, I'm going to refer to my discovery by the name of my only child, Oscar. You'll understand why as you watch this tape.

"Now, if Oscar got me, then, honestly, I guess that represents some kind of universal justice since my inattention to detail led to his death. No, strike that. I'm not entirely sure he is dead. Maybe he is. Maybe he's just been absorbed and has become something other than human. I guess I don't know. Even after all my experiments, there's a lot I don't know about what I discovered.

"Anyway, if I am dead, and you are the authorities here to investigate my death, first, I hope you have closed and locked the metal door at the entrance to my lab. If you have done so, then you should know that you can move freely around my lab. There are no traps, no surprises. I built this fortress for one reason, to survive long enough to finally understand what took my son from me and research how to reverse it, perhaps present it to the public, or kill it."

They watch as Martin's shoulders droop in resignation, and he finishes with "Which is just another failure on my part." He stops speaking for a moment and reaches for a small box with several buttons on it. Holding the box, he pushes a button on a controller attached to the camera or recorder, and Martin's visage freezes.

The tape begins playing again, and they all see and hear Martin chuckle. "Sorry, I had to get a drink. What follows will mostly be my scientific opinion. I will try to leave out any emotional context, but I make no promises. What you are dealing with is, in my estimation, a perfect, living, radioisotope thermoelectric generator without the nuclear signature. It is pure perfection; the only downside is you die if it touches you, which is pretty much a huge downside. I believe that this thing must have existed in a pure liquid environment in its own universe, which is why it likes the bayou so much.

"I said you were safe inside, and you are. However, there are things in my lab that can kill you. I was able to section and freeze pieces of the original, and they are in the walk-in freezer set into the wall. I have fifty or so shavings I made from the organism before it attacked my son and was lost.

"By the way, Oscar, my son, was not kidnapped. I was distracted by a phone call and stupidly left him alone in my lab. Honestly, it was the worst kind of parenting I can imagine. While I was out of the room, he broke the container where I had the creature secured. The best way to describe what happened after the attack is that Oscar was consumed, eaten, something like that. If you are the authorities, you can close the case on my son's disappearance."

Clint and Jerry share a look.

"Good luck putting that in a report," Jerry says without a tinge of his usual mirth.

"Yeah. I wasn't sure this could get any weirder, but there it is," Clint mutters.

"The organisms are in the freezer behind you. They are stacked and labeled *1* through *50*, all inside sealed specimen containers. I must warn you, do not thaw them. Each one is capable of growing into a lethal killer of truly epic proportions. After my experiments with a few of them, observing and cataloging their reactions to stimuli, I sometimes wonder if this is how the dinosaurs disappeared. Maybe we all arrived in a meteorite and just happened to become the dominant species. Who knows?

"Anyway, if you are local law enforcement investigating my demise, or something similar, I guess you could stop this tape and immediately go to the military. However, I would caution you against doing that as well. Why? Because once they get their grubby little hands on these creatures, I'm sure they would figure out a way to unleash them on our enemies, only to have them turn and consume us once they've killed everyone else."

Martin pauses, takes a swig of water, and then continues.

"That is not a joke. These things are voracious eaters, yet I can find no evidence of a waste product. They're like the perfect little machine. However, it's only the soft tissue and marrow of their meals that they consume. They can't digest bones or any inorganic material. I would also caution you about the electricity for this facility. The slides in my freezer are in some kind of hibernation, or stasis, because of the cold. I theorize that is how they survived in deep space."

Martin looks off into the distance for a moment as if pondering an important question or point. He then smiles and resumes speaking.

"I have always wondered, since encountering the first one in my bayou, just how old it was, or how long it was up there, in space. I guess it could be hundreds, thousands, millions, or even billions of years old. Unfortunately, it's so foreign that there's really no way to tell. Maybe a NASA scientist, with access to a government-funded lab, might be able to determine its age or more details about it, but I'm not even sure we are that advanced yet.

"Okay, a word of warning: if there hasn't been any power in a while, and you hear thumping from the freezer, don't open it, okay? That would be very bad. If you hear thumping in the freezer, run."

Martin smiles at that last remark.

"I guess I can joke around a bit since I'm probably dead, right? Okay, here is the short version of what happened. There was a flash of light in the bayou behind my house and a slight tremor. Before I could investigate, a local redneck, Timmy Johnson—who, by the way, was a victim of Oscar's appetite—called me about seeing a meteorite in the sky above his trailer. I looked out a window towards the bayou, and sure enough, there was evidence of an impact. I geared up, investigated, found it in about a foot of water, and took it inside my lab.

"As I carefully examined it, I found a crack in the structure, and out plopped this thing that kind of looked like a brown golf ball without dimples, or like one of those Silly Putty eggs you'd give a kid for Christmas. It was small but somehow sensed my presence because it took refuge under a cypress log I'd put inside the container.

"I was excited and scared. This thing wasn't like any animal I'd ever seen, heard of, or even imagined. And it wasn't something from inside my bayou. Luckily, I didn't try to scoop it up with my hand, or I guess I'd have been its first victim, and none of what you're seeing would exist. I designed a plan to observe it and then experiment on it—infrared light, cold, heat, sound, chemicals, and stuff like that. After a few days, I figured maybe it needed to eat, so as an experiment, I tossed in a frog. It shot what looked like a tentacle out from under the log, grabbed the frog, and left only the frog's bones minutes later.

"I gave it a steady diet of frogs, fish, things I could find around here. When I saw what it did after that first meal, I started taking serious precautions around it. I correctly theorized that if it could do that to a frog, it could certainly do the same to me. Since it continued to leave the bones of what I was feeding it, I figured that its digestive system couldn't do bones for some reason. Of course, this detail also reinforced my belief that I was dealing with an extraterrestrial organism of some kind."

Martin pauses, and they watch as he leans partially out of frame. He returns in a few moments with a bottle of whiskey in one hand and a glass in the other. They watch as he pours himself a double shot.

"This is the hard part, which is why I need this," he says, downing the glass of amber liquid with one gulp. Thus fortified, he resumes. "Everything was fine until Oscar came to visit a few weeks after I discovered the creature. I hadn't had the time to try and understand it. I had warned him in the past not to play with anything in my lab, but somehow, while I wasn't in the room, he tipped over the glass case, and it broke into a million little pieces on the floor. When I rushed into the room, the creature had already attacked Oscar and was covering his face. Oscar was having trouble speaking, so I believe it was already going down his throat.

"I ran to get an oxyacetylene torch, to try and fry it off of Oscar. But as I came back to the house from the garage, I saw Oscar, or what once was Oscar, running down to the bayou. He paused and looked back at me. I have always wondered if at that point, when he turned around and looked at me, maybe there was still some of human Oscar alive. But that is just my wishful thinking.

"Even though I wanted to kill what was left of the creature in my freezer, I did not. Instead, ever since the accident with Oscar, I've been experimenting on the slices I saved from the original, working on a theory that maybe there is a way to undo what it did to Oscar."

He stops, pours, and takes another drink. They see the alcohol beginning to take effect as he starts speaking again, his tone much more subdued.

"I know this is a lot to take in. I will say this. If you're inside my place and have engaged the negative-pressure chamber, then at least, somehow, I was able to tell you how to be safe. I hope that goes in the 'good' column on the balance sheet of my life. So, over there"—Martin points towards the opposite wall—"near the door, that large box underneath a piece of burlap? Remove it, and you will find that it covers the bulletproof case. If you look closely, you'll see the cypress log I spoke of earlier. One piece of the original creature lives under it."

Hearing this, Clint and Jerry jump up and move away from where Martin is pointing.

On-screen, Martin laughs.

"I'm sure you just about flipped out, but you are safe, as long as the lid is closed and locked, which it always is unless I need to get into it. What I'm about to tell you is very important, so you must follow my instructions perfectly. If you've decided not to tell the military, then I need you to kill everything—the pieces inside my freezer and the creature in the glass case. Let me explain what I need you to do, but first, here is what I know about the organism.

"I can't prove it, but I believe the primary building blocks of my creature's life are polycyclic aromatic hydrocarbons. These are uncharged, nonpolar molecules with distinctive properties due to delocalized electrons, which means their electrons are not associated with a single atom. Many materials with these characteristics are found in coal and oil deposits. They are also produced by the decomposition of organic matter, like in engines, incinerators, or forest fires. Interestingly enough, NASA researchers believe they are abundant in interstellar space! I could have told them that, but whatever.

"One theory is that they formed as early as the first couple billion years after the Big Bang. I've read peer-reviewed journal articles by experimental physical cosmologists—people at NASA who study the origin of the universe—who believe they are critical to the formation of new stars and exoplanets. So, if things like this creature have been around since the Big Bang, then it may contain the starting materials for abiotic syntheses of materials required by the earliest forms of life! Think of it! What splashed down in my bayou might be as old as all life in the universe!"

Martin looks pretty happy with himself.

"I've always wondered why we stopped the moon missions in 1972 after spending so much time and money to make them happen. What if—and bear with me while I speculate, which is something I don't normally do—what if my little space-rock critter is just one of many, and the astronauts either encountered one on the moon or brought one just like mine back to Earth?

"I've contacted them a couple of times to find someone there who might talk to me, but they all treated me like I was one of those UFO flakes. Imagine if they'd listened closely enough to believe me when I told them I had an alien in my bayou and that I've been experimenting on pieces of it for more than a year!"

He pauses, scratches his chin, and resumes.

"Just hearing myself say that kind of still freaks me out. I guess if I'd have shown up at NASA, the guys in the white suits would have taken me to a padded room."

He frowns, pours, and takes another sip. "Sadly, what is in my bayou and that glass case is absolutely an unflinching killer. Even after losing significant pieces, it can survive, and thrive. I know that scientists worldwide would love to examine it. There must be ways to determine how it survived in space for so long, how it exists without breathing, how it eats without producing waste, stuff like that. It's the most important thing ever discovered, and now, I must tell you exactly how to destroy it."

He pauses once more, starts to take another drink, then stops midway.

"Anyway, if I am dead, it is imperative that you destroy it. And by that I mean kill what remains of it. All of it. I can't be more serious when I say that what is inside the bulletproof case can never be allowed outside this facility. And you should also know Oscar can never be allowed to survive either, but we'll get to that in a second.

"First, if you look at the glass case, you will see several different boxes I have added. One is labeled *Kill Box*. In the freezer, you will find an experimental mixture of creosote and other chemicals. I don't know how this thing breathes, but I do know it can be smothered and killed.

I've done it, and that's what I need you to do. Go to the freezer, pull out the container labeled *Kill*, and wait for that concoction to thaw fully. It may take a day or two. Just leave it outside, and the Louisiana heat should do the trick.

"Now, I warn you, the one that lives under the log exhibits some sort of ability to know, or intuit, what is happening outside the box, so it may sense what is about to happen and try to get out. But don't worry. The way I built the addition you'll be using will make that impossible. I caution you to not fiddle with it or try to alter the box because it is the only thing that has kept me alive. It's also keeping you alive for the moment. Okay, now I want you to press the pause button. I'm sure you might have some things to discuss. I'll be right here."

Without hesitation, Jerry pushes the pause button and turns to Andrew and Clint. Andrew scratches his head for a moment. Clint and Jerry look shell-shocked and remain quiet.

"Say, Jerry, if you don't mind, I'm guessing there might be quite a bit more tape to watch, but can you rewind it to the beginning? I'd kind of like to watch the entire thing up to where you just stopped it and take some notes. I might ask you to do this a few times."

Jerry shrugs and says, "Sure. I guess that's a good idea" as he rewinds it and pushes play. "But I'm gonna freak out at the same place each time."

"Yeah, me too," Andrew replies.

After the third time, before Jerry starts the tape, Clint turns to Andrew.

"Is he just crazy? Do you believe any of this?"

"I might not have believed it six hours ago, but after what we just went through, I have become a believer. I'm interested in what else he has to say."

Martin smiles as the tape begins to play again.

"Thank you. I guess, whoever you are, you've talked about it and decided I'm not a raving lunatic. I assure you, I had the very same reactions the first few times I interacted with my creature. No matter what secrets these things might hold for the future space exploits of mankind, they all must die. For your safety, if it is raining, I want to emphasize that you must stay inside until the rain stops or the sun is shining. Then, go to the freezer, remove the solution as instructed, wait for it to thaw.

"Once it is thawed and you are ready to proceed with the other steps I'm about to give you, someone will need to return to the freezer and retrieve the slides. That person will pour the frozen specimens into the box using the little sliding access I built into the side. You should look at it now. It's got a label on it that says, *Kill Box*.

"It's simple. You'll insert the slides, push it, and twist the handle. This will dump them into the box. Then, bring in the container of the unfrozen liquid, and put it on the table next to the box. You will attach the hose built into the side of the box to the container, making sure to keep both stopcocks in the closed position until you're ready to proceed. When you are ready with the other preparations, someone will need to be here, inside, so they can open the stopcock on either side and let it fill the box fully.

"I would urge caution around the box as you dump the slides in, as well as the chemical. Like I said earlier, I don't exactly know how aware the one under the log is, but I bet it will try to survive once it figures out you are killing it.

"Now, what I'm about to tell you next is very important. After taking care of what's in the box, you need to get ready to do the same to my lab and then to the bayou behind the lab. If it isn't raining, if it is another beautiful, sunny North Louisiana day, go into the shed outside, the one that looks like a something off a container ship. It is, by the way. The keys to it are hanging by the front door, on a key chain with a metallic cutout that looks like David Bowie. You'll need those keys to open the container. Go outside, unlock and open the doors. Once the doors are open, you'll see twenty cylinders in specially constructed racks. The cylinders should be full. I inspect them every week.

"It is critical that you look for the date I have written on the paper tag attached to each cylinder. If it's within a couple of weeks of the current date, the tanks should be full, primed, and ready to use.

There are twenty pressurized tanks, all connected to each other by a nonconductive pipe. They have one main pipe connected to the lab through an underground delivery system. When the time has come to kill everything, one of you needs to be inside to open the discharge-line valve located over there. It's the bright-blue valve on the wall. And then be prepared to run for your life."

Martin stops talking and points off-camera to a valve built into the side of his lab, located just inside the pressure chamber.

"You're wondering where I'm going with all this: well, I've thought about this question a lot, so bear with me. If I could blow up the dam, would that force the one in the bayou out into the open and provide an opportunity to kill it? I believe so. However, it's not even possible to test this theory without actually blowing up the dam. Some of the experiments I've conducted with the creature in the glass case have been around how it survives on Earth. It is an alien organism, and yet it thrives here. How does it do this?

"Like I said earlier, I have determined that the water, at least fresh water, is the perfect home for it. Salt water hurts it but does not kill it. Also, sunlight is, for some reason, as hurtful as salt water. Every time I've exposed a small slice to the sun, it withers and dies." Martin chuckles a bit and continues, "I know that must sound crazy, but it's true. Maybe it has something to do with the star in its original home being different than our sun. Maybe it's a light-wavelength thing. I don't know. However, the turbidity of the bayou water provides cover for it and presents opportunities for sustenance. Since there is still animal life in and around the bayou, this leads me to believe that it possesses some measure of intelligence not to fully deplete the food sources in its home territory. There is some measure of harmony in how it lives.

"I believe when it is not raining, the creature spreads out over the floor of the bayou to minimize its potential exposure to the sun and to rest. I have replicated this through experimentation with my captive ones and have proven that this is more than just a theory. Therefore, if the bayou were to be filled with dirt, forcing it up from the bottom,

I believe it would lose the cloak it depends on for survival, at least in the bayou. So, if I'm dead, and you need to close the book on this situation without involving the military or those idiots up in DC, then I implore you to follow my guidance. Bear in mind that it needs to be done immediately and in conjunction with what I'm instructing you do with the blue valve. When you're ready, I suggest you take notes. I'm going to pause the tape and resume in a moment."

Andrew, Clint, and Jerry pause the tape as well, to stand and stretch.

Jerry speaks first. "I don't know about this. If what Martin says is true, how are we supposed to deal with this thing?"

"Maybe he does have it figured out. He's pretty sure that whatever it is, he can kill it. Let's hear what else he has to say about it," Clint says. Jerry nods, leans forward, and pushes the play button once again.

"Welcome back. I guess you're still with the program. Good. Now, what I'm about to tell you must be followed exactly as I lay it out. You must not deviate. Once you decide to undertake this course of action, there is no going back. First, you must open the blue valve inside my lab. As soon as you do that, leave the building, and close the doors as you leave.

"Next, go around the lab to the container where you'll find the cylinders. Each one has a handle on the top, and you must move the handles from 'blue' to 'red.' Without hesitation, you will need to move the lever on the floor of the container from 'closed' to 'open.' Once you do all these steps, it cannot be undone. Let me emphasize that point. When the liquid in the cylinders begins to flow under its own vapor pressure towards the blue valve inside, which you will have already opened, it cannot be stopped."

He pauses and points a finger directly into the camera. "I cannot emphasize this point more forcefully: do these steps exactly as I have just described and in no other order or out of sequence. If you do, you will die. It's just that simple."

Martin stops again and chuckles.

"I'm sure you are curious about what's in the tanks. Well, it is chlorine trifluoride, possibly the most flammable substance on Earth.

It doesn't even need an ignition source; it will ignite on its own. It even burns nonflammable items. Chlorine trifluoride is a component used in rocket fuel and the processing of nuclear fuel rods for nuclear reactors. It's cool stuff. Just don't ask me where I got it!"

He chuckles again.

"Which would be impossible anyway. I'm dead! Once the chlorine trifluoride enters the lab through the system I've designed, this place is gonna burn like you've never seen. The chlorine trifluoride is used in processing nuclear fuel, so it also produces harmful gases when burning. You're not gonna want to be anywhere close or downwind.

"Before you do all this, I also need you to go to the concrete room I built outside the lab. It sticks out behind the container full of the chlorine trifluoride cylinders.

"Inside that room, you will find—well, the best way to describe it is a thick, long, white hose that looks like something NASA would attach to a rocket. It is. I got it on the black market. Attached to the hose is a nozzle made of pure tungsten. With a melting point north of six thousand degrees Fahrenheit, it is critical to what I need you to do next.

"This hose has been treated to withstand the chlorine trifluoride for just long enough to start the process going; then it will disintegrate and cause the fire to spread. It is already connected to the cylinders that will deliver the chemical into my lab. I need you to stretch it out to the bayou and attach the twenty-pound weight, which you will find on the floor of the container, about ten feet from the end of the hose, and throw the final twenty feet into the water and then go back to the valve inside the container.

"I must stress that what I'm about to say is the last thing you do before you open the valve and start the flow of chlorine trifluoride. Once the chemical comes into contact with the bayou water, it will react explosively, and by that, I mean the entire bayou will explode in flames. The reaction will also create large amounts of hydrofluoric and hydrochloric acid as a bonus. I'm fairly certain that the fire will destroy whatever Oscar has become."

Martin shrugs slightly, "At least, I hope it does."

He looks wistful and then sad.

"It's not lost on me that the compound I'm using to kill the thing that must have come from outer space is one of the compounds we use to reach outer space." Martin smiles, and the serious look returns to his face. "Karma is a weird thing, isn't it? Anyhow, I do expect the fire department will respond, but tell them not to use water-based suppression on the fires. On the table over there near the door, in the green binder, you will find the manufacturer's data sheet for the chlorine trifluoride. You must take it with you and give it to the fire guys who show up."

He stops again, wipes a tear from one eye, and finishes with "One last thing . . . I'm sorry. I guess Oscar has killed people, perhaps even me, and now I'm asking you to clean up my mess. I once had a life full of promise, a good family, and the love I'd dreamed of having. Somehow, it didn't end well for me and others, and I'm sorry for my part in it. Now, I have told you how to stop the one thing that could have made me impossibly rich and famous because it can also end the world as we know it. I hope this helps. If you can, please take this tape with you when you leave, or, if you just want total deniability, leave it, and let it burn too. But if you choose to do nothing, it'll only be a matter of time before Oscar comes calling."

Martin looks into the glass of whisky and not into the camera. He finally lifts his head and starts talking again.

"I know I must sound like I know what I'm doing, but, honestly, I've made mistakes in dealing with whatever this thing is. I am confident that the steps I've outlined to kill everything in the freezer and the one in my box will work. The one in my bayou is the outlier. The last time I observed it through the windows, it was the size of a large human. In my estimation, doing what I have described, in the exact sequence outlined, should kill it. If you're the military or law enforcement, maybe you should talk to NASA before opening the glass box, the freezer, or setting fire to Webster Parish."

Martin gives a half-hearted wave and nods as he chugs what is left of the glass of whiskey. "I never thought about my future. If I'm dead, I guess I should have. Anyway, I bid you goodbye and good luck. You're going to need it."

He raises the remote controller for the recorder, looks directly into the camera, and pushes a button. The expression on his face as the video freezes is too much for Jerry, who stops the tape and begins to rewind it. "Wow."

"Yeah. What in the world do we do now?" Clint asks. "I kind of agree with him about calling the military to try and capture it. If this thing is as deadly as he says, then we can't let it fall into the wrong hands."

Andrew nods in agreement. As he begins to speak, he is surprised to note that the sun has started to rise. "Unless NASA already has one in cold storage somewhere, studying it as Martin did for a year. But we can't act on what-ifs. In my mind, there is only one course of action: we carry out the plan Martin just described to destroy the lab, the bayou, and hopefully the creature."

"Is there another choice? I mean, I wouldn't even believe it . . ."

Daylight breaks through the canopy as the sun crests the dam holding back the lake water above them, and further musings are interrupted by the sounds of a piece of metal or wood on the outside door. They all recognize the musical "Shave and a Haircut" call.

"Did it grow hands solid enough to knock the secret code?" Clint asks.

"Would it even knock? I wouldn't if I was a monster," Jerry offers with a smirk.

"Answer it," Andrew prompts.

Jerry uses a metal set of keys and raps "two bits" on the metal door of the negative-pressure chamber, and they wait.

A man starts announces their names over a police car public address system. Andrew hits the red button, and when the pressure is equalized, the door on the negative-pressure chamber pops open. Clint rushes to the steel door and calls out, "Who is this?"

"This is the sheriff! Open the damn door! Do it now!"

"Wait," Andrew says as Clint moves to unlock and open the door. "Martin is gone. We need to agree on a story. We say we let him go since he was in our custody when Jerry's deputy was killed."

"What about the fact we've been here all night?"

"We took Martin to the bus station and came back to begin executing the terms of our search warrant and simply lost track of time because our search was so meaningful."

Clint shrugs, as does Jerry.

"Just blame me somehow," Andrew offers.

"Alright, but we've got to get rid of them. We need to finish the job today or tomorrow," says Clint. Jerry nods. Clint takes hold of the handle on the door, turns the mechanism, and pushes it open.

"Man, we thought you guys were dead!" Sheriff Hancock says. He glances over their shoulders and asks, "Hey, where's your suspect?"

Jerry motions back towards Andrew and answers, "Mr. Federal Government there thought it'd be a good idea to let him go, since my deputy was killed while Martin was in custody. It was clear to us that he wasn't our killer." Jerry pauses, then continues, "He's gone and won't be coming back. Since we had time still, we decided to go ahead and search his lab."

"Find anything?"

"Lots of notes. There's a camera in there, but no videotape. The walk-in freezer is full of stuff. We still need to catalog it all."

"You spent all night here?"

"All night. I guess time got away from us. We were too focused on trying to understand exactly what Mr. Landry was doing here."

"Hey, Sheriff?" they all hear one of the deputies call out.

The four men walk ten feet to the east, giving them line of sight around the corner of the building. Andrew, Clint, and Jerry are not happy to see the deputy standing where Martin disappeared into the mouth of the monster, a set of handcuffs dangling from his left hand.

"Hey! There's a set of handcuffs here, still double-locked! And these look like someone's clothes, just lying right here next to a set of . . ."

"Let me guess," the sheriff interrupts under his breath.

". . . bones," both men say at the same time. Turning to Andrew, Clint, and Jerry, the sheriff squints as he speaks. "I'm not sure what happened here, but if, as you say, Mr. Landry is out of my parish and not coming back, then as far as I'm concerned, the book is closed."

Jerry takes the initiative. "Well, Sheriff, I do believe that after last night, we all have seen the last of Mr. Martin Landry."

Sheriff Hancock smiles a crooked smile, says nothing, and nods as he says, "Men, let's get outta here. Back to Minden!" They watch as five deputies jump into their cars. The sheriff rolls down his window, winks at them, and waves slightly as they leave.

Clint shakes his head and laughs.

"He thinks we chopped him into gator-sized pieces and tossed him into the bayou, doesn't he?"

Andrew's expression remains unchanged as he answers. "Something tells me he would be fine with that."

"So, what is our next step?" Jerry asks, looking up at the clear, blue morning sky.

Andrew chuckles. "As long as it's not about to rain, then I think we go back inside and watch the tape again. I suggest that we write down the instructions for using the, what was it, the chlorine trifluoride stuff as Martin gives them, and then, we burn this place to the ground and kill his space monster before it eats any more Americans."

"Couldn't have said it better myself," Jerry offers as he turns and retreats into Martin's lab, followed by the other two. "Though, I have an ex or two I might like to introduce to Oscar."

Clint laughs and slaps Jerry on the shoulder. "No. You are not feeding your exes to the monster."

"Let's get going, guys, before Jerry gets more funny ideas," Andrew says. He turns and takes two sets of keys from the wall, smiling at the large, metal David Bowie keychain. Then he uses a large key from the other set to lock the lab's front door.

One minute later, Clint pushes play on ce again.

25

Back at Jerry's office, Jerry leans forward to address his primary concern regarding their plan for Martin Landry's lab.

"Alright, so, Martin was pretty clear that what's in the freezer and the glass box are all the organisms he has in the lab. But what do we do about the one in the bayou if it doesn't die from the fire?"

Clint returns Jerry's look with silence. Jerry shrugs and, in turn, looks at Andrew, who inhales and starts to formulate a plan out of thin air.

"Well, I guess we need a contingency plan. What were some of the chemicals or compounds Martin mentioned in the lab notes or on the videotape?"

Jerry thumbs through the notes he made and stops at the page labeled *Killer potions*.

"On the videotape, he said the most success he'd had was with coal-tar creosote. The hotter, the better. What are you thinking?"

"Can we get our hands on some?"

Jerry responds with a chuckle. "My friend, this is Louisiana; if we can't get it or make it, it doesn't exist. Plus, there's a couple of good ole boys I know who can cook us up a batch of anything we need."

"Off the books?" Andrew questions.

"Absolutely," Jerry replies, though he doesn't look enthusiastic.

Clint knows his friend and mutters, "Whatever it is, Jerry, spit it out."

"Okay, if we blow up the dam . . . isn't that a bad idea? Won't we flood the homes across Dorcheat Road? Shouldn't we evacuate them? I don't want to kill a bunch of people, and I know neither of you wants to either. How do we take care of them?"

Clint contemplates Jerry's question. "Well, we do have to warn them; maybe make it part of the plan to say Martin has mined the area with devices, and if the dam goes, they'll be in danger. I think we can accomplish this through the sheriff.

"So, if we blow the lab just like Martin described, which begins with the line from his chemical container out to the bayou, I'd prefer we do this on the brightest, sunniest day possible so that whatever is on the bottom of his bayou doesn't come up and try to eat us."

Jerry laughs, "I'm generally not very digestible. Hopefully, I'd give it a terrible case of indigestion."

Clint nods and replies, "For sure."

Andrew is amused. "Well, I say we do everything to avoid Jerry giving the alien monster indigestion. We do exactly as Martin laid out in the video. First we kill what's in the freezer and the glass box. Then we blow the dam, the bayou, and lab at about the same time."

"That leaves the possibility of us waking up the sleeping monster and facing it."

Andrew nods and holds up one finger.

"Yes, one more reason to do all this on the hottest, sunniest, non-rainiest day possible. Martin said the fire will burn incredibly hot and create a toxic cloud. And according to him, water only makes the chemical burn hotter. His idea to blow up the dam and use the influx of water to increase the temp of the fire sounds like a great option."

"And as a result of the explosion, dirt and rocks from the dam will fill in the bayou, denying the creature the bottom?"

"Yes."

Jerry whistles and Andrew continues, "When the fire is finally out, we hit the entire area with your redneck concoction of coal-tar creosote. Can they mix in a bunch of salt, too, since Martin says salt is also toxic to it?"

"I'll make sure they do."

"Alright. So, if we draw on my former skills, one gallon of gasoline can have the explosive force of fourteen sticks of dynamite under optimal conditions. Dynamite is rated by weight strength, which is the amount of nitroglycerin it contains. A normal stick of dynamite is between twenty to sixty percent nitro. The rest is called 'dope.' This is the absorbent storage medium mixed with a stabilizer and any additives.

"Now, if I can get my hands on military-grade dynamite, that contains seventy-five percent RDX, which is a more energetic explosive than normal TNT. It also has about fifteen percent TNT, and the rest is cornstarch and motor oil. But it might not be possible to find unless you guys know someone who knows someone who can acquire things that fall off military trucks, and if you do, I don't want to know about it."

Clint is quiet for a heartbeat. Jerry and Andrew can see the gears working behind his eyes. "What's up, Clint?" Jerry asks.

"Well, the ordnance factory. We talked about it the day they found Timmy's bones."

Andrew interrupts before Jerry can respond.

"Oh, that's right! It's over on Highway 80! I've driven by it headed up here to the lake. Sorry to interrupt; what were you going to say?"

Clint nods. "The last time I looked up the current Louisiana code on explosives, if I remember correctly, any police force is covered regarding the manufacture, storage, transportation, use, and handling of explosives and blasting agents, provided they are used within their respective official capacities and in the proper performance of their duties. So, while blowing up the dam might not fit into someone's ideas of our official duties, if we had to tell them the whole story, I bet they'd say, 'Blow it up!' and let us do it."

Jerry chimes in. "Yep, I remember the ATF guys laughed, talking about how it was good that we didn't know about the code. Otherwise, we'd have been using dynamite on all the drug or motorcycle gang houses."

Andrew is intrigued.

"Is the ordnance plant still producing matériel for the military?"

Clint nods. "Yep. Military grade. No lie."

"Great. Who do we know there, and how can we get our hands on about three hundred pounds of military dynamite? I'll need some other stuff too."

"How would you get the explosive into the dam?" Clint asks.

"Dig some holes at the top, middle, and bottom of the dam and drop in the dynamite. The dirt and rocks used to construct the dam will become missiles and rain down on everything within a few hundred yards, by the way."

Clint and Jerry are silent, contemplating the weight of what they are planning, which could easily be considered an act of terror in virtually every legal sense.

Jerry chews his lip for a second.

"Look, we have to do this. We talked yesterday about figuring out how to blame Martin. I think that might be easier than we think. If we can do the same with the dynamite, like, he had the dynamite hidden and it just exploded, then I believe that's also what we should do."

"It'd be our luck if the conservation police were on the lake when we blow the dam, doing boat safety checks, and show up, wondering what the heck is going on."

"That would not be a good thing."

"Agreed." Andrew makes some notes on a sheet of lined paper. Looking up, he asks, "Say, what was it that Martin said killed those small ones he'd thawed out?"

Clint flips through another notebook and finds the appropriate entry.

"He thought it was something called 'bioaccumulation.' It looks like he went to the LSU-Shreveport library and cut a bunch of pages out of books, gathering information about the topic. Several pages appear to be from scientific textbooks."

"What is bioaccumulation?" Andrew asks.

"Says here that it's the process by which an organism takes in chemicals through ingestion, exposure, and inhalation. One of the more studied organisms is a mollusk, and Martin has written in the margins that his creature reminds him of a mollusk. You guys have seen mollusks that attach to the wooden marine pilings. Says here studies have been done trying to determine how direct contact with the creosote preservative affects the mollusks. One study was about mollusks in a contaminated environment shown to have bioaccumulation of up to ten times the concentration of the chemical compounds in creosote pilings compared to a control species."

Jerry reads a section that Martin highlighted while Andrew and Clint wait. When he finishes, he exhales. "You guys need to hear what scientist boy underlined several times. A chemical reaction called oxidation-reduction allows some compounds to be broken down into new forms of more toxic molecules. Studies have shown oxidation-reduction reactions of creosote-preservative compounds yield compounds that are listed as environmentally hazardous. So, not only are the initial compounds in creosote hazardous to the environment, but the byproducts of the chemical reactions are also environmental hazards."

"So, by using it to kill the monster, we also might kill the ecosystem."

"Yep. We're not run-of-the-mill terrorists. We're also eco-terrorists."

"Great," Andrew says, not entirely under his breath. "Look, what you both said about the neighborhood downstream concerns me. We can't get branded as the bad guys for what we do. I just can't allow that to happen. So, here are my unsolicited thoughts; Jerry, contact your good ole boys, as you called them. Get every drop of whatever you think they have made. They can either produce it or retrieve it if it's stashed somewhere.

"Clint, you and I are going back to Shreveport to have two conversations. One with your superintendent, the other with my US attorney. We'll bring the videotape with us and show it. If we have to fly down to Baton Rouge tomorrow after our talk with the US attorney, then that's what we'll do. Hopefully, the videotape and our experiences with the creature at Martin's will convince the powers that be this is a true national emergency, and they'll do three things: first, believe us; second, evacuate the locals; and third, give us whatever we need. How does all that sound?"

Clint and Jerry nod their approval.

"But what if it leaves the bayou before we can execute our plan?"

"Risk we have to take, which is why I want to move quickly. Martin believed the creature uses the bayou as home base. I recall he said that his theory was the bayou reminded the creature of where it came from, wherever that might have been, which is why it stayed there or returned there even after leaving to seek food. Maybe he was right. Who knows, perhaps some part of his son is still inside, absorbed by the creature but missing the place he knew as a safe location.

"The weather forecast calls for rain the next two days, but then a stretch of sunny weather. So, we may have more people disappearing at night if it rains hard before we can act, which means we have to step it up. Let's get all our notifications and planning done and, in three days, meet back at your office, Jerry. Does that sound like a plan?"

Clint and Jerry nod. "Sounds like the only plan," Clint says.

"I agree," says Jerry. "And I'm glad you're going to at least run what we're planning by someone much higher up than us. I think that is prudent, and once they see the videotape and hear what you tell them, I don't see how they could come to any conclusion that differs from ours. I hope they don't decide the military option is the only course of action."

"Exactly," Clint and Andrew say as Jerry locks up the marshal's office and they head outside to the parking lot. They hear thunder in the distance and share a collective look of concern.

Jerry says, "Well, gentlemen, the past couple of days have been interesting. That thunder tells me we need to do this as soon as possible. If something happens tonight, it's still on Martin." Jerry stops for a moment, then finishes with, "Good luck with the higher-ups. Andrew, I expect you to let me know if I need to prepare for the witness protection program."

"You got it, Jerry. We all might need to prepare." Turning to Clint, he says, "You know where the US district courthouse is over on the corner of Edwards and Fannin?"

Clint nods, and both men wave goodbye to Jerry as he pulls out of the lot.

"Great. Meet me there tomorrow morning, bright and early? Just come up to my office. I'll contact an AUSA I'm friendly with tonight and inquire about his boss."

"Okay. I'll see you tomorrow, Andrew," Clint says. He cranks his car, pulls out, and joins all the other traffic headed out of town.

Andrew sits in his car for a minute, saying a quiet prayer that their plan works. *It will or it won't. But, somehow, it has to work.* Andrew starts his Plymouth and heads back to Shreveport. His mind races ahead, organizing his arguments for and against what they are planning.

He grits his teeth. Pressing on the accelerator with a bit more force, the V8 responds, hurtling Andrew McLean towards an uncertain destiny as lightning illuminates the world around him and rain hits his windshield.

"No," he mutters, looking up at the dark sky. His mood darkens with each drop. "This must be how Martin felt every time it started to rain." He refocuses on the road as the sprinkles transition into heavy rain. He knows that Oscar might be rising off the bottom of the bayou, searching for an easy meal. Andrew slaps the steering wheel in frustration, hoping the heavy rain will put a pause on anyone venturing outside.

Looking through the windshield, Andrew growls, "Enjoy it while you can, Oscar, cuz in three days, your reign as killer king of the bayou ends."

26

Jerry shields his eyes from the bright morning sun and looks on as Earl connects fifty feet of three-inch hose to the tanker truck. Built to empty and transport sewage from septic tanks, Jerry commandeered it from a buddy who was reluctant to let him have it without knowing what it was going to be used for but finally relented. Jerry watches Evan pull the cord on a commercial-grade, submersible sump pump, which coughs to life. With the motor running, the liquid begins to transfer from the underground tank into Jerry's truck.

"So, you guys thought you'd make a million dollars with this stuff, huh?" Jerry inquires, curious about how they even mustered the brain cells to come up with the idea. Having dealt with Evan and Earl before, he understands the limits of both their abilities and intellects.

Earl answers.

"Yeah, Marshal, me and Evan figured there was a market for a new kind of pesticide that also could act as a wood preservative. Turns out we was wrong. We appreciate you not going to the sheriff about this stuff. I didn't know it was illegal to produce, and we are grateful for you helping us out and everything. I promise to get you something useful soon on them drug dealers we was talking about. Tit for tat; you're helpin' us, we're gonna help you. That's a promise."

"Just keep what we're doing here with this stuff to yourselves. I don't want to hear any talk around town that the Black city marshal helped you dispose of your illegally produced chemicals. Are we clear about that?"

Both men nod. "Yes, sir, we got it."

Jerry steps up and reaches into the truck cab, retrieving a wide-brimmed hat. He pulls it low on his forehead and takes a seat in the lawn chair offered by Evan.

"Thank you, Evan. Say, this looks like it's gonna take a while. Think I'll relax a bit. If I fall asleep, you boys wake me up when it's done." Before closing his eyes, though, he watches, intrigued, as Evan produces a well-worn dobro resonator guitar from the back of a pickup truck and spends a few minutes tuning it. When he's satisfied, he fishes a glass Coricidin D sinus medicine bottle out of a pocket. Sliding the bottle over his left middle finger, he smiles and looks over at Jerry.

"Don't mind if I pick a few tunes, do ya?"

Jerry shrugs when he answers. "Guess not."

"You like the blues, don't ya, Marshal?"

"I suppose."

"I thought all you people liked the blues. I could play a little Huddie Ledbetter—you heard of him, right? You know, Lead Belly. He's from over in Shreveport." With Jerry's noncommittal response, Evan tries again. "Here, lemme play you a new song I just learnt, sung by the group Lynyrd Skynyrd. It's called 'Curtis Lowe.' I know you'll like it."

Without moving, Jerry responds, "Okay, Evan, but first, what you just said is pretty damn racist. I don't want to hear you call us 'you people' ever again, okay?" Evan nods quickly, suddenly aware he's stepped over a line he didn't know existed. Satisfied, Jerry settles back in the chair. "And second, sure, play me something nice on that fancy metal guitar."

Evan smiles in relief and begins to play. Much to Jerry's surprise, Evan is actually a talented musician. "Nice," he mutters, and closes his eyes.

Two hours later, Evan hears the motor begin to whine at a slightly higher pitch and knows that means the tank is empty. He gently shakes Jerry awake.

"Hey, Marshal, I think it's finished."

Jerry sits upright and removes his hat. He stretches and completes a giant yawn. "Did I snore?"

Evan laughs and replies, "Yep. So did Earl."

"I always snore," Earl offers as he bends down to remove the hose from the underground tank. He lies on his stomach, clicks on a flashlight, and peers into the tank. His voice echoes with a metallic resonance when he calls out, "She's empty." He stands and begins to take apart the hoses. When finished, he turns to Jerry.

"That's it, Marshal. That's everything we had in the tank. I figure you got about four thousand gallons."

Jerry claps his hands together and tries to look serious as his voice adopts a stern tone. "Alright, men, thank you for your cooperation. Now, as I said earlier, zip it. Not a word regarding this stuff and my involvement." He stops for dramatic effect. "I'm dead serious about this. There's a reason I've not told you what I intend to do with it, and it's best that you don't know. I hear otherwise, we're going to have a very unpleasant conversation."

Both men nod, their heads bobbing up and down like they're attached with slinkies.

"Marshal, we got you. It ain't lost on us that you're doing us a serious favor. We won't tell no one. Me and Earl is done with the chemical stuff, think we'll stick with just shine." Evan realizes he's just admitted to a lawman that he makes illegal liquor and tries to walk it back. "I mean, uh . . ."

Jerry holds up his hand and chuckles. "Evan, I don't care if you're making shine out here. I don't care at all. You do you, brother. If shine is your thing, stick with that and try to make the best shine you can make. Just, no more playing around with dangerous chemicals, got it?"

Evan removes his Richard Petty ball cap and wipes his forehead. He'd heard this new marshal is a fair man, and now he knows the rumors are true. He was afraid when Jerry came to them, asking if it was true that they were dabbling in some new kind of chemical preservative. Evan just knew it meant jail time. So he was pleased when the marshal offered to take the chemical off their hands, without any questions or repercussions.

"Yes, sir, I believe we can stick to shine. We're pretty good at it. And, of course, our regular jobs."

Jerry smirks at the phrase "regular jobs" and finishes with "Of course you are. Evan, say, you're pretty talented with that guitar. Maybe that's what you should be doing. Something to think about. See y'all later." He cranks the engine and shoves it into gear, then leans out the window with a slight wave and drives away.

As he waves in response, Earl shoves three fingers into his shirt pocket. Eventually, he finds the joint he rolled that morning. He pulls it out, attaches a small clip to it, lights it, and inhales deeply. With his eyes closed to enhance the high, he passes it over to Evan. Earl exhales finally and asks the only question he's been wrestling with for the past hour.

"What you figure he gonna do with our chemical?"

Evan takes a hit off the joint, holding the smoke in for a moment. Then, he blows the smoke forcefully into the air and shakes his head. "Wondering about that myself. I don't know, but I bet someone's day is about to get pretty screwed up. I admit, when he was elected, I was concerned 'bout having a Black lawman in town, but now I think I mighta been wrong on that."

"Yep," Earl replies. "He treated us right. I know we can't tell nobody 'bout what we did here, but we can at least let some of our buddies know that our new marshal is a perty decent man."

"Agreed," Evan says as he gives the joint back to Earl. "Plus, he likes my playin'. Well, come on, let's get the hose and soap going. We gotta clean this thing out real good. It'll make a helluva weed hidey-hole."

"Even though we just told the marshal we'd stick to shine?"

"Well, we cain't be one-trick ponies, can we?"

"Guess not. Can't we wait til we finish this joint?"

Evan nods approvingly. "Oh yeah, fer sure we're finishing this joint. It's good stuff! It's grown from seeds my brother-in-law brung back from Mexico."

"Well, it's Louisiana weed now, not Mexican weed. Maybe we should call it something cool. How 'bout Cajun Cripple?"

"But, Evan, we ain't Cajuns."

"Don't matter; we can be whoever we want to be now. We know people!" Evan makes the point by raising his arm towards the spot where Jerry and the tanker truck disappeared. "How bout we call it Redneck Ripple?"

Earl smiles. "Now, that's a name I can get behind!"

They return to the lawn chairs, which creak as they settle in.

"Here ya go, bro, to chase the weed," Evan says, opening a cooler full of ice. He digs around and hands Earl a beer, then sits back as Earl pops the top off a cold Coors, takes a healthy swig, and burps loudly. He examines the can.

"Say, Evan, ain't Coors illegal in Louisiana?"

Evan smiles. "That awful word, 'illegal'—it ever stop us before?"

"Reckon not. I'm getting hungry. We finish our beer, we should go hit Cotton's Fried Chicken! I feel the need for some onion rings and chicken."

"Why wait until we're finished?" Evan says, beginning to move, but Earl holds out his arm to stop Evan from rising out of the lawn chair.

"Wait a sec, just hang on. Let me at least enjoy my buzz before we leave?"

"Good idea," Evan says, sinking back down.

"I wonder what the marshal is gonna do with that stuff?"

"Stop thinking about it, Earl; it don't matter."

27

Clint glances up at the cobalt-blue sky and smiles. He is momentarily distracted by motion near the middle of the dam; Andrew tosses a spearhead shovel aside and inserts something into the hole he's just dug. Behind Andrew, an array of wires cascades down the grassy hill and joins two others that stretch out from the trunk of Andrew's car. Andrew stands, surveys his masterpiece, and waves Clint's direction. As Clint exits the car, he admires the systematic placement of the high explosives. *It's like a pyramid. Guess that's how you bring down a dam.* He turns and sees that both steel doors have been removed and are on the ground beside Martin's lab.

"Man, I hope all this works. With those strong, metal doors gone, that building is no longer the refuge Martin designed it to be."

He peers at the bayou. The cypress trees stand resolute, unaware of the danger lurking just beneath the surface. Spanish moss hangs from every limb and sways in the slight breeze. An involuntary shiver runs up his spine as he recalls the night Martin was killed. Clint is acutely aware that inside that beautiful bayou lives something not of this world, a thing capable of killing them all without hesitation or emotion.

He hears a noise from behind the lab and walks towards the container of chemicals to his left. Jerry is dragging the white hose Martin spoke of in his video towards the bayou, made more difficult by the twenty-pound weight Jerry has tied to the end of the hose. Clint points at the weight and holds up both arms. "What the heck are you doing with that weight, Jerry?"

"It's to sink the hose so that the chemical fire starts as deep as possible."

"I saw the video too, remember? But why not get the hose to the boat first, and then tie on the weight?"

Jerry continues to drag the hose and mutters, "When did you get so damn helpful?"

Clint laughs as he bends down to lift a section off the ground. "Here, lemme help. It looks like you might need some assistance with that," he says. "We don't want to get a rip in it."

"Yes, I know. Any holes in the hose will result in the chemical escaping before it hits the bayou, changing the dynamic and making it less effective. It could also put the fire somewhere we don't want it."

"I'm glad you were paying attention. Makes me feel better."

Both men walk the unwieldy hose to the edge of the water. Clint holds it as Jerry puts the weighted end into a small johnboat. Jumping in, Jerry grabs a paddle and rows about twenty feet out into the bayou while Clint helps by feeding the hose out, making sure it doesn't kink or twist. Jerry's not too worried, given the bright, sunny day, but in the back of his mind is the visual of Martin disappearing into the monster's mouth.

The newcomer senses movement and would like to reach out to explore. However, emerging is impossible, given the hateful red dot in the sky and its filtered death through the muddy water, so it relaxes and tries to understand what is happening above.

"Say, Clint, if this thing decides he likes sunlight and comes up to chomp on ole Jerry, do me a solid and shoot me first?"

Clint laughs and pauses before answering.

"Jerry, if that's what you want, I would happily shoot you."

Jerry drops the weighted hose into the water and watches it sink. He raises his eyebrows as he considers Clint's response. "I think you said that with a tad too much enthusiasm."

Clint doesn't answer immediately, but the smile on his face tells Jerry that Clint is thinking of an appropriate way to acknowledge his statement. He doesn't have to wait long.

"Well, if I was the one dropping the hose that will release a deadly chemical and cause an explosion of unknown potential, hopefully killing an alien creature that is living on the bottom of a bayou, I'm sure you'd do the same for me."

"You forgot the part about said creature having the power to dissolve your body, leaving only hollow bones."

"No, it was implied. I just didn't feel the need to say it."

Jerry looks unhappy but manages a lopsided smile.

"Sometimes, I wonder why we're such good friends. And you felt it necessary to remind me that thing is down there somewhere, didn't you?" he grumbles, watching the hose disappear into the murky, tannin-filled water. "I wonder how deep the bayou is out in the middle."

"None of them are very deep. Maybe ten, twelve feet deep. I bet Martin's little space alien is sizing you up for a snack right now," Clint ribs his friend.

"As I have said before, I'm beginning to suspect that, on occasion, perhaps you don't have my best interests in mind," Jerry shoots back as he rows to shore. A burst of energy in his rowing denotes his desire not to become a snack for Oscar. When the metal bottom of the johnboat scrapes up onto the sandy beach, Clint grabs the handle on the front lip of the boat and pulls it out of the water.

The twenty-pound weight settling to the bottom of the bayou confuses the newcomer. It explores and finds this new and foreign thing has no taste. The color is pleasant, but there is foreboding evil in its design. The newcomer retracts and flattens out, covering the bottom more thoroughly in anticipation of some new calamity. The red dot above continues to mock it.

On land now, Jerry rubs his hands together, clearing sand and water off.

"All done. I hope this works."

"Me too," Andrew says from around the corner. "If it doesn't, we'll have to get people with far more power than we can muster involved. And I don't even want to consider that, given the possibility the military might step in and try to keep the darn thing, or something equally stupid." He quickly changes the subject. "So, Jerry, that tanker, is that what I think it is?"

"Yep. I got the truck from a buddy, and this morning, I acquired the stuff from the two knuckleheads who made it. This plan better work. I hear the Forest Service cleared the entire campground up on Caney, some excuse about a toxic issue over here at Martin's lab. I figure the media will get wind of it eventually."

"I hope they don't show up. Luckily, on a weekday, there weren't that many people at the lake or the campground. The biggest issue was the boaters and fishermen on the water."

Jerry nods. "Sheriff told me last night that they did a cautious evacuation of all the families downstream."

"Yeah, clearing the campground was someone up in DC's idea. They figured we'll empty the lake, or the dam will collapse. Can't have anyone around to witness it, so the US attorney made some calls, and the result was the Forest Service ordered the evacuation."

"How about the sheriff or fire department?"

"I was told there'd be a conversation with the sheriff and the fire chief. With regard to the five families downstream, if the water reaches them, they'll be compensated somehow. Not my department."

Jerry looks doubtful. "When this place goes up, I bet Sheriff Hancock comes out. He might not ask us questions, but I know he'll have some. You know, Clint, your girlfriend might come out too," Jerry adds.

The humorous expression on Jerry's face alleviates Andrew's knee-jerk concern. "I'm guessing we're talking about Diane Chase?" he asks.

Clint nods. "Jerry, did you call Diane Chase and tell her to meet us here?"

Jerry laughs as he responds. "That was not on my list of things to do today. I thought you would do it since you guys are such tight friends now."

Andrew decides to get in a few licks too. "When she called my office, my deputy just told her I was engaged in a life-and-death struggle with an alien invader that was eating humanity one at a time and that I'd have to call her back after I'd saved the planet. Again."

Sharing a good laugh breaks the tension. Then Jerry turns a complete circle. "You don't think she's out there, watching and filming us right now, do you?"

"If she is, might as well prepare for a life on the run, because no doubt she'll not be showing our best sides . . . and you do realize they don't use film anymore, right? Remember Martin's camera and tape machine? That's what most of them use now."

Jerry mock glares at Clint and responds, "It's just an expression. What can I say? I'm old." He shrugs. "Back to my original question, I guess when we set this thing off, it's going to be a serious fire, right?"

"No doubt in my mind."

Jerry considers Andrew's answer. He knows this plan will kill lots of wildlife if the fire gets out of control, and he dislikes killing innocent things. He watches a box turtle start to make its way from one side of the yard towards a stand of bamboo, so he runs over, picks it up, and walks it to the other side of the road. Clint smiles when Jerry returns from his mission of mercy.

"Jerry, you are a kind individual."

"Thanks, Clint. I just couldn't stand to see that poor thing get eaten by that monster or killed when we burn this place to the ground. And don't tell anyone."

"Your secret is safe with me." Clint points towards the dam. "So, Andrew, explain what you've got rigged here if you don't mind."

"Sure, follow me," he answers, heading towards his car parked across the road from Martin's lab. He stops at the trunk and starts to explain. "I guess getting a call from Washington was helpful for your guy at the ordnance plant because he was able to put together more than enough high-grade explosives to bring down the dam. When he delivered them, he wanted to stick around and watch, but I was finally able to shoo him away.

"Without a detailed examination of the dam, I called an old Navy buddy who still does this sort of thing for the Army Corps of Engineers. Needless to say, he had a whole lot of questions about my questions. Finally, though, he gave me some good pointers on how to bring down a large dam. I have placed the explosives in spots I think should weaken it to the point of failure. I tried to do one deep-core sample at the top, middle, and bottom. All I found was mounded-up dirt and rocks."

"Does that make it easier?"

"Yes. I was able to sink the explosives more than six feet deep in every instance, which is critical at the bottom of the dam. You'll notice the holes are in an hourglass shape with lots of holes at the top and bottom. It may look like random placement, but the charges face downward, making them more effective."

"What exactly are you using?"

"The explosive your guy provided is military grade, based on explosive compounds that expand at a very high speed—more than twenty thousand feet per second. I'm not trying to disintegrate the dam, just move some of it out of the way and let the volume of water do the rest. I have concentrated on the top and bottom, where the high-velocity pressure should slice right through it, splitting it in half. Though I need rocks and dirt coming down, I'm not entirely able to force the dam and its material to go in one direction. But I figure if I blow the dam properly, lots of water will be coming towards the bayou and the fire."

"How will you ignite it? I'm guessing we can't be very close when that chlorine stuff hits the bayou water, or we'd be incinerated, right?" Jerry asks, concerned.

"Right. My initial plan was to be all the way out by Dorcheat Road, but after considering the flow of the water, I think it's more prudent to be up the hill, away from both the water and the fire."

Jerry chuckles. "Yeah, I'm, uh, all in for not drowning or getting blackened like a good piece of catfish."

"Me too," Andrew says, also with a chuckle.

"The fire won't ignite the explosives?" Clint asks.

"Sadly, no. Contrary to what you see in movies and on television, military-grade explosives are very stable. The fire won't ignite them, so I will apply a severe shock using blasting caps, also called primer charges, connected by wire to my detonator."

At that point, Andrew opens his trunk, and they see three medium-sized metal boxes, each with positive and negative posts protruding from the top.

"These are ten-cap blasting machines. That means each machine can handle setting off up to ten dynamite loads. My plan, and how I have the wiring designed, is to blow the middle first, then the top, which will hopefully weaken the dam enough to cascade down on its own. I will then blow the remaining ten I have sunk into the floor of the dam, to the left and right of the cascading water and debris. This should result in its total collapse. I'm counting on the fire and debris to distract the . . . what are we even calling it?"

"Well, Martin called it Oscar. So, I'm good with Oscar if you two are," Clint offers.

"Works for me," Jerry says.

"Alright, Oscar it is. Well, I'm counting on Oscar being injured by the fire and potentially disabled. The chemical Martin acquired, the chlorine trifluoride—I read the data sheet on this stuff, and, man, it's all bad, all day. The water we release when the dam blows will make it burn even hotter. I bet it even melts the dirt. Everything here is going to burn."

"What about the lab? I see you've removed the doors," Clint says.

"We going to draw short straws for who goes in?"

"I'll go. I guess I need to also kill the freezer and glass container critters, though, don't I?" Clint asks.

Jerry pretends to be relieved as Andrew nods. "Yes, you need to do them first. Then, open the valve. After you kill what he has stored in the freezer and the glass box and open the blue valve, you run the hell outta there. We crank up the cars and make a fast getaway. I have put several cans of gasoline inside the building and a few extra sticks of explosives too, all tied to a separate detonator, which will go when the chemical hits it. The whole building should disintegrate."

"Nice," Jerry mutters approvingly. "What if Clint runs out of the building after getting attacked and infected by one of those things?"

Clint looks worried as Andrew answers with a matter-of-fact "Well, I've reserved a few boom sticks for any emergency. I guess one of us will have to take care of him."

"Uh, guys, please only blow me to smithereens if you're one-hundred-percent sure I'm a monster."

"You betcha," Jerry says with an evil smile.

Andrew continues, "Clint, as soon as you run out of the lab, Jerry will be in the container where he opens the valve, starting the flow of chlorine trifluoride into the bayou and the lab. We beat it up the hill and hunker down. I expect the creature will appear and somehow try to escape, but I hope Martin's plans work and that it can't escape the dirt, the heat, and explosions. It helps that it's a bright, blue-sky day."

Jerry voices a concern. "Do we need to have the fire department on standby, just in case we kill this thing and the fire stops burning as a result of the chemical additive and just burns because the forest is on fire?"

"Yeah, I thought about that as I rigged the explosives. But from what I understand, the chemical will just have to burn itself out. Once that's done, and it's just a fire, then yes, the fire department will need to be called. But I'm all for waiting to let things take their course before we jump on the radio and place a call to fireboard. Especially since we still have to douse the creature with the chemical from Jerry's redneck scientists after the fire. Questions? Thoughts? Speak up now because once we start, there is no going back."

Jerry turns to face the lab, bayou, and dam.

"Well, I would never be in favor of burning down a section of my parish or destroying the only local recreation area." He turns to face Clint and Andrew. "And there is no doubt in my mind that what we have planned will destroy the lake. The Army Corps of Engineers will have to build a new dam at some point, and fish and wildlife will have to restock the lake with fish, frogs, turtles, etcetera. However, we have seen what we're trying to kill and what it can do. Short of getting the military involved to nuke the place, I don't think we have any other choice." He goes quiet. Clint and Andrew remain silent, waiting for him to continue. They see the conflict on his face. He finally shakes his head.

"Well, Martin's research and notes all say that this is the only way to kill it. I hope he was right because if he wasn't, we are going to have bigger troubles to deal with than blowing up a local dam."

Andrew wades in with "The data and the research Martin did tells me it burns with such fierceness that very little can withstand it. Seems it is too volatile for its own good. Even the Nazis in the war were unable to handle it successfully without lots of collateral deaths.

"His notes on the smaller versions of the creature are pretty clear. First, he found that they need moisture to exist and thrive like virtually every type of life we know of. His idea was to deny the creature moisture through the use of the hottest fire he could acquire. After the fire, he tried to prevent the reanimation of the cells through the destruction of the cell material. For some reason, creosote kills its cells, making it impossible to survive. He watched as they died, suffocated somehow. I guess he never got the opportunity to fully examine the mechanism of their deaths. Of course, he also never figured out how it survived in our nitrogen/oxygen atmosphere either."

Andrew stops so that Clint and Jerry can consider the gravity of the plan. Finally, Jerry hits on the proper response.

"Well, looks like the three amigos, the three musketeers, are riding in to save the day! I say we steal a phrase from NASA and light this candle!"

"Okay, let's get to it. I'm going to finish stringing my two detonator cords up the hill; then I suggest we don't delay." Andrew adds with a bit of irony, "Plus, what's that old saying about the weather?"

"If you don't like it, stick around; it'll change in five minutes?" Clint offers.

"Yep. And I don't want the weather to change to the advantage of the alien we're trying to kill."

"Ten-four," Jerry says. He is interrupted when they hear a pickup truck cross the railroad tracks, headed their direction. His heart sinks a bit as the sheriff pulls into Martin's driveway.

"Oh man, this can't be good."

28

"Howdy, boys," Sheriff Hancock says through the open driver-side window. He turns off the engine and steps out. "I wasn't sure if the attorney general was pulling my leg or what. I didn't even believe it was him at first. But it didn't take him long to prove his bona fides."

"William Saxbe called you?" Andrew inquires incredulously.

"The one and only. Called me at home and had me drive from Minden to Barksdale to get on a special phone, something called a 'stew,' and only then did he tell me the entire story. Said I was to find you three and offer every bit of support my office could muster. I thought I'd get out here without putting anything out on the radio since, well, you-know-who might be listening."

The sheriff walks past them to get an unobstructed view of the bayou and shoves one hand into a pocket while resting the other on his holstered sidearm. He asks the only question that matters at the moment: "Is what he told me true?"

Andrew moves up to stand beside the sheriff.

"Well, Sheriff, the 'stew,' as you called it, is the *S-T-U*. That is a secure telephone unit. And it is so top secret that we barely even acknowledge its existence. That the attorney general of the United States told you to go to Barksdale and use one should convince you. Yes, he told you the truth. Clint, Jerry, and I have seen what this creature can do. It's worse than you can imagine, given we're not even sure we can kill this thing. All we have are the notes, the results of Martin's experiments on it, and the directions he left for us."

"This thing, it got Martin, didn't it? He's not on a beach somewhere, is he?"

Andrew just nods. Sheriff Hancock nods as well. "Well then, I guess the only thing left to do is kill it before it tries to kill the rest of us."

"Oh, trust me, Sheriff, it wouldn't try. It would succeed, which is why we plan to follow Martin's directions to the letter. Martin might have been crazy, in a mad-scientist kind of way, but I trust his scientific calculus on this thing."

"Tell me how I can help."

While Andrew explains the plan, the four men are unaware that up in the tall grass on the dam, Diane Chase and her cameraman have been recording every move they've made. That lack of knowledge goes both ways, though, since Diane doesn't know that they are less than ten feet from the tip of Andrew's triangle-shaped set of explosives. Quickly dodging the portable barrier across the road, the cameraman drove into the Caney Lake recreation area and parked at the boat launch next to the dam. Squatting and low crawling through the grass, they stopped at a convenient spot to set up a tripod and start recording.

"You sure this is alright?" he nervously asks. Typically, he'd be fine going around blocked-off or gated areas. But with four of the most senior lawmen in North Louisiana down below, he's not real keen on losing his job or going to jail.

"Story of the century. Maybe the biggest story in all human history. We'll win awards for what we're doing here for the next ten years. Just keep the tape rolling. Are you sure the parabolic mic is working?"

"It's working, but they're so far away, and they keep moving, so the audio goes in and out. It won't be great, but we'll still have video and natural sound."

"Great. No matter what happens, keep that concrete building in the frame. I hear those idiots plan to blow it up and try to kill whatever kind of exotic zoo animal it is that Martin Landry was experimenting on down there. A source down in Baton Rouge told me that Landry viewed himself as a modern Dr. Moreau. Sounds like he was trying to create some kind of monster using radioactive stuff from a meteorite, and he died as a result. It's caged right now, in that lab, but they can't let it get out into the world. So they're going to blow it up and then set it on fire."

"But the doors to his lab are open. Is it still inside the lab?"

"Yes, but I was told that part of it is also in the bayou below us."

This news isn't at all helpful in tamping down the cameraman's fear, instead pushing him much closer to the edge.

"It's in the bayou? There's some kind of killer animal in the bayou that's not a gator? In the bayou below us? What the hell have you gotten me into!"

"Oh, calm down. No, it's not a mutated gator, as far as I know. And we're still alive, aren't we? And the same source that alerted me to this said that whatever it is only comes out in heavy rain. Look above our heads—another beautiful, sunny Louisiana day. Stop worrying. Don't be such a wimp."

Diane makes a mental note to ask for a different cameraman next time. *Maybe there won't be a next time. This one is gonna project me into the stratosphere! Network, here I come!*

"Hey, they're moving. The trooper went into the lab. The marshal has some kind of wires."

"I guess that'd be the detonation cord to the explosives they're going to use on the concrete building," Diane says. The cameraman zooms in all the way and watches as Andrew connects more wires to a spool sitting on a rack in the trunk of his car. Curious, the cameraman follows the strand of wire leading directly into the concrete building. Retracing this movement, he then follows the other wires but loses sight of them because of their size and the slope of the dam.

"Say, I can see one wire going into the lab, but there's another set of wires that goes somewhere else, and I can't follow it because of the dam. Where do you think those wires go?"

Diane considers the question for a heartbeat.

"Hmm. Not sure. I only heard about the plan to blow up the lab. Maybe into the bayou? Look back down there; tell me what they're doing now."

In the lab, the newcomer in the glass box senses much more movement and is curious. It extends feelers into the area of its incarceration. Feeding time? Perhaps some new form of torture to endure? It believes something is different. The creature that approaches has an odd mass and is moving unusually. Then, the newcomer is no longer alone, though it knows that the new additions to its home are deep in stasis. They emit a cool sensation when introduced into the warm environment of the bulletproof box, filling the enclosure with moisture as they begin to thaw. The coolness is something new and painful, so it adjusts, trying to minimize the danger. Different vibrations indicate it is feeding time, though it is confused. Why are these new ones here? It cannot feed on them. This would kill them all.

Fear rises, as does a sudden rush of anger.

Clint is careful when dumping the frozen slides into the bulletproof box. He watches with surprise and interest as tiny tendrils emerge about two inches from underneath the cypress log and begin to explore what he's just added to the box.

"Sorry, little buddy, but this is the end for you. It was just your bad fortune to crash into our planet. Unfortunately, we can't have you getting out. I hope you understand. It's not personal. I like my planet and want it to stay just like it is."

With meticulous care, Clint tightly attaches the hose to the container of thawed chemical. Without hesitation, he opens the valve that controls the flow and watches as the dark material fills the tube, inching its way towards the open valve of the kill box.

The newcomer underneath the cypress log wonders about this new activity. Then, it knows more anger, then pain, as Martin's mixture fills the box. The hatred for this world grows with each part of it that dies. Finally, with nothing to do and no escape possible, it stops trying. The others of its species introduced into the box succumb quietly without ever waking. It tries to survive, but it cannot. This is its last act on Earth.

Satisfied, Clint turns his attention to the blue valve. With some effort, he uses the purpose-made wrench hanging on the wall to open the valve all the way. When the nut stops moving, he drops the wrench and sprints out of the building.

"Jerry! Open the blue valve!" he yells.

Using the zoom lens, the cameraman sees Clint exit at a full sprint.

"Hey, something's going on. The trooper just ran out of the lab."

"Keep rolling!" Diane says with some force.

"The city marshal is running away too! He was behind the lab, at that container thing. He and the trooper have jumped into a truck, and the sheriff is right behind them. Looks like they're leaving. Man, they just peeled out like they were stock car drivers! That US marshal is leaving too, but he's driving more slowly, and he's trailing three long wires out of his trunk.

Diane makes a poor decision and stands. Below her, the chlorine trifluoride begins to spew out of the blue valve and into the lab, igniting the jugs of gasoline Andrew placed next to the bulletproof box. The explosive wave of fire makes her stagger back as the bulletproof windows bend inward, implode, then explode. The entire building heaves for just a moment, then disappears in a blinding ball of fire. Simultaneously, the chemical in the white NASA hose hits the depths of the bayou and explodes. Virtually everything the chemical touches is consumed by the fire. That blast knocks Diane and her cameraman into the grass, which is already engulfed in fire as they regain their footing.

"What the hell?" the cameraman yells. The heat is almost unbearable as he stands. He yanks the camera from the tripod, slings the padded strap on the recorder unit over his shoulder, and, camera in hand, rushes in the opposite direction of the fire. He intends to leave, even if Diane Chase burns to a crisp behind him.

On the bottom of the bayou, the billion-year-old newcomer knows genuine pain for the first time. Just as Martin had imagined, the chemical fire is enhanced by its contact with the water and burns so entirely that it is inescapable. The newcomer tries to rise and leave, but it finds that its entire world is overcome by the immense destructive power of the chlorine trifluoride. Somewhere, deep inside its body, the human genetic memory to scream whenever injury or pain occurs tries to emerge, but vocal cords have never survived the initial absorption.

It changes shape a thousand times, losing an eye, gaining an eye, more fluid than solid, but nothing helps. It tries breaking into millions of tiny pieces, but it's too late; each individual piece is too small to survive, so it retrieves what remains alive and continues upward. Some of it burns and disappears, never to live again. The newcomer's alien metabolism is already on the downward slope. Knowing this, and with some effort, it travels through the flames to the surface, where it endures a pain like no other as it grasps onto the charred remains of a burning cypress tree. Like the burning water of the bayou, its rage boils. The dark smoke blots out the sun, so it feels a measure of safety in rising to the surface.

This is the moment it decides to sacrifice everything in hopes that something can remain. In the rushing water and fire, it musters every ounce of strength and concentrates its life force to enable the survival of one small piece, no larger than a quarter. In that small piece of the whole is the only remaining mechanism capable of survival not damaged beyond repair. It snaps off and floats away.

The sense of self-preservation in this tiny, immature newcomer overrides every other sense, and it suppresses its resentment at its premature separation and attaches to a submerged piece of fiberglass blown into the bayou from the lab. It wraps around the fiberglass and flairs out, a motion akin to unfurling a small sail. This action works to move it away from the conflagration that consumes its parent and into the churning water. Carried through the woods by the flood, this new life-form must feed to grow, but there is no sustenance close that resembles a meal, so it waits, riding the current to a new home.

The original newcomer, now devoid of the option for life unless it can feed, turns its attention to the things that hurt it. There is still time to inflict injury on those responsible. It wonders how all this is still happening, given its recent acquisition and absorption of its original captor. The bottom of the bayou is no longer available, so it rises fully out of the remaining few inches to the surface. The drive to find those responsible for this pain and to make them stop is the only reason to exist.

One far-off memory remains. After being kidnapped by the supermassive black hole that killed its parent universe, it once wondered if its existence would be easy, or one filled with pain, sacrifice, and hardship. It now knows the answer to this question.

Diane, transfixed by the visual of fire everywhere, screams. Her cameraman turns, hoping to find her on fire. He sees her pointing towards the bayou, so he looks. He wishes he had not. In the middle of the inferno is something out of a horror movie. It is brown, with an odd-shaped, yellow eye. A large, dark-rimmed mouth is open as if it is trying to scream. It is entirely on fire, and a thin brown arm appears to be flailing in agony. The other arm is wrapped around a burning cypress tree. Diane and her cameraman stand, spellbound by a sight neither was prepared to see.

Then, something in the lab explodes with enough force that it knocks Diane to the ground once again. A deadly hailstorm of pulverized concrete rains down.

"What the hell is that? That is not some mutated zoo animal!" the cameraman yells as he holds his camera above his head like an umbrella. Diane does not get a chance to answer him because they are thrown into the air when Andrew pushes the plunger for the first ten sticks of high explosive buried in the dam.

Fury is all the newcomer knows now. The very second the dam surrenders, its anger overtakes its will to survive. Entirely out of the water, it senses movement and turns. It sees two targets. Perhaps they are the source of its pain. Somehow, it must go there and punish them.

But before it can move, the nearby mound of dirt disappears, obliterated by some invisible force. Chunks of the structure fall from the sky. The fire rages even hotter. It must survive! It has done so for more than a billion years in the deepest reaches of space. It hates this planet and wants every living organism on it to die.

But Martin's fire is as efficient as planned.

It tries everything it knows to survive, but the newcomer is now more sad than angry. Nothing can stop the path to nonexistence. What is left of its life force dissipates with each lick of the distasteful, unending flame. It knows that the end has already begun. Whatever this evil is cannot be stopped. It looks towards the woods, hopeful that its little one has escaped and lives. It stretches out its damaged senses, searching. It brings every sense to bear and focuses. Relief floods in. The little one is alive.

Up the hill from the lab, Andrew twists the next plunger, and ten more charges explode. Diane and her cameraman are almost off the dam as it collapses into the bayou, spreading lake water across the entire property once occupied by Martin and his bayou. It overflows the woods next to the lab and reaches the railroad tracks. Soon, everything is on fire.

Diane screams at her cameraman, "Hey! Stop! Turn around! Why aren't you getting this?"

"Screw you! I don't know what that is down in the bayou, but it looked right at me, and when it saw me, if it could have killed me, I know it would have. The look in its eye was one I'll never forget! If we hadn't moved, we'd be dead right now! They blew up the dam, for God's sake!"

"I told you they were going to do something crazy, didn't I?"

They watch water and debris from the ruptured dam tumble into the bayou. Residual chlorine trifluoride creates a new tornado of fire that swirls around the brown thing with the yellow eye. Both of them see the thing wrap both arms around a burning tree stump.

"Oh my God. The fire is rotating in place around that thing like an opening to hell trying to suck a demon back home," the cameraman yells. He turns and, with new resolve, races towards the news van.

Andrew tears the wires from the plungers and slams his trunk shut. Clint and Jerry stand silent as thick, black smoke streams into the sky. Andrew nods at Sheriff Hancock, who then speaks into his radio.

"Webster One."

"Webster One, go ahead, Sheriff."

"Alert the fire department. We have a chemical fire burning off of Parish Road 116. It is at the Landry concrete house. The building is demolished, the dam on Lower Caney is breached by explosives left as a booby trap by Mr. Landry, and water and fire are spreading into the woods. Tell them to bring the special trucks that Barksdale brought over this morning. Also call fish and game and the state with the same message. Copy?"

There is a pause as the dispatch center tries to fully grasp what the sheriff has just said.

"Uh, Sheriff? Are you serious?" the woman asks, doubt evident in her voice.

"Webster One, ten-four. Tell them to be prepared for environmental hazards of unknown chemical origin. Have Barksdale bring everything they've got. Now hurry, get them started in our direction. Have everyone contact me on this channel, but tell them they must stage on Dorcheat Road and wait for my signal when the scene is cold. The scene is very hot right now, so the fire department needs to stage and be ready to come in when I give them the all clear. That is critical. Make sure they stage and do not just come right into the scene of the fire. Copy?"

"Webster One, we are ten-four. Alerting the fire department with your instructions."

The sheriff looks at Andrew, Clint, and Jerry.

"Okay, I did my part. That tape you guys sent up to DC got them so worried that the secretary of defense called Barksdale and had them run some stuff out to us that can be used to fight a fire such as this one. What's next? I guess that the big tanker Jerry has parked out by the railroad tracks is the next item on the hit parade?"

"Yes, sir. The tanker is full of the chemical Martin identified as deadly to our little alien visitor. He tried it dozens of times, and it always worked. He believed the creature was living on the bottom of the bayou, only emerging to feed on whatever was close.

"As he designed it, the plan was to burn the lab and bayou, weaken the creature by drawing it out into the open on a sunny day, then blow the dam, which would serve two purposes. First, the dirt and debris would deny the bottom as a safe refuge by filling in the bayou, and second, the water influx would make the chemical fire burn hotter. He theorized that the combination of raining debris down on it and letting the chemical fire burn would kill it. Then, we use what I have in the truck, spray it all over the bayou after the fire has died down a bit."

"Do we have to wait?"

"Yes. We have to wait because as the chemical we used burns, it produces hydrofluoric acid and hydrochloric acid, both of which can kill humans. So, we let it burn a bit more, then we apply the creosote compound over the entire area, especially where the creature was living."

"Okay. Say, next time you guys decide to blow up a significant recreation area, maybe go over to Sabine or Claiborne Parishes?"

"How about we try to make this the last and only time," Clint says through gritted teeth.

"What do we do now?" Diane's cameraman asks as he throws his gear into the back seat of the Chevy van.

"What do you mean, what do we do now? Sheriff Hancock is down there, the state trooper, the city marshal, and that new US marshal from Shreveport. We're going where they are."

"Oh, hell no we're not," he spits out.

He never sees the slap. But as Diane's hand leaves his face, he staggers briefly and almost balls up his fists to slug her. As the sound of the slap resonates inside his eardrums and his adrenaline begins to subside, he hears her yelling at him.

"We are not going back without this story! This is huge! Huge, I tell you! We are the only ones with the story! *Exclusive*! How can you even think about leaving without knowing what is going on? You need to man up and get your crap together. We're going down there and confronting those men!"

"You are crazy. I don't know what that thing in the water was, but it wasn't an exotic, modified zoo animal, as you were led to believe. It was something else. Something I never want to meet or think about ever again. I do not want to go down there, and you can't make me!"

"Watch me," Diane growls. In a quieter voice, she adds, "Give me the keys. I'm driving. If you know what's good for you, you'll shut the hell up and do exactly as I say. You can thank me after we win a Nobel Prize for journalism."

Cowed by Diane's aggression, the cameraman doubts such a prize exists, but he is unwilling to challenge her. He reaches into a pocket and tosses her the keys, then trots dejectedly around the van and jumps into the passenger seat. The tires squeal as she puts the van into drive and careens out of the boat-launch area.

29

"Is that it?" Sheriff Hancock asks quietly, pointing towards the newcomer engulfed in flames. For the second time, Andrew, Clint, and Jerry see the creature out of the water.

"Yes. That's it! Now that it's out in the open, we need to hurry!"

The sheriff coughs as the wind blows smoke from the fire in his direction. Clint reaches into Andrew's car and hands the sheriff an air-purifying respirator. Andrew, Clint, and Jerry don theirs while Sheriff Hancock puts his on and adjusts the straps to ensure a tight fit around his large face.

While the four men watch the fire consuming the bayou and hopefully the newcomer, Diane Chase and her terrified cameraman are racing south on Dorcheat Road when they see the first piece of fire equipment stop at the intersection with Parish Road 116.

"Why aren't they turning? They can see the smoke, so the fire is still burning. What's the matter with them?" Diane's unwilling accomplice screeches. Both see a fireman in yellow bunker gear standing in the middle of the road. He appears to be about to stop all traffic, but Diane isn't going to be stopped.

"I don't know why they're not turning, but I am. I'm not about to let a bunch of firemen interfere with my story."

"Diane! He's waving for you to slow down and stop!"

"I don't care what he wants me to do!" she screams as she slows just enough to fool the fireman and then swerves the van around him. He yells at her, but she turns onto Parish Road 116 anyway, a satisfied smile crossing her face.

"That's right, boys, you can't tell Diane Chase what to do. You can just sit on it," she says, using a phrase from her favorite television show.

As the news van clears the intersection, the deputy fire chief shakes his head, swears, and picks up his radio.

With their eyes fixed on the newcomer, Andrew, Clint, Jerry, and the sheriff hear his radio squawk to life.

"Sheriff, this is the fire chief. The fire department is staging as you requested. But you have a news van headed your way. We tried to stop them, but they drove around our roadblock and could be at your location in a couple of minutes. Copy?"

With a look of disgust and some admiration, he replies, "I copy," He slams the door to his truck and yells, "You guys hear that? We got incoming. Looks like a news crew."

Jerry's reaction is a practical one. "Should one of us go intercept her? I still need a ride back to my tanker truck. If she sees the truck, she might stop there. I bet she'll have questions about it."

Sheriff Hancock chuckles. "I bet she has lots of questions about everything. Especially if any of her moles fed her information on what we're doing here, which is why she came out in the first place. It looks like I might need to figure out who in my organization is a leaker."

He turns and motions to Jerry. "Jump on in. I'll give you a ride to the tanker. And then I'll have a little chat with Ms. Chase." As he pulls out of the driveway, the sheriff jokingly yells to Andrew and Clint, "Don't go and try to make friends with it, okay?" Andrew and Clint

turn and watch for any indication the newcomer might be coming
for them.

Over on Parish Road 116, Diane and the cameraman slow to a
crawl as they drive past the tanker truck parked near the railroad tracks.

"Why is that tanker truck parked here?"

Sniffing a connection to the fire story, Diane hits the brakes and
backs up. She stops when the van is behind the tanker.

"Do you think it might be connected to whatever they're doing
here?"

"Could be." Curious, the cameraman is once again fully engaged
in the story. "Let me out for a second so I can get a quick shot of it."

Diane shifts the van into park, and her cameraman jumps out. He
opens the sliding door on the side of the van and retrieves his camera
and recorder.

She admonishes him, "Alright, but be snappy. I don't want to miss
anything."

"Yeah, I know you don't," he says to himself as he flicks the switches
to turn on the camera and recorder. He focuses on the entire truck and
rolls off two minutes of videotape. At the back of the truck, he spots
brown liquid dripping from a hose attached to what looks like an
electrical pumping mechanism designed to spray pesticides. He records
the dripping and more establishing shots of the railroad and truck.

Every second he stands with the camera on his shoulder, his stress
level rises. He knows that Diane is stewing like a pressure cooker in
the front seat, angry that he's taking so long. *She should learn how to
do this. I'd like to see her lugging around a twenty-five-pound camera and
fifteen-pound portable videocassette recorder.* He puts the camera down
on the roadway and searches for a stick, then rubs it on the dripping
liquid. Holding it close, but not too close, he takes a tentative sniff.
The odor almost overwhelms him, and he throws the stick away as he
dry heaves. Diane, who has been watching his actions in the rearview

mirror, yells out of the driver's side window, "What is it? Is it toxic? Some kind of poison? Are you okay?"

Grabbing his camera and recorder, he returns to the van and tosses the equipment in the back seat. He gets a memory whiff of the chemical and begins to choke before getting into the passenger seat.

"What's wrong? What made you so sick?"

"The tanker is full of something that smells like liquid creosote. We had a plant nearby growing up in south Shreveport, and the stench from that place, when they were treating the telephone poles, was almost too much to bear. I'd know that smell anywhere." He considers his discovery. "Do you think it's connected to what they're doing down here?"

Diane flips down the sun visor mirror, raises her eyebrows, brushes some residual grass and dirt off one cheek, and says, "Well, let's go find out." She turns the ignition key, bringing the motor back to life.

About to put the van into drive, Diane sees a vehicle headed in their direction. "It's the sheriff; roll tape!" she says. Her cameraman jumps into the back seat, shoulders his camera, and pushes the button to start recording. Sheriff Hancock stops at the cab of the tanker truck, and they watch Jerry jump out.

The sheriff slows to a stop beside the open window on the news van. He nods at Diane, getting her attention, and gives her an order in a very calm voice.

"You two stay right here. I tell you this for your protection. Do not go past this point until I return. The fire is burning off toxic materials, and you guys can be killed if you inhale them. Stay here. I will be back in just a second, and we'll talk then about getting you into the scene."

With that, he accelerates past them.

"Wow, the sheriff seemed a bit miffed, but at least he said maybe we can get access," the cameraman says, putting down his equipment.

"Yeah. I guess we've crashed their little party, and they're not too happy about it."

In front of them, Jerry jumps into the truck. He has no way to know how long Sheriff Hancock will be, so he starts the engine and flicks the switches that power up the compressor system he's attached to the dispersal hose. He jumps down and goes to the back of the tanker. Waving at Diane and her cameraman, he takes down the hose, holds it tightly, and does a test spray into the woods.

"Are you getting this? Why is the marshal spraying that stuff into the woods?" Diane wonders aloud.

The cameraman hits record again and, hoisting the camera to his shoulder, starts shooting video through the windshield. "I'm on it."

"Good. Keep rolling."

With the sprayer working perfectly, even with the thick creosote mixture, Jerry is confident it will do the job. "Oh yeah," he says as if speaking directly to the monster. "If the fire has weakened you, this hideous stuff should finish you off." Satisfied, he puts everything back in place, and with a wave towards Diane, he returns to the cab and shifts the truck into first but doesn't remove his foot from the brake.

"Looks like the marshal is going to leave," Diane hears from the back seat.

She hesitates for a second and shifts the van from park into drive a couple of times.

"Don't do it," the cameraman warns. "The sheriff was pretty clear that he didn't want us to move. We're not in Shreveport, where we might have some power. We're in rural Webster Parish. I'd rather not wake up in the Webster Parish jail tomorrow morning."

Diane knows for once her cameraman's hesitation may be right, so she shifts the van back into park, though she is not happy about it. She wishes she'd paid more attention to the press shield law in Louisiana when she got her press credential from the Caddo Parish Sheriff's Office.

One mile to the east, less than an inch below the surface of the still-burning bayou, a small measure of life remains in the newcomer. The rocks and dirt from the destroyed dam have filled in the bayou completely, leaving no bottom on which to hide, and very little surface water remains in which to live. Barely clinging to life, it repeatedly tries to flex and spread, which would help it heal, but it also badly needs sustenance, which is key to repairing the injuries it has suffered. However, in its weakened and wounded state, taking the necessary nutrition is impossible. Nothing remains of the treasure trove it has called home. In all directions, there is nothing but devastation and death. The extreme nature of the fire has done precisely what Martin had hoped: killed virtually all life in the bayou.

The newcomer knows it cannot survive but does not accept this fact easily. Enduring for so long on so little during its journey through the cosmos, it still has hope for a future. It wants to take revenge on the inhabitants of this place that have caused it so much hurt. It tries to find the strength to go into stasis, but the wind kicks up again, moving the clouds in a new direction. Doing so brings direct sunlight into contact with the water, which accelerates the harm. A rivulet of burning chlorine trifluoride snakes towards what is left of the newcomer. The impossible is unobtainable. It relents and, against its innate will to live, stops trying to heal itself. Instead, it focuses on another option and releases the tree trunk.

Out on the road, Jerry is relieved to see the sheriff roaring his direction, emergency lights on and siren blaring. He needs Sheriff Hancock to delay Diane, so he puts the truck back into park and jumps out. When the sheriff pulls up next to Jerry, he leans in and has a conversation, pointing towards Chase several times. Jerry then runs to the tanker, cranks it up, and drives away. The sheriff gets out of his car and approaches Diane's window, which is still down.

"Okay. The marshal and I have come to an agreement regarding you two. You can follow me in, but you have to stay as far away from the fire as possible. There is still the possibility of toxic smoke and other hazards. Just like before, I need to hear you two say that you understand my rules and that you'll abide by them. Only then will I allow you inside the perimeter. Park somewhere out of the way; stop about one hundred feet back to give the fire department room to maneuver. Film whatever you like, just don't get underfoot, and once the fire department does get here, for sure don't get in their way."

Chase nods. When Sheriff Hancock leaves, she looks over at the cameraman. "We're so getting the story of the century. You got video of whatever was in the bayou, right?"

"I think so, but with the fire and the whole dam exploding, I can't be sure until I get a chance to throw the tape into the playback machine to check it."

Andrew and Clint are relieved to see Jerry's tanker truck. They'd begun to wonder what the holdup was.

Clint jumps up on the running board as Jerry rolls down the window. "I think you should take it around back as close as the fire will let you get to what's left of the bayou."

"You got it; hold on," Jerry says and shifts the truck back into gear, driving slowly around the concrete blocks and rebar, hoping not to blow a tire. As he avoids the debris field, Diane and her van roll to a stop at the edge of the Landry property. The forest on both sides of the road is still on fire. Diane and her cameraman cough.

"Stop. Back up about twenty feet or so. I don't want the van to catch fire," the cameraman says. "The tires are what I worry about. They'll catch fire easily, and if that happens, the whole van will go up in flames."

Diane takes his advice and backs the van up. Both jump out.

"Shoot as much of the fire as you can. Get as close as you can to where the concrete structure was—"

He interrupts, "Hey, whatever was in the bayou might still be there. I'm good to set up and shoot lots of angles, but I will not get in anyone's way. And I'm for sure not going anywhere near the concrete building or the bayou."

"Yes, you are," Diane mutters with resolve. "You'll thank me later."

Jerry pulls the tanker truck up to the edge of what once was the bayou, jumps out of the cab, and runs to the back, where he begins pulling hose from a large spool.

"How far can we spray with that nozzle?" Andrew asks.

"I did a trial run, and I can get a good thirty feet, which should get us about where we believe that thing was living. How deep do you think the water is now?"

Both men look up at the ravaged dam with the large, V-shaped swath of material missing from the middle. Muddy water and dirt continue to slosh through the lowest break in the dam, and parts of it tumble into the bayou, adding to the material already there.

"I bet it's no more than a few inches deep. Most of the water was displaced by rock and mud or burned off. Not to mention the destroyed carcasses of all the cypress trees are in the water too."

"What's the holdup? I thought you were going to start this party," the sheriff says, joining them.

"Couple of things. We're curious about how deep the bayou is now. When the fire started, it came to the surface. We hope it's still there, but we're not anxious to see it again. We know it was living in the bayou. We just wonder exactly *where* it's living in the bayou."

Sheriff Hancock smirks and points over his left shoulder. "How about I tell Ms. Chase to go check it out? She can be like our canary in a mine. I bet the creature would love to meet her."

Jerry laughs and puts one hand to his left ear like a TV reporter during a live telecast, speaking with a deep, sonorous voice. "This just in, loveable and perky reporter Diane Chase was eaten by an alien while on assignment in Minden. Film at eleven!"

They all share a laugh. The cameraman sees Jerry and laughs too.

"Look, I think he's pretending to be a news anchor. But why are they wearing masks? Shouldn't we have them on too?"

"Do you have a mask?" He shakes his head. "Yeah, I didn't think so. I don't care what he's doing. All I care about is why you aren't rolling tape."

The cameraman shakes his head and coughs, which draws a look from the men.

"You told them to stay back, right?" Jerry asks. "Do they need masks? I didn't bring any extras."

The sheriff shrugs. "That's on them. If they start vomiting, maybe we'll tell them to move."

"Okay. Time to spray?"

"Time to spray," Clint agrees.

Jerry pulls a pair of hip-wader boots down from a metal bar on the back of the truck and slips them over his pants. "I'm going out as far as possible. Don't start the pump until I give you the high sign. I need someone to help me control the hose."

"I'll help," Clint says.

Andrew volunteers to man the compressor and help feed out the hose.

"And I'll keep an eye on Ms. Chase and her cameraman, and call the fire guys in with their foam when you're ready," the sheriff offers, happy to not be anywhere near the bayou.

"Okay," Jerry says with a smile. "Wish me luck."

"Don't get eaten. I kind of like you," Clint jokes to break the tension.

"I ate brussels sprouts and asparagus for breakfast, so I hope that makes me far less tasty than normal." Jerry makes his way towards the bayou.

"Whatever he's doing, make sure you focus on him. I get the feeling that this is important," Diane says over the cameraman's shoulder.

"Of course it's important. That monster we saw must have lived in the bayou. I suppose they're trying to capture it or something like that."

At the very edge of its continued existence, the newcomer senses vibrations. Something approaches. The precipice of darkness beckons, but it resists. Perhaps there is hope after all. The deadly orb in the sky darkens briefly. The sustenance to rebuild is close. Maybe it will be possible to regenerate, to repair the extensive damage caused by the hateful things. Then, it can rejoin the little one, regain its former self, and begin a new life. It would welcome the opportunity to rid this otherwise perfect world of the things that have hurt it.

It gathers what strength it still has and tries to rise. The fire scorches and hurts, but it must continue. Above, the clouds part, and the bright, deadly orb returns. The newcomer knows excruciating pain, but it must try.

"What the hell is that?" Diane yells. "Do you see that?"

"Shut up, Diane. Of course I see it! That's what I saw when the dam exploded. That thing looked right at me, and it knew I was there. It must be why they blew up the dam, set the fires, and are doing whatever it is they're doing now."

"Well, keep rolling; no matter what happens, keep rolling," she says through clenched teeth.

"Shut up," he says again. "You're screwing up my nat sound."

Bringing all its reserves to bear, the newcomer disregards the immense pain and continues rising. It tries to rebuild its eye to see its prey, but the toll taken on it is so great that the effort seems impossible.

Jerry sees something covered in brown-and-red mud moving the water. *Maybe a cooked nutria?* A bump appears. Jerry stops his foray into the water, which now covers the tips of his boots. The mass of brown and red is less than ten feet away. "Turn it on!" He waves in fear towards Andrew, who throws the switch to start the flow. "It's right here in front of me!" Jerry screams as Evan and Earl's creosote mixture courses through the hose. He plants both feet shoulder-width apart and aims the nozzle at the alien.

The newcomer knows there is danger, but a primal need has overtaken its other senses. Then a new taste begins to rain down from above—but not the sweet liquid it has come to love; instead, this taste is quite deadly. In its weakened state, there is no recourse available. It frantically searches every spare molecule that strikes it for something it can use, but there is nothing in the foul liquid to sustain it. Every atom in its body is assaulted as it is smothered. It tries to divide once again and survive, but this new threat has erased any residual power to do so. It musters what remains of its energy to at least confront the thing killing it. Perhaps it can still survive.

Then, success! A small eye is born. But the resources and effort to create it mean certain death. Finally, out of the water far enough for the eye to focus, the newcomer blinks and sees the one attacking it.

"Tell me you're getting this," Diane screams through pursed lips as something brown rises out of the bayou. "Is that an eye?"

The cameraman smiles. He hopes she's terrified. He certainly is.

The newcomer tries to extend and touch Jerry but is unable to muster the strength. There is movement, and shrill, painful noise pierces the air. The eye settles on the hideous creature making the noise—one unlike any other it has ever encountered.

"It's looking right at me!" Diane screams.

Jerry continues to spray, praying that Martin was right about creosote finishing the job.

The newcomer begins its slide into darkness. Before the eye closes forever, it sees something that gives it hope. Above, in the shocking blue sky that means death, it sees the white planet it encountered after being kicked out of the comet's tail that brought it to this awful place. A small part of it recalls that members of its species are there, covered in cosmic dust. Though they exist in stasis, they are alive.

The last thought that flashes through what is left of the newcomer's mind is aimed at those of its species still living in this hostile universe. The thought is exceptionally direct and very human.

Avenge me.

The molecules of the newcomer's body scream as they are destroyed, piece by billion-year-old piece, until nothing remains. Angry with the futility of its life, the newcomer surrenders to the precipice and plummets into the abyss of nothingness.

"Oh man, I'm rolling, but no one is ever going to believe this," Diane's cameraman murmurs to himself, hoping his pronouncement wasn't caught on the microphone.

"Told you to stick with me and I'd get you the story of the century, didn't I?"

Everywhere the liquid hits, new fires burst out, consuming what remains of the already scorched bayou. Finally, the compressor whines at a higher pitch, and Andrew shuts it off.

"That's it!" he yells to Jerry.

Jerry retreats to where the others are standing. Tentatively, they remove their masks.

"I hope that did the trick. Did you see it? I think it tried to get out of the bayou once. I even saw that yellow eye for a few seconds."

"I think you're right. That brown bump was it, right?" Sheriff Hancock asks.

"Yes. I bet that's what was left of it after the chemical fires and dam collapse." Looking over his shoulder, Andrew continues, "I'm certain they saw it too. And if they got that on camera, I wonder what people will say once they air the video footage on the news tonight."

More concerned about his parish at the moment, the sheriff looks to Andrew and asks, "Do you think it's okay to have the fire department come on in to try and contain the rest of this fire?"

"Yes."

"Webster One."

"Go ahead, Sheriff."

"Tell the fire department the scene is cold. They are to proceed in and begin addressing what is left of the fire."

"Ten-four."

Minutes later, they hear the whine of the sirens. Several large trucks from Barksdale and neighboring jurisdictions pull into the driveway. A combination of firemen and airmen, all in yellow fire-resistant suits, many with self-contained breathing apparatuses strapped to their backs, swarm over trucks that don't resemble fire trucks at all. Rows of silver canisters with bizarre placards crowd the backs. Hoses are deployed, and soon they're spraying something over the entire area.

"Sheriff, we need you guys to step back," an airman from Barksdale says. He points at Diane and her cameraman. "Them too."

Watching the crews spring in action, Jerry is impressed.

"I guess they knew what to bring."

The sheriff nods. "Yep. I asked this morning about it, and the fire chief told me they already knew what kind of fire they were about to fight. It was lucky Barksdale had the right combination of things to assist."

The fire chief approaches, and Jerry can't help but inquire about what they are using to fight the fires; none of it resembles foam or water.

"What is that stuff?"

"We were told to prepare for a chlorine trifluoride fire. According to NASA, the Air Force, and OSHA, once we apply liquid nitrogen to the area, that should retard the fire's growth. All those big canisters you see came to us this morning, special delivery from NASA."

"How does it work?" Clint asks.

"First, the stuff is crazy cold. Its boiling point is negative 320 degrees, so the cold alone is a huge fire deterrent. Second, by spraying enough of it, we will displace the oxygen that feeds the fire. If we displace the oxygen, we remove one of the legs of what we call the fire triangle."

"The fire triangle?"

"Every fire must have three things: heat, fuel, and oxygen. Hence, the fire triangle."

"I see. That makes perfect sense." Jerry is about to put another question to the chief when something distracts him. They all turn as a car pulls up, and a large man gets out. He stands silently and makes no attempt to get closer to the action. "Say, who is that?"

Sheriff Hancock shakes his head. "Oh man, what the hell is John Lambert doing here?"

"*The* John Lambert?" Andrew asks.

"Yep. I guess I better go see what he wants."

"We're coming with you," Andrew says, which elicits a nod of agreement from Clint and Jerry. The four men head up the slight incline to where the man stands. The sheriff speaks first.

"Good morning, Mr. Lambert. I'm Sheriff Hancock."

"I know who you are," Mr. Lambert says, nodding slightly to acknowledge the sheriff. He also nods at Clint, Jerry, and Andrew. Taking this as a sign he should continue, the sheriff asks, "Sir, how did you get in here? I have law enforcement stationed to prevent unauthorized entry."

Leaning against the front door of his large, four-door Cadillac, Mr. Lambert shrugs and smirks. "Sheriff, you of all people know that money buys access. Besides, one of your guys is a distant cousin. But there's not much that can be done to stop a determined man, and I was very determined to see and understand what happened here." He holds up both hands. "Look, I'm not here to cause trouble, but I do have questions." He points at the destroyed concrete house. "First, is Martin still alive?"

"Martin is dead," Andrew interjects quickly, which draws a squint and a forceful exhalation from Lambert.

"Good. He got my Oscar killed, didn't he?" Seeing no reaction, he presses forward. "Do you know what happened to Oscar? Before Martin died, did he confess? You men have been here, so you must have all the answers. I have to know. Oscar was my only hope for a future, the only good thing I had left in my life, and that bastard Martin took him away from me."

"Sir, I am very sorry for your loss, but there is no way we can settle the issue for you right now. Perhaps, one day, it may be possible. For now, sir, you really have to leave. It's not safe here for you."

Mr. Lambert's shoulders droop, and he seems smaller and much less intimidating. Andrew opens the car door and gently guides Lambert into the driver's seat. He hesitates a second, then takes one knee beside the open door and speaks in a voice so low that only Lambert can hear it.

"Mr. Lambert, I am US Marshal Andrew McLean."

"Yes, I know who you are and all about you."

"Then I'm sure you know my reputation as a truthful and reliable man."

Mr. Lambert nods just enough to signify he understands, so Andrew continues. "Good. One day soon I will find you and tell you the details of what happened here. All of them. I will leave nothing out. The truth will be hard to hear and maybe even harder to believe. And once you know the truth, you can never reveal it to anyone. Ever. This is a personal favor that I will do for you. In return, one day, I will come to you and ask that you return my favor, and you cannot deny me. Agreed?"

Mr. Lambert sits, silent. Then, with a slight pause in his breathing, he turns, looks directly into Andrew's eyes, and grasps his extended hand. The bond formed between the men is more like a ritual treaty between two former enemies than anything else. Releasing Andrew's hand, Mr. Lambert nods, shuts the door, starts the car, and disappears down the road.

Sheriff Hancock looks at Andrew curiously. "Don't know what you told him, but whatever it was, it's in stone. His handshake is stronger than any promissory note or notarized document, or so I've heard."

Turning back towards the firefighting efforts, Jerry blurts out, "Hey, what's going on with those two?" He points towards Diane and her cameraman, who seem to be engaged in a heated argument. They watch in awe as she tries to slap him, but the cameraman dodges left, and her attempt goes wide. He stands back and puts his hands on his hips for a few seconds as if mentally trying not to reciprocate her slap. They see him bend down and push a button on top of the recorder unit.

"I think he just ejected the videotape," Andrew says, with some measure of certainty. "I didn't realize it until now, but their gear looks just like the gear Martin had. Guess they shop at the same store."

Andrew, Clint, Jerry, and the sheriff watch in amazement as the cameraman rips the videotape out of the recorder, winds two feet of tape around the body of the videocassette, holds it above his head, and throws it into the nearest smoldering embers.

"Oh my. Did that just happen?" Jerry asks.

They watch Diane scream at the nearest fireman, trying to get his attention. The plastic case begins to melt, and the tape inside flares up just as the fireman trains suppression foam onto it. Another fireman holds Diane back when she tries to jump into the foam to retrieve it. As the fire dissipates, the fireman turns his attention elsewhere, and Diane does try to grab the videotape. She burns two fingers in the process and finally gives up and instead begins swatting at it with a still-smoldering tree branch. Whatever was on that videotape is no longer useable.

"Guess I won't have to steal that tape during the traffic stop I was planning," Sheriff Hancock says with a muted smile.

Clint walks over to the cameraman, who doesn't seem fazed by what he's just done.

"What happened? We all saw her try to slap you. Did you just burn your videotape?"

"Yes. Everything from today was on that tape. I saw that thing in the bayou, and it saw me. There was no way I was going to let her profit off of it. And her trying to slap me? Back on the dam, she connected with one. It hurt. This time I was ready. I've had it with snooty reporters who only think about themselves and getting to the network. I'm done with this job, too. It's all about the blood and the guts. I mean, I have a college degree. I guess it's time I start figuring out how to use it."

Clint is quiet for a minute, then he smiles. "Ever thought about a career in Southern law enforcement?" He turns to point towards his compatriots. "Including myself, there are four men here who appreciate what you just did and will be more than willing to help you, should you express any interest."

The cameraman doesn't hesitate. "I always thought law enforcement might be a fun career. Can we talk after I get back to Shreveport and resign?"

Opening his credentials, Clint extracts a business card and hands it over.

"Absolutely. Here's my card. Call anytime."

"I will. Thank you, sir," the cameraman says as he shakes Clint's hand.

Walking back to the other three, Clint resists giving them a surreptitious thumbs-up and instead just smiles while Diane tries to figure out how to work the camera.

Two miles to the west of what once was Martin's lab, far away from the chemical fire and suppression gases, the water from Caney Lake washes over the landscape. However, the levels have diminished significantly as it flows into the various bayous, cattle ponds, and streams of northwest Louisiana.

The immature newcomer, unsure and alone, hugs its fiberglass lifeboat and rides the fastest current. Due to the contours of the land, the water eventually finds its way into Caney Creek and then Bayou Dorcheat. Soon, the tiny newcomer's water highway brings it into the clear, cold water of the Dixie Inn gravel pits. Its young senses aren't yet capable of surviving in the cool water, so it continues onward, and it's not long before the fiberglass and its tiny alien sailor are deposited into Lake Bistineau, a 15,550-acre impoundment recreation lake just south of Minden.

It might as well be an all-you-can-eat buffet to the infant newcomer. The warmth of this place is an ideal selection for a new home, so it releases the fiberglass and hugs the bottom while it searches for a large rock under which it can rest. When it finds a suitable one, it contracts and settles in.

It likes this new place. Soon, it plans to satiate the hunger it feels.

30

The silent flight of newly hatched mayflies, attracted to the Coleman lantern burning brightly less than ten feet away, fascinates Colin. He shivers a bit in the cool mountain air as darkness moves to cover the Ouachita Mountains. Glancing up, he sees the first stars, their meager light poking holes in the dimming canopy of the sky. He returns his attention to the mayflies and holds out a hand as several come to rest on his outstretched fingers and palm.

"It's like they don't even exist," he murmurs. "They're so light and fragile."

Andrew smiles and responds, "Yes, son, they are beautiful, aren't they? Look how their wings are almost completely translucent."

Colin parrots the word, splitting its syllables into parts as he holds up his hand and looks. "Translucent? What does that mean, Dad? Lucent means light, right? And trans, like, they transmit light? But they don't. Instead, they are kind of see-through. Is that what it means?"

"Smart guess, son; that's good intuition on your part. Yes. The light is diffused. The wings are not thick enough to block light like a bird's wings. Instead, if you hold up your hand and put the mayflies between you and the lantern, you'll be able to see through them even though they have a small amount of brown and green in their wings." He turns his attention back to the telescope and makes some final adjustments.

When he looks through the eyepiece, he smiles and points towards the lantern. "I think we're all set up, so go ahead and turn the lantern off so our eyes adjust to the night sky. Just be careful."

"Okay, Dad," Colin replies as he carefully grabs the round knob that controls the flow of gas to the two glowing mantles. He turns the knurled knob until the light sputters completely out and says, "I just gotta remember not to touch the glass or metal after the light goes out cuz it's very hot."

As the lantern extinguishes, the fast-approaching darkness is interrupted only by the sounds and lights visible across the water in the camping area. The smell of a dozen campfires fills the air. Andrew inhales and replies.

"That's right, son. You and I have our share of scars from this thing. Let's not add any more. Besides, your mother would get pretty upset if we came back to camp and needed some bandages or had to run into town to see a doctor about a burn."

"Yep. Mom always says I have visited that doctor up in Perryville too many times. At least she wanted to come here to finish our vacation before school starts again. I know she was upset when we had to leave Caney Lake so quickly. She didn't say a word the entire ride home."

Andrew is grateful his face is no longer illuminated by the lantern. Serious emotions tied to the events of the past couple weeks play across his face. He recalls the drastic measures he, Clint, Jerry, and the sheriff took, and they bring a shudder to his body—born out of a combination of disbelief and relief with some measure of pride. His smile changes to a smirk. *Why couldn't Martin's hungry little monster land on the lawn in front of the Capitol? I bet most of us would have been okay with him munching on those losers.*

Seeing his father quietly in thought, Colin nudges him with his foot. "Whatcha thinking about, Dad? You worried we'll see some moon aliens in the telescope tonight and that maybe they'll see our telescope pointed at them and decide to come down here and start something?"

Andrew chuckles at his science-fiction-obsessed son's comment.

One day, I'll have to tell Colin just how close to the truth he was with that. But not tonight. Tonight, we'll just look at the planets. "No, son, I hope the clouds stay away and we get to see the rings of Saturn or the craters on the moon."

"That'd be cool." Now that his father is finished setting up the telescope, Colin notices that it's different from the one he trained on last year. "This new telescope is pretty neat. It's bigger than the one we had, right?"

"It is bigger and better, but it's made by the same company. This is the eight-inch Cave Astrola. The one we owned last year was the six-inch. Do you know the difference?"

Colin thinks for a moment before he replies. "The larger one can gather in more light. That means we can see more things, right?"

Andrew nods. He holds up a piece of equipment that looks like the top part of a camera tripod. "With this attachment, we can even take photographs using my camera. You just attach it right here," he says, manipulating a thumbscrew through the middle of the metal plate. "The camera then sees everything that you can see through the telescope."

"Is that why you brought your Nikon camera?"

Andrew nods. "Yes. If it's a clear night, I thought maybe we'd try to get a few shots of the moon."

Colin nods eagerly. "Sounds good to me." He sees where his father has aimed the telescope. "But it's not a full moon tonight, right?"

Leaning into the eyepiece on the telescope, Andrew manipulates the focus knob, making a slight adjustment, and the moon comes into focus.

"You are correct. The full moon was last weekend. Tonight, the moon is what's called waning gibbous. If you look at it right now, it's not pure white like normal. It's kind of reddish. That's reflected light from Earth." Andrew moves away from the telescope. "Have a look for yourself. Hurry, though, the moon is moving, just like us, so it'll be out of frame in a minute or so."

Colin bends down towards the eyepiece and holds his breath for a second, trying not to nudge the telescope with his head. He blinks, and the moon comes into focus. Colin strains to see movement on the surface, hoping to be the one who discovers something new. He leans back from the eyepiece and asks the question many amateur astronomers eventually wonder.

"How many people might be looking at the moon tonight?"

Andrew considers the question for a minute. "I'm not sure. I'm sure some amateur astronomy clubs are out tonight, and some observatories connected to universities are always studying the sky, things like that. I bet the number isn't very large."

"So, we're in a small, kind of unique group then, right?" Colin asks, his voice rising. He likes the idea that they are different than most.

Andrew smiles and chuckles as he answers.

"Yes indeed. You and I are in a unique group."

Colin stands and looks at the moon.

"When we landed astronauts on the moon, I wonder what they saw up there. Do you ever wonder if we found anything or anyone on the moon? Maybe the Russians or Chinese beat us up there, and no one ever told us?"

Andrew recalls some of the notes from Martin's lab and stays quiet for a moment. He wonders if he can ever tell his son what Martin theorized about his creature, that it arrived on Earth purely by accident, like a lost intergalactic tourist. That it had probably been riding in the tail of one of the comets that transect the human solar system every year for millions of years, and somehow got kicked out of the tail. Martin also theorized that two things must be true: First, the moon, and virtually all the planets in the solar system, have been struck as well. His second truth was even scarier—that more creatures probably exist somewhere else on Earth.

Andrew shakes his head at the thought of every planet in the solar system infested with hungry Oscars. Since blowing up Caney Lake, he has wondered whether there is another "Oscar" out there, quietly wreaking havoc, and they just don't know it yet. *Some under-the-radar, unsolved murders.* He glances back at the moon and completes that train of thought. *Colin's question is on point. What did NASA find when we went to the moon, and why did we stop the moon program so suddenly?*

"Well, Dad, do you think there is anything, or anyone, up there? On the moon?"

Thinking back to the mayflies that landed on his son's outstretched hand, Andrew has a disconcerting thought: *Humanity is just like those mayflies. A fragile and short-lived species.* He clears his throat and, without moving his gaze from the moon, tries his best to answer without answering.

"I don't know, son. I just don't know."

31

Clint slides the sheaf of paperwork into the two-hole punch. He pushes down on the handle, and a satisfying *kerchunk!* follows. He lightly taps the papers on the desk to get them even, looks up as Jerry enters the room, and slides the newly created holes home onto the metal retaining clips at the top of the manila file folder. Without missing a beat, he greets his buddy.

"Hey, Jerry."

"Clint," Jerry replies matter-of-factly. Pointing to the folder, he asks, "Is that what I think it is?"

Clint holds up the file. "Yes. Right here, I have my version of the most bizarre case I have ever worked."

With his back still turned, Jerry asks, "Did you call it Oscar?"

"Well, I couldn't decide if calling it Oscar was appropriate. So, where it was necessary to refer back to the creature, I used something more descriptive. To me, it was like one of those critters that sits on the bottom of the bayou, like a carp or catfish, just waiting for its next meal."

Jerry nods in agreement. "Yes. 'Bottom feeder' certainly sounds better than 'Oscar.' Would make a great movie, though. I wonder who'd play me? Cleavon Little? Redd Fox?"

"More like Richard Pryor," Clint says with a laugh.

"I'm sure I play a starring role in your little report, right?"

Clint pantomimes hitting his forehead with his open palm. "Oh man, maybe, but I bet I spelled your name wrong. It's with two *T*s and one silent *PH*, right?"

Jerry chuckles as he answers, "Yes, but we only use the silent *PH* in formal settings."

"Of course, you play a critical, though supporting, role."

Jerry lets that slide. "Probably the best parts, though, which I appreciate. What about Andrew?"

"Yes."

"Diane Chase and her cameraman?"

"Yes, they are there as well."

"Evan and Earl?"

With mock exasperation, Clint responds, "Yes, Jerry." Then, not hearing more questions, Clint has to ask, "Is the interrogation over, or is it going to continue?"

Jerry zooms right past Clint's question and forges ahead. "Now, Clint, regarding this alleged report of yours . . . are you sure you want to even put all that on paper? We killed an entire lake, fish, and all. Filled in a bayou, started a fire, and contaminated a large section of national forest with a deadly product. Then we blamed it all on a dead guy, who, by the way, was eaten by an alien—a bottom feeder, as you call it. Any idea what's going on out there? I've driven by a couple of times, but the whole area is cordoned off. Even the roads are closed."

"The federal government has mobilized something called the National Oil and Hazardous Substances Pollution Contingency Plan to deal with the containment and cleanup."

"That's quite a mouthful! What does that do?"

"It's some kind of government response plan for oil spills and hazardous substance releases. It is like our MOU for mutual aid. Every federal government department has some responsibility for the umbrella plan that was developed. They also share in a national response network. I guess that is a pretty good idea, to have a coordinated approach to cope with spills or hazardous situations that require cross-agency assistance or cooperation."

"Or bottom feeder aliens who think of us as giant beef sticks," Jerry says with a smile.

"Exactly. It's a soup-to-nuts kind of plan. They do the accident reporting, spill containment, and cleanup. I understand it went all the way up to the president."

"Mr. 'I am not a crook'?"

"Yeah, I guess it was one of the last things they told him. Now Mr. Ford is the one who doesn't believe it."

"Well, both of those conversations had to be very interesting. Especially in the middle of all this Watergate mess."

"Andrew told me that they copied the tape and sent it to some eggheads over at NASA, then they put the original on a fighter jet out of Barksdale and flew it up to DC. A very select group in the White House viewed the tape. It was all very hush-hush. Top secret and all. They clamped a lid on it so tight because they didn't want the Russians getting wind of it, something about spies in the US would try to capture it, make more of them, and use them against us."

"In other words, pretty much why Martin didn't want us to go to the military?"

"Yep. So, the boss was clear: put everything in my report, leave nothing out, then deep-six the file. Second, when I called Agent Beldon over at ATF 'bout an hour ago, I thought I would be clever and see just exactly how much she'd been told."

"And?"

"She let me know, without saying so, that she's already gotten briefed by the acting head of ATF, after he'd been briefed by the secretary of the treasury. She made mention of the failsafe devices the raid team found that triggered the explosions in Martin's lab and all over his property. She was kind of angry that no one called her office since the word 'explosives' is in their title."

"They're saying that the raid team found them and inadvertently set them off?" Jerry asks, curious if that story will hold up to scrutiny.

"That is the official story. And don't fret about it. I can guarantee it's not going to hurt us. They just needed deniability for some reason. Kind of makes me suspicious, but whatever."

Jerry looks doubtful for a minute but still responds, "Okay, if you say so. What about the creosote?"

"Oh, she knew that story too."

Jerry shakes his head. "Someday, someone may ask what we did to stop the bottom feeder. I mean, we don't even truly know what was in the bayou, do we? All we have are Martin's claims that it was an alien. But, I mean, how can that be true, and how can anyone even prove it? It's not like we know it came from space, or the moon, or Mars. What if it was just a natural thing and not an alien? In fact, I still don't believe it, and I was there." Jerry looks out a large picture window and mutters, "Makes you wonder. At least, it makes me wonder."

Clint nods. "The first few minutes of that first day, everything seemed normal. Just another abandoned car. Then came the report of the body. Then more bodies. Then Martin. Then everything else. And now? Who knows what normal is."

"Yeah. The world had to go all crazy on us."

"True."

"No more of those things, right?"

"Swear to God, I hope not."

"Good. It would seem that in the bayou, there is no mercy, even to visitors from other planets, or solar systems—heck, maybe even other universes or other dimensions. Who really knows?"

Clint nods in agreement and repeats, "Who knows? I mean, even Martin didn't know for sure, so we'll never know either." Clint walks to a file cabinet in the corner. He manipulates a cipher lock and opens the drawer, then drops the file into an accordion folder marked *Clint's Ridiculous File.*

"You headed out soon?"

"You trying to get rid of me?" Clint responds with a laugh. "I saw you skulking near the door marked *Armory and Equipment* a few minutes ago. I know you must have some hair-brained scam cooked up to peruse the inventory in there while I'm not looking. I can only imagine that there's something in there that the city marshal from Minden will try to arrange to be transferred to said city marshal."

"Now, that is a great idea, but, no, I was curious if you wanted to go to that new Mexican place out on Airline Drive."

"We've met, haven't we? When have I ever turned down Mexican food?"

"Never, so let's go! I've worked up an appetite trying to get you to spell my name correctly."

"Is that what you were trying to do?" Clint chuckles as the public address system comes to life.

"Captain Ward, if you are still in the building, please call the front desk." Clint looks pained and, in his best Elvis Presley imitation, says, "Just like Elvis, Clinton Ward has left the building, thank you very much," which elicits another hearty laugh from Jerry.

"That call might be important," Jerry says through his smile. "Could be the president."

"Which one?" Clint asks as he sits back down and hits the speakerphone button on the phone, dialing 0. It rings twice, and Nicole, the desk sergeant, answers.

"Captain Ward? You have a call holding from the sheriff down in Bienville Parish. This is a transfer from the superintendent's office. The caller is asking for you specifically. He won't say what it's about."

Clint looks at Jerry while he speaks into the phone. "Thank you, Nicole. Did the sheriff say his name?"

"Last name of Miller.

"Which line is it?"

"Line three," she says; then, with very little humor in her voice, she finishes with "It's the only one blinking."

Even though Jerry is concerned about this new call, he can't help but snicker.

Clint flashes the international "you're number one" hand gesture towards his buddy.

"Hello, this is Captain Ward. How can I help you, sir?"

Clint hears nothing for a moment and wonders if he's gotten disconnected. Then, someone on the other end coughs and begins to speak.

"Captain Ward? This is Sheriff Miller down here in Bienville Parish. Say, I'm going to get right to the point. I had a long conversation with my fellow sheriff, Homer Hancock, up in Webster Parish a few minutes ago. Then I spoke with your superintendent, who said I should get your input about something we got going on down here. I understand you just finished working a case that was, well, kind of, let's just say, not the normal kind of homicide case."

By pure muscle contraction, Clint snaps the pencil he's holding into two pieces. His heart skips a few beats.

"Uh, if you don't mind, Sheriff, how exactly did you hear about my case?"

Jerry sits slowly and strains to hear both sides of the conversation.

"People talk, Captain; you know, the redneck telegraph is a powerful tool if you just listen. So, I'm hoping you can help me."

With no response from Clint, Miller continues. "I'll git straight to the point. I've had a couple of fishermen go missing, and now there's something over at the state park that, well, to be blunt about it, might resemble a case you just finished working. I've spoken with some people, and from what I have been able to gather, there's a whole bunch of unexplained disappearances and some unusual murders that stretch across the entire middle portion of the state and up to Oklahoma and the Mississippi line. I'm not sure, but we may have ourselves a very prolific serial killer or an entire group of serial killers."

Clint's brain works on how to frame and grasp this new information. A minute passes without a word said between them; then the sheriff clears his throat.

"I guess you're curious why I called."

Clint's effort to keep his voice even is only marginally successful. "Yes, sir, you could say that. Don't know how I can help, but I'm happy to assist with any information you think I might be able to give you."

"Well, this is something new. We get plenty of your regular, garden-variety murders. People disappear in the woods, rivers, and the lake all the time. Some turn up dead at some point, and some just never turn up. But these? Tell me about a killer who leaves only bones. Perfectly cleaned bones, with a slight tinge of red in the most porous ones. Almost like someone soaked them in a vat full of acid, bayou water, and mud. Does any of that sound familiar?"

Clint is unsure if the earth is spinning, or if he is. His concept of the passage of time is altered, and as far as he is concerned, the universe has stopped. Goosebumps appear on both arms, and his vision clouds.

"Captain? You still there?"

Finally, Clint manages to croak out, "Only bones, you say?"

Jerry hears the phrase "Only bones?" and knows this can't be happening. Not again. "No. I refuse to believe there's another. No way. Not possible," he says softly.

On the phone, the sheriff answers Clint's question in the most direct way.

"Just bones. Nothing else. Some clothes occasionally. No tissue, no muscle, nothing left on the bones. They are completely smooth. As if the killer tumbled them in one of those rock tumblers kids get for Christmas. I've sent some of the evidence to your main lab in Baton Rouge. Honestly, at first glance, we all thought the bones had been boiled and stripped. Any of this sound familiar?"

Clint lets that question hang for a few seconds while his brain argues with his soul. Both openly debate his potential responses. Clint puts the phone over his shoulder and rubs his eyes for a moment. He can't bring himself to look at Jerry because there is no way to answer Jerry's silent, question-filled stare. Finally, he brings the phone back up to his face, inhales, and says, "Sheriff, if you give me a second, let me grab my case file."

"Certainly."

Clint finally looks at Jerry and points towards the file cabinet. "You know the cipher code?"

Jerry shakes his head. "I'm pretty damn sure I don't want to know the damn cipher code."

Clint doesn't even pause as he covers the mouthpiece with his hand and whispers, "Five, twenty-one, forty. Reach back in there and hand me that folder. Sounds like we might need to get the team back together."

Even though he doesn't want to, Jerry goes to the cabinet. One word Clint said sticks out.

"We?" he grouses under his breath as he retrieves the file folder. "*We?*"

EPILOGUE

Doctor Gerald Ross, director of a secret facility funded through black operations in the Department of Defense budget, sits patiently. He shifts his body and wonders why all government-issued office chairs are so uncomfortable. *Maybe they're designed like that on purpose—to keep the sitting-while-getting-paid experience from being too enjoyable or restful,* he thinks with a smirk. He peers over his reading glasses at his colleague Carol Madison, PhD, as she quietly reads the single-spaced, typewritten document he gave her twenty minutes ago. Her reputation as a speed-reader is well known, and he tries to follow her eyes, left to right, left to right, left to right, but he finally gives up.

She's already read the entire thing twice. The motion of her eyes is hypnotic. It begins to lull him to sleep. To keep focused, he creates a mental game designed to categorize her potential reactions, awarding points by how frequently her forehead and face muscles change. As her reactions go from incredulous to anger, to disbelief, back to incredulous dozens of times, he loses track of his score and reluctantly stops. Watching her reactions gives him a measure of comfort, given his similar reactions, though on a slower scale. He glances down at his desk and realizes he's unconsciously making twirling doodles on a piece of paper, so he stops, puts away the pen, and throws the paper into the "circular file" on the floor under his desk.

He returns his focus to Dr. Madison as she exhales loudly and finally closes the folder with bright-red stripes and large letters that spell *TOP SECRET* emblazoned all over it.

"Well?" he asks.

"Do you believe it? I mean," she sputters, which is accompanied by her shoulders shrugging vigorously, "is it even possible?"

"You tell me; you're the exobiologist."

Madison, still shaking her head, tries to compose an answer that doesn't sound like the rantings of a lunatic. It takes her a few seconds to array her thoughts into sentences she can clearly articulate.

"I, uh, would like to speak with this US marshal, the gentleman who wrote the report. I'd also like to talk with the other two who were involved. If Washington gave them everything necessary to carry out the extermination of the alien entity, then even they must have thought it was legitimate. I'm also curious about exactly why they even let us have access to this information. Seems like something the government would want to bury. Forever."

Ross nods and interjects, "I agree. And I'm guessing they made that determination after watching the videotape the marshal references."

"I would love to see the alleged videotape confession of Dr. Landry. But still . . . I am beyond shocked. This is huge!" She thinks for a moment and adds, "And I am saddened at the same time. If true, just to get my hands—well, my robotic hands—on that organism. With our technology, imagine what we could have discovered about it that Dr. Landry wasn't capable of discovering."

"Such as what was up with the red tint on the bones."

"Absolutely. Perhaps the tinting was some part of the digestive process."

"I agree which is why I have requested that the bones be transferred from state custody to us," Ross says as he holds up a plastic case the size of a videotape cassette and continues, "Should we go get some popcorn from the commissary?"

"Gerald, is that what I think it is?"

Ross nods. "Yes. And I thought the conclusions the marshal drew were quite interesting. Especially when he mentioned the Apollo moon missions."

Madison shifts in her uncomfortable chair. "Yeah. But when we stopped going to the moon, that decision *was* budget-driven, right? The public had lost interest in our moon shots, thought of them as routine and uninteresting. We, uh . . ." She pauses as something clicks in her mind. Her blood pressure jumps, as does her pulse. She leans forward just a tick more. "We have some of the moon rocks downstairs, don't we?" She shifts her posture again, thinking about the largest moon rock ever collected, nicknamed "Big Muley" by the Apollo crew who found it and brought it back. She already knows the answer to this question but asks it anyway.

"I requested Big Muley last quarter. Has it been delivered? If so, have we X-rayed it? I wonder if . . ." Her voice trails off as she contemplates the possibilities.

Ross smiles as he answers.

"Yes. I checked just before you got here. It's downstairs. And it's not the only one we have, just the largest. The Lunar Rock Depository finally sent it over last week. No surprise that it's been forgotten and in cold storage since Apollo 16 brought it back. And you wonder, what? If our X-ray or other imaging can see inside it? If the folks over in Houston examined it thoroughly enough to rule out something we've missed in the years since it was brought back from the moon? It wasn't mentioned, but what if the creature they fought over in Louisiana is invisible? If one of—what'd the marshal call it—the bottom feeders is inside our rock downstairs?"

Without hesitation, Madison answers, "Yes!" with gusto.

"Since reading that report, I've been curious as well," Ross admits. "To that end, just to be cautious, I had the rock moved to our containment lab. However, given that the creature the marshal described consumed almost every living thing it encountered, I'm not sure if I want to find out—"

Ross is forming the last word when he is interrupted. Above him, the fluorescent lights blink once, twice, dim, and then brighten. A red bubble light above the door leading to a hallway begins to revolve, casting a V-shaped red shadow onto everything. Klaxon sounds reverberate through the entire complex, and a metallic voice announces the beginning of their worst nightmare.

"Attention! There is a breach in containment. Repeat. There is a breach in containment. All groups go to alert level one. Repeat. There is a breach in containment. All groups go to alert level one. This is not a test."

Ross hesitates for a moment, unsure. He pushes back from his desk.

Madison does the same, but her chair topples to the floor as she jumps to her feet, further scaring her. She turns towards the door, then looks back at Ross, a mixture of fear and uncertainty racing across her face.

"The bottom feeder?"

Afterword

First, thank you for reading *Bottom Feeder*. I hope you enjoyed it and are looking forward to the next installment (yes, there are at least three more).

The chapter where Colin and his family go camping is from my childhood. From May to September, my father, mother, younger sister, and I would camp on the weekends. Sometimes at Caney Lake, just north of Minden, Louisiana, or another campground in northern Louisiana. When not in Louisiana, my family could usually be found in the Ozark or Ouachita Mountains of Arkansas. We started our camping adventures using a WWII, Army-surplus canvas tent (which leaked like a sieve) and eventually progressed to a pop-up trailer (which I fell out of one night and rolled all the way down to the edge of the Cossatot River in Arkansas). Then, one spring day, Dad came home with a Shasta "Starflyte" trailer. Sort of a knockoff of Air Stream trailers.

I slept in a cozy loft bunk above a foldout dining table, the metal of the trailer just a few inches above my head. During heavy rain or thunderstorms (it was Louisiana, after all, where rain falls all the time, all year-round), the metal roof of the trailer would make a tremendous amount of noise as the raindrops pounded down. That noise kept me from deep sleep, and in the REM sleep cycle, the place where bizarre dreams and nightmares grow, mine were always vivid and colorful.

The one that stuck with me all these years generally followed the same pattern and was the kernel that grew into this novel. In that nightmare, some kind of monster lived on the bottom of the lake, and when it rained, the monster would rise up, mud and slime dripping from its body, and go searching for people to eat. Thus the name bottom feeder.

With my nightmare never far from my mind while camping, I learned how necessary it was to visit the pit toilets before bedtime at a very early age. Conversely, I also learned how to hold it until daylight arrived. Rarely did I open the ventilation windows on either side of my loft, given my belief that the monster might reach in and snatch me through the window screen.

Thank you to my advance readers: Catharine Gibson; Rick Ware, retired city marshal of Bossier City, LA (Clint is based on Rick); E. A. Coe (an award-winning author of noir fiction in his own right); Mark Muse; Elizabeth Cottrell; Heather Rosenker; Peggy Finarelli (NASA, Ret.); and Lynne Perler.

My writing mentor, L. Y. Marlow, has been the greatest coach and fan of my writing that I could have wanted. L. Y. is the talented author of three very influential books. If you've never read *Color Me Butterfly*, *A Life Apart*, or *Don't Look at the Monster*, you should.

The encouragement, attention to detail, love, and support from my wife, Ann, as I sat at the dining room table, hunched over the glowing screen of my MacBook Pro or thumbing through reference books, was unending and unwavering. Thank you, Ann.

About the Author

James Davison is the author of two previous books, the nuclear thriller *Trinity 3.11*, and the fictional memoir of the oldest man alive, *I Am Lazarus*.

Davison draws inspiration from his years as a journalist, a public information officer in the federal government, and his experience in local law enforcement to give his books realism. A native of Louisiana, he is also an accomplished cook, a musician, an avid fly fisherman and competitive powerlifter. He and his wife live and work in Virginia.

Of Note

The Fouke Monster

In Arkansas folklore, the Fouke Monster is said to have been seen in and around the city of Fouke, which is located in Miller County, Arkansas, during the early 1970s. The creature was accused of attacking a local family. Initial sightings of the creature were concentrated in the Jonesville/Boggy Creek area, where it was blamed for the destruction of local livestock. Later, sightings were reported several hundred miles to the north and the east of Fouke. It has never been caught, and the mythos surrounding it only grows with every unexplained disappearance in southeastern Arkansas. If you'd like a couple of decent movies about it, I can recommend *The Legend of Boggy Creek*, and *Creature from Black Lake*. https://en.wikipedia.org/wiki/Fouke_Monster

The National Oil and Hazardous Substances Pollution Contingency Plan

This plan was developed in 1968 by the US government in response to a massive oil spill off the coast of England. To avoid the problems faced by response officials involved in the incident, the government developed this coordinated approach to cope with future spills. The plan provided the first comprehensive system of accident reporting, spill containment, and cleanup. It also established a response headquarters, a national reaction team, and regional reaction teams (precursors to the current national response team and regional response teams). The plan was strengthened and broadened under the Superfund Act, the Clean Water Act of 1972, and the Oil Pollution Act of 1990.

https://www.epa.gov/emergency-response/national-oil-and-hazardous-substances-pollution-contingency-plan-ncp-overview

"Run a 29"

The abbreviation for the police ten-code 10-29. If an officer requests a "29," they are usually asking the dispatcher to contact their teletype operator and verify or inquire if there are any open/active warrants for the individual.

https://policecodes.net/ten-codes/

"Big Muley"

Otherwise known as Lunar Sample 61016, "Big Muley" is a lunar sample discovered and collected on the Apollo 16 mission in 1972 in the Descartes Highlands, on the rim of Plum Crater, near Flag Crater (Station 1). It is the largest sample returned from the moon as part of the Apollo program. The rock, an 11.7 kg (26 lb) breccia, consists mainly of shocked anorthosite attached to a fragment of troctolitic melt rock.

https://en.wikipedia.org/wiki/Lunar_Sample_Laboratory_Facility

CPSIA information can be obtained
at www.ICGtesting.com
Printed in the USA
LVHW021531120522
718422LV00005B/78